Love is
a time of enchantment:
in it all days are fair and all fields
green. Youth is blest by it,
old age made benign:
the eyes of love see
roses blooming in December,
and sunshine through rain. Verily
is the time of true-love
a time of enchantment — and
Oh! how eager is woman
to be bewitched!

WISTERIA HOUSE

Emily Frobisher had been adopted by Stephen and Mary Larby, who had brought her up in their beautiful home, Wisteria House, in a sleepy village on the Sussex Downs. Throughout her idyllic childhood, Emily was great friends with Peter Stuart, the son of the local doctor. In her late teens, she meets and falls in love with one of Peter's old schoolfriends, Hugh Mallory, and they are engaged to be married. But the outbreak of the Second World War brings irrevocable changes, and it is to be many years before Emily finally finds the contentment she seeks.

PAMELA HULTON

WISTERIA HOUSE

Complete and Unabridged

ULVERSCROFT
Leicester

First published in Great Britain in 1995 by
Navigator Books
Ringwood
Hamphire

First Large Print Edition
published 1997
by arrangement with
Navigator Books
Ringwood
Hampshire

British Library CIP Data

Hulton, Pamela
    Wisteria House.—Large print ed.—
    1. English fiction—20th century
    2. Large type books
    I. Title
    823.9′14 [F]

    ISBN 0–7089–3702–0

Published by
F. A. Thorpe (Publishing) Ltd.
Anstey, Leicestershire
Set by Words & Graphics Ltd.
Anstey, Leicestershire
Printed and bound in Great Britain by
T. J. Press (Padstow) Ltd., Padstow, Cornwall

This book is printed on acid-free paper

Acknowledgements

Such research that was necessary in order to write this book was done the easy way — simply by seeking from my friends the information I required.

I would like therefore to acknowledge my gratitude for their considerable help and encouragement. Those who are kind enough to read Wisteria House once it is in print, will no doubt, recognise certain paragraphs that will be familiar to them. In particular, I would like to express my grateful thanks to my proof reader, for the immense amount of time and trouble that he has spent on helping me with the task of checking and re-checking every line in the book.

I should perhaps mention John Gordon Davis, the author of The Years of the Hungry Tiger, whose vivid account of the riots that took place in Hong Kong during the 1970's has helped me to describe the incident with a greater degree of accuracy than would otherwise have been possible. Finally, to a friend who enjoyed reading Wisteria House sufficiently to want to show it to a publisher, my very grateful thanks.

List of Main Characters

James and Victoria Frobisher
Emily's natural parents

Stephen and Mary Larby
Emily's adoptive parents

Andrew and Elaine Stuart
Local doctor and his wife

Peter Stuart
Their son, and Emily's childhood friend

Teresa Mallory
Emily's school friend

Hugh Mallory
Teresa's brother and Emily's first husband

Christobel Blair
Owner of hat shop and Emily's employer

Joshua Frere
Christobel's artist brother

Nicholas Frensham
An older man-of-the-world with whom Emily has a brief affair

Myra Fingleton
Peter's American wife

Elsie Stokes
James Frobisher's one time mistress

Meg (Stokes)
Elsie's and James' illegitimate daughter and Emily's half sister

Martin Stuart
Peter and Emily's son

Cara Stuart
Peter and Emily's daughter

Maisie (Stokes)
Meg's illegitimate daughter who is adopted and brought up by Peter and Emily

Charlotte
Martin's wife

Paul and Gregory
Martin and Charlotte's twin sons

Madelaine Gale
Cara's lesbian partner

Hugh McNeil
Maisie's husband and Teresa and Robert's son. Emily's nephew by her first marriage

Fleure and Simon
Hugh and Maisie's children

Part One

1912 – 1945

1

SURROUNDED by gently rolling countryside, the sleepy, picturesque village of Applefold lay tucked away in a hollow of the Sussex Downs. With a population of less than three hundred people, the village boasted a church, a few shops, a school and a pub. In the centre was the village green, where old men would sit in the shade of an ancient oak, contentedly smoking their pipes and reminiscing on days gone by; where small boys, clutching their jam jars, would gather round the duck pond to fish for newts and tadpoles, and where courting couples would stroll, hand in hand, often as not to exchange a surreptitious kiss from behind the shelter of the giant oak tree.

At one end of the village stood an old, stone built house. Known as Wisteria House, it had derived its name from the mass of long, pendulous strands of lilac blue flowers that shrouded its grey walls in bountiful profusion.

The house had once belonged to one Matthew Larby who, on the untimely death of his only son, had left the small property to his eldest grandson. Stephen Larby now lived there with his young wife Mary — the daughter of a country parson — whom he had married in the summer of 1912, shortly after the death of his grandfather. Lit by oil lamps and warmed by open log fires, the house had an air of peace and tranquillity about it, a warmth and friendliness that conveyed itself to all who crossed its threshold.

The garden with its well-kept lawns, carefully tended flower beds and long-established specimen trees and shrubs, spoke of generations of loving care and thoughtful planning. At the bottom of the garden was an orchard, beyond which was an expanse of open country that stretched across the South Downs towards the coast a few miles away.

A short distance from Applefold was the country town of Hurstborough, where Stephen was a partner in a family firm of solicitors. Messrs. Larby, Bodger and Scott had originally been founded by

Stephen's grandfather around the middle of the last century and, after coming down from Cambridge and completing his articles in London, Stephen had joined the firm as a junior partner.

Stephen and Mary had been married for barely two years when their life was disrupted by the outbreak of the Great War. In common with many other patriotically minded young Englishmen, Stephen had immediately enlisted in the army, joining the Royal Sussex regiment, and was fortunate enough to have survived the war with no more than a minor leg wound.

Mary, with no family responsibilities, had spent the war doing voluntary work with the Red Cross, and now, thankful to have her husband safely home again, was beginning to pick up the severed threads of her life, ordering her household, taking part in village activities, entertaining their friends and more than adequately fulfilling the role of an affectionate and loving wife. She loved her husband dearly and the only thing missing in her marriage was that, after seven years of marriage, she was still childless. Now in her late twenties, she had become almost reconciled to the fact that she was unlikely to conceive a child all these years later. The only person with whom she had ever discussed the matter was her girlhood friend and confidante, Victoria Latham. The two girls had been at school together and over the years a warm and close friendship had developed between them.

In looks as well as character they were complete opposites. Victoria, perhaps the more striking of the two, was tall and slender with fair, honey coloured hair, and a naturally lovely complexion. Carefree and full of life, she was impulsive, warm and generous, as well as being an intensely loyal friend. In contrast, Mary was small and dark, her wide-set, expressive brown eyes perhaps her most distinctive feature. She was placid and reserved by nature, but beneath the calm exterior she was a woman of sensitivity and compassion.

Since Mary's marriage, Victoria had become a frequent visitor to Wisteria House. Stephen, always deeply concerned for his wife, welcomed her visits, knowing how well the two girls got on together and how much Victoria's warm and exuberant personality seemed to revitalise Mary. Besides which he was genuinely fond of her, looking upon her more as one of the family than a guest.

The war had been over for almost a year when, on a bright and sunny autumn morning, Mary sat at the dining room table, going through her correspondence. She was halfway through breakfast before Stephen appeared.

She looked up and smiled as he entered the room. "Hello darling. What happened to you this morning?"

"Sorry I'm so late," he apologised. "Lost my collar stud and couldn't find the damn thing anywhere." He helped himself to bacon and eggs from the sideboard and sat down opposite Mary.

"Anything interesting in the post?" he asked as he cast a casual glance at the pile of correspondence on the table.

"Not much really, a couple of invitations and a few bills," Mary replied, "but there is also a letter from Victoria. She wants to know if she can come for the weekend."

"Oh good, you'll enjoy that."

"The only problem is that we are dining with the Fletchers on Friday evening, but I don't suppose they will mind an extra guest, will they?"

"Why not give them a telephone call?" Stephen suggested.

The telephone had only recently been installed and Mary, used to writing short notes when she wished to contact any of her friends, found it difficult to remember that she now had only to lift the receiver to get an instant reply.

As he finished his breakfast Stephen said, "I'd better make tracks. I've got a fairly early appointment with a client this morning." Mary accompanied her husband to the front door and after kissing him affectionately, watched him wind the starting handle of his Morris Cowley before he climbed into the car and with a cheerful wave of his hand, drove off in a haze of exhaust fumes.

She stood outside for a few minutes enjoying the autumn sunshine. 'The season of mists and mellow fruitfulness', she mused. Then, deciding it was about time she went in search of Mrs. Soames to discuss the day's meals, she reluctantly went indoors.

Mrs. Soames was her cook and had been with her from the time she had first come to live in Applefold. A woman in her middle forties, Mrs. Soames both liked and respected her young mistress. She was aware of how much Mary would have liked to have had children and felt a great sympathy for her when, as the years went by, there was still no sign of a child. Mary in turn had a considerable fondness for this large, kind-hearted woman who, although a tyrant in the kitchen, never wavered in her loyalty and was a good worker besides being an excellent cook.

As she crossed the hall, Mary heard her say impatiently, "Now then hurry up, Lily. It's high time you had finished that job. Madam will be coming in at any moment." Mary smiled to herself, feeling a little sorry for Lily, a young girl from the village. Lily had been with them for only a few weeks, and was still in the process of being trained into the ways of the house. Before the war there had always been an indoor staff of three with additional daily help from the village. Nowadays Mary ran the house with Mrs. Soames and Lily and a Mrs. Brown who came in for three mornings a week to lend a hand about the house.

Mary opened the green baize door that led into the kitchen. She greeted her staff with a cheerful "Good morning, Mrs. Soames. Good morning, Lily. How were your parents when you went home yesterday?"

"Quite well, thank you, M'm", Lily replied, "but Alf's got the chicken pox."

Mary said that she was sorry to hear that. She knew there was a lot of it about. She then turned her attention to her cook. "Now, Mrs. Soames, what about lunch today?"

Ten minutes later, the domestic details attended to, she was about to leave the kitchen when she remembered Victoria's visit.

"Oh! Mrs. Soames, I nearly forgot. Miss Victoria will be coming for the weekend. Will you see that Mrs. Brown gets her room ready for her?" Mrs. Soames knew most of the Larby's friends, but Victoria was by far and away her favourite. She had a very

10

soft spot for the tall, elegant young woman who, whenever she came to stay, always popped into her kitchen for a chat and never failed to enquire sympathetically after her various aches and pains.

"That will be very nice, Madam," she said, "I'll make sure everything is ready for her."

* * *

Mary stood by the front door, her arms outstretched in welcome as Victoria drew up in her open two seater.

"Hello darling," Mary greeted her, "have you had a good drive down?"

"Simply marvellous, thank you. The countryside was looking absolutely beautiful with all the leaves just beginning to turn."

Victoria climbed out of the car and warmly embraced her friend. "Darling Mary, it's simply gorgeous to see you again. You look wonderful! How is Stephen? I hope he didn't mind me inviting myself again quite so soon after my last visit; and Mrs. Soames and all her rheumatics? And the funny little Lily?" She prattled on without waiting for an answer in her obvious pleasure at being back in the relaxed and familiar surroundings of the peaceful old house among people she cared for.

Mary laughed. "We're all in very good order, thank you. As for Stephen, he's been looking forward to your visit almost as much as I have." She tucked her arm through Victoria's and led her indoors. "Let's go and have some tea. Mrs. Soames had made one of her special sponge cakes that you like so much, so I hope you've got a good appetite to do it justice!"

Over tea they talked non-stop, catching up on each other's news.

As she settled into the depths of an armchair, Victoria kicked off her shoes, and curled her feet up underneath her. "It's so good to be back, Mary", she said wistfully. "You've no idea what London is like these days, with so few of one's old friends about the place. Things just aren't the same any longer."

During the war Victoria had worked

as a voluntary aid detachment nurse, known as a VAD. From having led a fairly sheltered life as a young girl, all at once she had found herself exposed to the sight of dead bodies, amputated limbs, the nauseating stench of festering wounds, and heartbreaking cases of young men returning from the trenches, blinded or suffering from shell shock. As she resumed her old life at the end of the war, she had quickly become bored and disillusioned by the social round she had once enjoyed. She envied Mary her happy and contented marriage. At the age of twenty seven, Victoria knew that, more than anything else, was what she wanted for herself. Years ago she had been very fond of a man called Bertie Drummond, but Bertie, in common with many of her friends, had been killed in the war. Since then she had not met anyone with whom she felt she wanted to spend the rest of her life. As Mary listened, she sensed Victoria's restlessness and despondency, yet felt powerless to help.

Stephen's arrival home brought their

conversation to an end.

He greeted Victoria with an affectionate kiss. "Well, how's life in London these days?" he enquired.

With some of her old exuberance returning, Victoria replied cheerfully, "Not too bad really. Actually, I've just spent the last couple of hours boring Mary to tears, with an account of how different life is in London since the war. I'm feeling a lot better now having got it off my chest!"

They sat talking for a while, until, looking at his watch, Stephen said, "Isn't it about time you two girls got changed? Darling, you have told Victoria that we're dining with the Fletchers?"

"Yes, Stephen," Mary replied, "but we're not invited until eight o'clock and it's only six-thirty. What about having a drink before we go upstairs?"

Later that evening, dining with Susan and Tom Fletcher, Victoria found herself sitting next to a tall, attractive man, who was introduced to her as James Frobisher. James, she discovered, was a weekend guest like herself. In his early thirties, he was clean shaven, with dark, thoughtful

14

eyes and a wide humorous mouth. Good looking, with an air of distinction about him, he was also witty and intelligent and a charming dinner companion. In the course of the evening, Victoria learnt that during the war he had served with a guard's brigade and was now back in his old job at the Foreign Office, where from all accounts — she was to learn later — he had a promising career ahead of him. What she was also to discover was that having been married for less than a year, James had suffered the traumatic experience of losing his wife as a result of a riding accident.

Victoria returned from the party with stars in her eyes. A few months later they announced their engagement and were married within the year. If ever a marriage was made in heaven, Mary had thought at the time, this must surely be it.

Some months after their wedding Mary received a letter written in Victoria's sprawling, schoolgirlish handwriting. Opening it, she read:

15

Knightsbridge
Feb 15, 1920

Darlingest Mary,

I am dashing this off to tell you the exciting news. The Doctor has confirmed that I am enceinte. Isn't it wonderful! We have been trying so hard to have a baby and now at last it's happened. You and Stephen simply had to be the first to know. We have decided to call the baby Henry (after James' father) if it's a boy, and Emily (after no one in particular) if it's a girl. I feel that I am being horribly selfish in telling you how thrilled we are at the idea of becoming parents, when I know how much you have always wanted to have children, but I know you will understand and be happy for us. Keep the news to yourselves for the moment, until I've had a chance to tell all the parents. James sends his best love.

Your loving,
Victoria

16

The following August, after a long and difficult labour, Victoria gave birth to a baby daughter, whom they named Emily Victoria. Their cup of happiness was brimming over, but fate decreed that their joy was to be short lived.

Mary never knew for sure what happened. Something went wrong soon after the baby's birth. Septicaemia set in and a week later Victoria was dead. The first Mary knew about it was when a telegram arrived from James saying, 'Victoria seriously ill. Please come at once'. She packed her suitcase and caught the train to London, but by the time she arrived it was too late. Victoria had died a few hours earlier.

Mary stayed on in London. She organised the running of the house, helped with the funeral arrangements and tried to bring some comfort to James — shocked and distraught by the events of the past week.

After the funeral, feeling that it was early days for him to be on his own, Mary said to him, "James, dear, have you thought about getting away for a short time? It might help to have a complete break. If you are anxious about leaving Emily," she added, "I could easily take her home with me for a while — and the nurse too, of course."

James looked at her gratefully. "You've been such a tremendous help already, Mary — I don't know how I would have managed without you — but I hardly like to impose upon your kindness any further, although, at the moment, I feel I would like to get as far away as I can from all that has happened here during this last week." He walked across the room and stood looking out of the window for several minutes. Then, turning back to Mary, he said, "Are you quite sure you could manage to have Emily? It wouldn't be too much trouble for you?"

"Of course not," Mary assured him. "There's plenty of room at home, and I shall enjoy having her." And so it was arranged. James went to stay with some old friends in Scotland and Emily, at barely three weeks old, came to live with Stephen and Mary in the old Sussex house that was destined to become her home for the greater part of her life.

After his return from Scotland, James came to stay for the weekend. Rather hesitantly, he asked Mary if she would keep Emily for a little while longer, until he had made a few necessary domestic arrangements. Mary agreed willingly, realising that he still needed time to adjust before taking on the responsibility of his motherless baby. She suggested thoughtfully that until he had sorted out his domestic affairs, he might like to join them at the weekends. But as the weeks passed, it soon became clear to both Stephen and Mary that James had no immediate plans to take Emily back to London.

One weekend he arrived much earlier than usual saying that he wanted to talk about Emily's future. Mary felt a sudden chill. She knew there could be only one explanation. James had obviously decided to take Emily home. She had always known that having the baby to live with them was no more than a temporary measure until James had managed to pick up the threads of his life again, but during the time that Emily had been with them, Mary had grown to love Victoria's baby more than she was ready to admit, even to herself. The thought of losing her now filled her with sadness. Her frequent visits to the nursery had become part of her daily routine. During the last few weeks the baby had begun to recognise Mary as soon as she walked into the room, her small face breaking into a wide, toothless grin, as she grasped Mary's finger in a vice-like grip.

Mary was in the garden dead heading the roses when James arrived.

She greeted him affectionately and led him indoors, saying in a detached, impersonal voice, "I'm so glad that you have decided to take Emily home James. She is so young that she will soon settle down, once she gets used to her new surroundings."

She continued to talk in much the same vein, in an attempt to hide the unhappiness she was feeling, until James, unable to stem the flow of words, put his arm around her shoulders and said to her gently. "Mary, you don't understand. I don't want to take Emily away. Quite the contrary. I've come to ask if you would have Emily to live with you — permanently, I mean." In a low, unemotional voice, he told her how, over the last few weeks, he had been considering Emily's future. He spoke first of his concern at not being able to make a proper home for her, explaining how his job was bound to take him abroad for a lot of the time; then went on to say that he had no wish for her to be brought up in the sole charge of a nurse for the whole of her childhood, or, for that matter, by elderly grandparents.

James continued in an impassive voice, "Watching you with Emily these last weeks, has made me realise how much more you have to offer her than I could ever give her."

He paused for a moment before adding a little diffidently — fearing that he might be treading on delicate ground — "I know from Victoria how much you have always wanted to have a child, and it is this, together with your obvious love for Emily, that has finally decided me to ask if you and Stephen would consider adopting her and bringing her up as your own child."

Bewildered by the unexpected turn of events, Mary said gently, "But James, you might decide to marry again, later on, I mean," she added hastily, "you would then be in a much better position to provide a home for Emily."

His voice was tinged with bitterness. "I shall never marry again, Mary. I don't seem to have much luck in my marriages; meanwhile there is Emily's immediate future to be considered. Believe me," he went on, "it's not been an easy decision, but I am satisfied in my own mind that it is the right one for her. Living with you and Stephen would give her the secure and happy background that she needs, and I know for certain that there would never be any shortage of love and affection in her life."

After Stephen returned later that evening, the three of them discussed the matter at length. Stephen urged James to wait a few months longer before making a final decision. He feared that James' judgement could be clouded by his grief and was more aware than anyone how much his wife could be hurt if later, James should have second thoughts. James, on the other hand, was firm in his belief that he had made the right decision and nothing Stephen or Mary could say would persuade him otherwise.

Emily was six months old by the time the adoption papers were signed. A few months later James left the country to take up an appointment at the British Embassy in Rome.

2

FOR the first three years of her life, Emily was looked after by a nurse. Nanny Spiers was a tall, rather gaunt looking woman, somewhere in her mid forties, who had come to Mary with excellent references. Going along to the nursery one morning, Mary opened the door.

"Good morning, Nanny. I've just come to let you know that I shall be taking Emily out with me this afternoon. Perhaps you would like to have a few hours to yourself to do some shopping . . . ?" She glanced quickly round the room. "Where is Emily, by the way?"

The nurse looked flustered. "Emily has been very rude to me, Mrs. Larby", she replied. "I'm afraid that I have had to punish her."

"But where is she?" Mary repeated.

"I have shut her in the broom cupboard on the landing."

Horrified, Mary exclaimed, "You've done what?"

"Well, she had to be disciplined, Mrs. Larby," the nurse replied defensively.

Mary, curbing her anger, said, "But she's only a baby — you don't discipline a small child by locking her in a dark, airless cupboard."

She hurried across the landing towards the house-maid's pantry and quickly unlocked the door of the broom cupboard. The place reeked of floor polish and brasso. Emily was sitting on the floor amid an assortment of brushes and brooms, mops, carpet sweepers and a vast vacuum cleaner. Her small face was white and tear-stained. Her clothes were creased and covered in dust.

Mary gently gathered the frightened child into her arms and carried her back to the nursery. She faced the nurse and said coldly, "Please bring me a clean dress and another pair of socks. After that you can go to your room and pack your bags. I shall not be requiring your services any longer."

As Mary changed Emily's dress she noticed that the child's arms were covered

25

in bruises. There was no need to ask how they got there. Finger marks were clearly visible. A closer inspection of her body showed that Emily's small posterior bore further signs of bruising.

Mary dabbed the angry red marks with some Pond's Extract. "Emily, has Nanny ever shut you in the broom cupboard before?" she enquired gently.

"She always shuts me in there when she says I've been naughty," replied Emily in a subdued voice.

"What did you do this morning that made Nanny shut you in the cupboard?"

"I put my tongue out at her."

Mary hid a smile. "Is that all?"

"Um . . . " There was a pause, "I did kick her too . . . " She looked up at her mother appealingly. "Just a little kick."

"Why did you do that?"

"Because she hurt me." Emily lifted her arm and showed Mary the dark red mark where the nurse had twisted her wrist as she had dragged her to the cupboard.

Mary was seething with indignation at the nurse's callous, irresponsible behaviour. Nevertheless she felt that Emily should at least be reprimanded for her own part in the affair. Very gently she began, "You know what you did was wrong, darling, don't you?" Emily nodded silently. "Well, if you promise me you won't do anything like that again, we will say no more about it." As she brushed Emily's hair and tied it with a fresh ribbon, Mary continued, "Emily, why didn't you tell me that you were being shut in the broom cupboard?"

Emily dropped her eyes. "Nanny said that if I told you, she would take Rosie away from me . . . " Rosie was a small rag doll and Emily's inseparable bedtime companion. Mary was appalled at what had been going on under her nose without her having any knowledge of it. The nurse's behaviour towards her small charge was both cruel and sadistic, and Mary was deeply shocked by what had occurred.

It was then that she decided to take over the responsibility of looking after Emily herself, rather than risk the occurrence of another such incident. She enlisted the help of a woman from the village to come in each day to do the washing and ironing and from then on, with Mrs. Soames' willing help, Mary took sole charge of Emily's welfare.

★ ★ ★

Mary had often pondered on the strange way in which this chubby little girl with her rosy cheeks and fair curly hair had come into her life. She loved Victoria's child with an intensity that she had never imagined possible. Nevertheless she brought her up in a firm and disciplined manner and guided her through her formative years with wisdom and resolve.

Stephen also adored his small daughter, and basked contentedly in the sunshine of her happy, light-hearted chatter and spontaneous laughter. He spoilt her outrageously, but if she were to upset her mother in any way, Emily was liable to receive the rough edge of his tongue.

After her parents, Mrs. Soames was perhaps the most important person in Emily's young life. She loved the kindly woman, who, regardless of how busy she might be, invariably had time for her small visitor. Emily always felt very much at home in Mrs. Soames' warm, cheerful, spotlessly clean kitchen. Her child's mind associated it with a mixture of delicious, mouth-watering smells, and Mrs. Soames' comfortable and reassuring presence. As Emily grew older, Mrs. Soames taught her how to make little cakes and biscuits, which Emily would proudly present to her mother at tea time. There were other occasions when, having been punished by her mother for some misdemeanour, Emily would run tearfully to the kitchen, and fling herself into the comfort of Mrs. Soames' arms. The kind woman would gather the weeping child to her ample bosom, and gently rocking her to and fro until the sobs subsided, would patiently point out to her that if Emily misbehaved, she must expect to suffer the consequences.

The conversation usually ended with Mrs. Soames saying, "Now, why don't you go and find your Mummy, and tell her you are sorry you've been naughty." Emily would wander off, a little reluctantly, in search of her mother, to do as Mrs. Soames had bidden her.

Then there was Lily. Lily was the

closest person in age to Emily, and was only too happy to play hide and seek with the little girl whenever she could escape Mrs. Soames' eagle eye. Mary would smile to herself, when she heard the shrieks of laughter that drifted across the garden, as her house-parlour maid, in her black afternoon dress, and white cap and apron, chased in and out of the bushes in her search for Emily. As the child booed out at her from behind a bush, Lily would exclaim in a high falsetto, "Ooh, you are a one, Miss Em, you didn't 'arf give me a fright!"

Emily had another friend in old Jessop the gardener. He was always referred to as 'Old Jessop' by Stephen and Mary, although he was not much over fifty. He was not a particularly good gardener, and spent much of his time in the tool shed doing, as Stephen succinctly put it, damn all. But Mary felt sorry for him and kept him on as she knew he would be unlikely to get another job in the village. Besides which he was very good at keeping an eye on Emily as she played around the garden, and on more than one occasion he had picked her up and carried her indoors when she had fallen and grazed a knee.

Outside her immediate circle, there was one other person who played an important part in Emily's young life. Peter Stuart was the only son of the local doctor. His parents, Andrew and Elaine Stuart, were close friends of Stephen and Mary as well as being near neighbours, and the children were perforce thrown together from an early age. Emily had known Peter for as long as she could remember. She idolised the tall, fair-headed boy, five years her senior. Peter, on the other hand, although secretly flattered by her obvious devotion, tended to treat his young companion in a somewhat cavalier manner. He looked upon her in much the same way any ten year old boy might regard a younger sister, for whom he had an affection, but not a great deal of use. As she grew older Emily began to take a more active part in his various interests and activities. She joined in enthusiastically with whatever he was doing, whether it was going birds' nesting — at which she soon became almost as proficient as

Peter — accompanying him on bicycle rides, or dangling a worm on the end of a line when they went fishing in a nearby disused gravel pit. Eventually, having proved herself to be a worthy companion, Peter learnt to accept her on equal terms and from then on, despite the disparity in their ages, they became firm friends.

★ ★ ★

At the time of her adoption it had been agreed that Emily should be told that she was adopted as soon as she was old enough to understand. Matters were brought to a head when, coming in from the garden one afternoon, Emily overhead a conversation between her mother and her Aunt Helen.

Helen was saying, "Mary, don't you think it is about time you told Emily that she was adopted? She is nearly four now, and if you leave it much longer, she is almost certain to hear it from someone in the village."

Mary replied coolly, "Stephen and I have discussed it, Helen, but neither of us feel she is quite old enough to be told just yet." Mary put a warning finger to her lips as she caught a glimpse of Emily crossing the hall and they changed the conversation.

Later, after Helen had left, Emily perched herself on the arm of Mary's chair. "Mummy, what does adopted mean?" Mary had always endeavoured to answer Emily's questions as truthfully as she could. She now found herself faced with a dilemma. She kept her explanation as simple as possible, telling Emily no more than she considered necessary. She stuck to the bare facts, knowing the details could be filled in at a later date. After she had finished speaking, there was a long silence then, as she jumped off the chair arm, Emily asked excitedly, "Can I go and tell Mrs. Soames?"

For the next few days Emily informed everyone with whom she came into contact that she had been adopted. She left no doubt in anyone's mind that she considered herself to be someone very special. But once the novelty of the situation had worn off, childlike she had dismissed the matter from her mind and the subject was not referred to again for several years.

★ ★ ★

During the time that James was abroad, Mary received an occasional letter from him. Brief and impersonal they told her little of how he was feeling, but, reading between the lines, she surmised that he was a lonely man, despite his busy social life. Then came a letter informing her that he was due back in England the following month. Soon after his return home he came to stay for the weekend. Mary was startled to see how much older he looked. His dark hair was beginning to grey at the temples and there were deep lines etched around his mouth.

As Mary introduced James to his daughter, she said quietly, "Emily, this is your Uncle James. Come and say how do you do."

Emily was suddenly overcome with shyness in the presence of this tall, distinguished looking stranger. Nervously she walked towards him and after politely shaking hands, she hastily retreated to her mother's side, from where she studied him with considerable interest. James had brought Emily a present of a beautiful china doll. Made in Italy, it was exquisitely dressed in hand-embroidered clothes. Emily had never seen anything like it before. Her present helped to break the ice and she lost some of her initial shyness.

Gradually her confidence returned. After they had finished tea, Emily sidled up to James. "Would you like to see my puppy?" she invited him shyly.

"I should very much like to see your puppy," he replied courteously. "Where does he live?" Emily slipped her small hand into his.

"You'll have to come with me." She led him to a small room at the back of the house where Mary arranged the flowers. Emily explained confidentially, "You see, Sam isn't quite house trained yet and Mummy says he has to live out here in case he makes a puddle on one of the carpets."

"I quite understand," James replied gravely. "How old is Sam?"

"He's very little still, he's only three

months old." She looked up at him — a small figure beside his six foot frame. "Mummy and Daddy gave him to me for my fourth birthday," she informed him. "He's the first puppy I've ever had."

The puppy, a small black cocker spaniel, greeted them with ecstatic delight. For a few moments dog and child romped together. Then Emily picked him up and offered him to James.

"Would you like to hold him?" Somewhat unwillingly James took the puppy from her and held it awkwardly in his arms. But the excitement was too much for Sam. Suddenly a large wet stain appeared down the front of James' immaculate grey flannel suit. Emily giggled nervously. For a moment she was uncertain what she should do. Then, with a flash of inspiration, she murmured, "I'll get Mrs. Soames," and disappeared in the direction of the kitchen. Seconds later she was back with Mrs. Soames in tow. Mrs. Soames took in the situation at a glance.

"Oh, dear me," she exclaimed sympathetically. "Never you mind, Sir, I'll have your clothes cleaned up for you in no time, if you would like to let me have them when you've changed." She looked down at Emily. "You should have known better, Miss Emily, than to give Sam to your uncle to hold. You know what that dog is like when he gets over-excited."

James saw the child's crestfallen face. "You mustn't blame Emily, Mrs. Soames, it really wasn't her fault. I should have known better than to have handled such a young puppy." He made it sound as if he had only himself to blame for what had occurred. Emily warmed to him. They exchanged a quick conspiratorial look and in that moment became friends.

The rest of the weekend went well and over the next two years James became a regular visitor to the house until he was once again posted overseas.

* * *

Emily was ten before she gave any further thought to the fact that she was adopted. She vaguely remembered Mary telling her years ago how her real mother had died soon after she was born and that her

37

father had had to go away, which was the reason she had come to be adopted. Now, for the first time, she discovered that she had a growing desire to know who her real father was. Prompted by a child's uncanny instinct, the idea began to formulate in her mind that James might be her father. Small, isolated incidents occurred to her, fanning her already inflamed imagination. She recalled the first time she had met him, soon after her fourth birthday, when her mother had introduced him as 'Uncle' James; and how, later, when Emily was older, Mary had explained that he was not her real uncle, but that he was a very close friend of the family. She thought of the many times that James had come to stay with them whenever he was in England, of the generous presents he always brought her, even if it wasn't her birthday. Once, during a conversation with Mary, she had heard him mention the name Victoria. Emily knew that Victoria had been her mother's name and she suddenly felt an urgent need to find out if James had ever known her mother. Her mind was filled with such an overwhelming curiosity that finally she decided to talk to Mary about it.

Mary was sitting at her writing desk when Emily came into the room.

She paused uncertainly in the doorway before going over to stand by Mary's chair; then, plucking up courage, she said, "Can I talk to you for a minute, Mummy?"

Mary looked up, her pen poised in her hand. "Darling, of course you can. What is it you want to talk about?"

Suddenly feeling awkward and embarrassed, Emily blurted out, "Mummy, is Uncle James my real father?" It took Mary a few moments to regain her composure after such a totally unexpected question.

She laid down her pen, got up from the desk and looked down at the child's anxious little face. She cupped it in her hands and said quietly, "I think you and I had better have a long talk, Emily."

And so, for the first time, Emily learnt the full facts, not only of the tragic circumstances surrounding her birth, but also of the great happiness her subsequent adoption had brought to Stephen and Mary. Mary went to great pains to stress that James' decision to have Emily adopted was taken in what he considered to be Emily's best interest, so that the child would not feel that she had been rejected by her father in any way. After Mary had finished speaking, Emily got up from where she had been sitting cross-legged on the floor, listening intently to every word. She went over to her mother, put her arms around her neck and hugged her tightly.

"Thank you for telling me, Mummy," she said quietly. As Mary held Emily's slender young body in her arms, she was conscious of a feeling of relief now that Emily knew the full story of her adoption and, what was more important, of her relationship to James.

Emily's immediate reaction was to wonder whether she would feel any differently towards James, now that she knew him to be her real father, but she found herself quite unable to imagine him in any role other than that of the much-loved avuncular figure he had always been to her. Stephen was the only person whom she could envisage as her father, and she knew that no one could ever replace the large, kindly, bespectacled man in her thoughts and affections.

3

PETER looked up from the task of tying a fly on to the end of his fishing line. He watched the young girl coming towards him across the lawn. She was tall for her age, slimly built, with merry, sparkling blue eyes and long, fair hair that she wore loosely tied with a ribbon at the nape of her neck. At the age of ten, Emily was already showing signs of great beauty. As she got closer, Peter noticed that her face wore, for her, an unusually serious expression.

"Hello, Em," he called out to her.

"Hello, Peter, are you busy?"

"Not really, let me just finish tying this fly on, then you shall have my undivided attention."

After Peter had completed his task, he carefully stood his rod up against a tree, then turned to Emily and said cheerfully, "What's up, Em? You look as though the end of the world has come."

It was the day following her talk with

42

Mary. Emily's mind was in a turmoil, trying to digest all she had learned in the past twenty four hours. She felt an urgent need to talk to someone, and instinctively sought out Peter.

Uncertain where to begin, she plunged in at the deep end, "I've discovered who my real father is." She paused for a moment to see what effect her announcement was having.

"Have you?" Peter was curious. "Who is he?"

Playing her trump card, she announced with a certain amount of satisfaction, "It's Uncle James!"

Peter was startled, "How on earth do you know?"

Unable to contain herself any longer, Emily told him from start to finish the story she had heard from Mary the previous day.

When she had finished, Peter said, "Gosh." Then, after a pause, he went on, "How do you feel now that you know the whole story? Does it worry you?"

"No . . . " Emily hesitated, "It's just that there's such a lot to take in all of

43

a sudden. I'm glad really, because I've been wondering for some time who my real father was, and I've had a feeling that it might be Uncle James. It hasn't really made any difference to how I feel about him, but I'm just sad my mother died like that, and that I never knew her. Mummy said that she was very beautiful and that she and Uncle James had loved each other very much. It must have been awful for Uncle James."

Emily felt better having got it off her chest. She had always been able to talk to Peter, telling him things that she sometimes found hard to talk about to her mother. She abruptly changed the subject. "When do you go back to school, Peter?"

★ ★ ★

From an early age, Peter had always known that when he grew up he wanted to join the Navy, and after leaving prep school he had gone to the Royal Naval College at Dartmouth. Now, at the age of fifteen, and in his second year, he felt his ambitions were gradually becoming closer to being realised. A very likeable boy, he had made several friends during his first year, among whom was a boy of his own age called Hugh Mallory. Hugh was the son of Admiral Sir Arthur and Lady Mallory and lived in an old Elizabethan Manor House, known as Dykes Manor, a few miles from the seaside town of Eastbourne. During the early part of the summer holidays, Peter had spent a few days with the Mallorys, and Hugh was now on a return visit.

Emily's nose had been a trifle put out of joint at the time. She and Peter were in the habit of seeing each other, for one reason or another, on most days of the week. Since Hugh's arrival she had set eyes on Peter only once, and that had been more by accident than design. Emily had been on an errand for her mother and as she came out of the village store with a laden basket in her hand, she had run into Peter, who was accompanied by a tall, dark-haired boy. Both boys were on bikes and were evidently off on some expedition.

Seeing Emily, Peter slowed down and got off his bike. He called out cheerfully,

"Hello, been shopping?"

"I was just getting some things for Mummy," Emily replied sedately.

Peter said, "Em, I'd like you to meet Hugh Mallory." He turned to Hugh, who had also dismounted. "Hugh, this is my friend Emily — Emily Larby — I was telling you about her the other day."

As he shook hands with her Hugh said, "Hello," rather abruptly. He then turned to talk to Peter, and took no further notice of Emily.

Emily returned home feeling hurt and slightly resentful towards the stranger who appeared to have completely monopolised Peter. She dumped her basket on the kitchen table and proceeded to air her grievances to a sympathetic Mrs. Soames, giving her a blow by blow account of what had happened.

Mrs. Soames said soothingly, "Don't you fret, Miss Emily, I'm sure Master Peter didn't mean anything by it."

"It wasn't only Peter," Emily complained in an aggrieved tone, "It was that silly boy Hugh whatever-his-name-is. He's got no manners at all. I can't think what Peter sees in him."

46

Mrs. Soames hid a smile. Recognising the little green eyed monster, she changed the subject and said to Emily, "Now, be a good girl and put those groceries away for me in the larder."

★ ★ ★

"Peter?" Emily prodded his arm.

Miles away Peter replied, "Sorry Em, what did you say?"

"I asked when you were going back to school."

"I go back next week, on Thursday to be exact."

"Oh." Emily hated Peter going back to school, and lived for the holidays and his return home.

Peter knew how she felt, and said sympathetically, "The Christmas term is a fairly short one, Em. I shall be back for half-term anyway." Seeing Emily's downcast expression he added, "Don't worry, it'll be much better when you start going to boarding school yourself. You'll find it a lot more fun than doing lessons with Miss Ponsonby."

Emily burst into giggles at the thought

47

of the governess she shared with another girl. Compared with Miss Ponsonby, with her mouse-coloured hair which she still wore in coils over her ears, her steel rimmed spectacles perched on the end of her nose, and her prim, staid manner, anything would be fun.

With a return to her usual good humour Emily said, "Oh Peter, you do make me laugh sometimes." Lying on the lawn they continued to talk aimlessly, until Elaine Stuart, looking out of the window, called out to them.

"Come on you two. It's time for tea."

★ ★ ★

Emily did not, in fact, go to boarding school until shortly after her thirteenth birthday, by which time Peter, now a midshipman, was stationed at the naval base in Portsmouth. Over the next few years they saw comparatively little of each other, meeting only when Peter's leave coincided with Emily's school holidays. In spite of Peter's assurances, boarding school did not altogether come up to

Emily's expectations. She found the strict, unvarying, daily routine both frustrating and irksome, and after taking her school certificate she left with few regrets.

At the age of eighteen she attended a domestic science course in Eastbourne, where she was taught the rudimentary principles of running a house; learning to cook, to sew, to polish and clean, as well as completing a short course in typing and shorthand. Here she enjoyed her life, savouring her first real taste of freedom, as well as making several new friends.

During her first term, Emily shared a room with a girl called Teresa Mallory. Teresa was a year older than Emily, an attractive girl, with short, dark, curly hair and an easy outward-going personality. From the start there had been a rapport between the two girls, and what had begun with a mutual liking and respect for each other, soon developed into a firm friendship. At first Emily was puzzled where she had heard the name Mallory before, but on discovering that Teresa's home was only a few miles away, she remembered Peter's school friend Hugh.

Pretty sure that not only was his surname Mallory, but that he also lived near Eastbourne, she asked Teresa if she had a brother called Hugh.

Teresa sounded surprised. "Yes, I have. How did you know? Have you met him?" Emily told her about her first meeting with Hugh, when she had been about ten years old, and how disconcerted she had felt at the time by Hugh's somewhat cavalier manner after Peter had introduced them.

Teresa laughed. "That sounds just like Hugh! When he was in his teens he used to get terribly embarrassed at the mere idea of being seen even talking to a girl!"

"I suppose he's in the Navy?" Emily asked.

"Yes. He's a sub-lieutenant, and although I say it myself, he's really rather dashing. You must meet him sometime. We'll fix up something during the holidays."

At the end of her first term, Emily went home for Christmas. A few days later Teresa 'phoned to invite her to a party at her parents house. Peter, who was home on leave over Christmas had also been invited, and he and Emily drove over together in his recently acquired sports car. Dark green in colour, the car was his pride and joy.

Dykes Manor lay on the outskirts of a small village, tucked away in a fold of the Sussex Downs. As Peter's car drew up outside the house, Teresa came running out to meet them. She greeted Emily warmly, then shook hands with Peter.

"I'm so glad to meet you at last Peter," she said enthusiastically. "I always seem to have been away whenever you stayed with Hugh; but I've heard so much about you from both him and Emily that I feel I almost know you!"

Peter grinned at her, "I hope it hasn't put you off too much! I too have heard a great deal about you, but I think I have the advantage as Emily has shown me some snaps she took on some picnic or other."

"Oh, that would have been on Beachy Head," Teresa laughed. "I remember it was a terribly windy day, and we were blown to bits — I must have looked an absolute sight!"

"I thought you looked terrific," he replied gallantly. Teresa gave him a quick glance. She decided that she liked this charming, easy going young man.

She led them indoors, and tucking her arm through Emily's, she said, "Come and meet Mummy and Daddy. They are both dying to meet you." She turned to Peter, "I don't know whether Hugh is down yet. I last saw him standing in front of a mirror, struggling with his bow tie!"

Emily immediately liked Teresa's father. The tall, lean, grey-haired man, greeted her with an air of old world charm and courtesy. Lady Mallory was a plump comely little woman with a reassuring and gentle manner that immediately put Emily at her ease. As she regarded the enchantingly lovely young girl that stood in front of her — her hands clutching nervously at her evening bag — Lady Mallory decided that her daughter had certainly not exaggerated her description of Emily.

At eighteen, Emily closely resembled Victoria in looks. She had the same golden hair, deep blue eyes, and flawless complexion. Yet the wide, gentle smile, and sensitive expression, was essentially that of her father. Her soft, shoulder length hair was held back from her face by a broad, velvet band that matched the blue flowered chiffon frock that she wore, the simple lines of which showed to perfection her tall, slender, gently rounded figure.

Lady Mallory held out her hand towards her. "Emily my dear, we are both so glad to meet you. Teresa never seems to stop talking about you. She is forever telling us about all the things the two of you get up to together and, of course, Peter has spoken of you too, so we don't feel you are a complete stranger to us." She smiled at Emily in a kindly fashion, "You have already met Hugh I believe?"

"It was a long time ago, Lady Mallory," Emily smiled, "I think I was only about ten at the time."

"Well, I expect you will both notice quite a difference in each other," Beth Mallory laughed.

She led Emily across the cosily furnished, oak panelled room to where a huge log fire crackled cheerfully in an open fireplace, "Come and warm yourself up, my dear," Lady Mallory continued, "you must be cold after your journey, and I want to hear all about your family. You're an 'only one' I believe?" For a few minutes they talked together, until Emily saw a tall, youthful figure walking towards them across the room. She knew from his remarkable likeness to his sister, he could only be Hugh. Her rather vague recollection of Hugh all those years ago, was of a dark-haired, lanky youth, who, she remembered thinking at the time, appeared to be slightly lacking in the social graces. Meeting him now, she was totally unprepared for the charming and attractive young man, with the wide boyish grin and the mop of dark, curly hair.

Lady Mallory said, "Ah! There you are at last Hugh. Wherever have you been all this time? Emily, this is my son Hugh."

Hugh smiled at her disarmingly, "Are you really Peter's little friend Emily? The girl with the shopping basket? I hardly dare face you! I gather from Teresa that I practically cut you dead the first time

54

we met. I do apologise. Will you ever forgive me?" Their eyes met and held for an instant.

Emily blushed prettily, "As long as you promise not to do it again!"

There were a dozen or so young people at the party, some of whom Emily already knew, and after dinner they rolled back the carpet in the large, spacious hall, and danced to gramophone records. Emily spent the first part of the evening dancing with the various young men of the party.

She had just finished dancing with Peter, and was sitting talking to him while she sipped a glass of lemonade, when Hugh, after putting on another record, crossed the hall towards her, "You've been so much in demand that I began to wonder if I was ever going to get a look in!" He held out his hand to her. "Will you dance with me?" Emily took his outstretched hand. She felt his arm encircle her waist and draw her gently towards him, and for a while they danced without talking, moving smoothly together in time to the music of a slow waltz. Emily was a good dancer and found Hugh to be a no mean performer himself.

Eventually Hugh broke the silence. "You dance well," he said.

"I love dancing."

"I can see that. Did you ever have dancing lessons?"

"Not in ballroom dancing, but I used to go to ballet classes in Hurstborough once a week until I was about eight or nine."

Hugh said, "Tell me about yourself when you were small."

"There's not really very much to tell," Emily replied. "I was adopted when I was only a few weeks old, as perhaps you already know?" She raised her eyebrows enquiringly.

He nodded his head, "Teresa told me. Go on . . . "

Emily continued, "I love both my parents dearly, they've been wonderful to me. I see quite a lot of my real father, James. He's more like an uncle than anything, and we get on tremendously well together. He's terribly attractive and good looking, and I adore showing him off to my friends! He's in the Foreign

Office and is abroad most of the time. I'm so lucky," she smiled at him, "because it's almost like having three parents!" She paused for a moment, "Do you still want me to go on?"

"Yes please."

"Well, I went to boarding school when I was thirteen. Until then I shared a governess with a girl called Brenda Thomas, whose parents lived in Hurstborough. Daddy used to drop me off at their house each morning on his way to the office." At the recollection of the plump, rather plain, pig-tailed girl, with a penchant for telling tales out of school, Emily giggled. "I couldn't stand Brenda. Somehow she always reminded me of that obnoxious child Violet Elizabeth in Richmal Crompton's Just William books. Did you ever read them?"

"Indeed I did," Hugh laughed. "I had an aunt who used to give me the latest Just William book for my birthday each year! Don't stop. Tell me about how you got to know Peter."

"Well, I've known Peter all my life." Emily paused for a moment. "We live almost next door to each other and grew up together really. Then he went to Dartmouth, and later I went to boarding school. Now we see each other only when he comes home on leave, which is very sad. The rest you know. After leaving school last year I went to Eastbourne, where I met Teresa. And that's my life story in a nutshell! What about you?"

"Pretty uninteresting really. Prep school. Dartmouth and straight into the Navy as a midshipman. Father retired a few years ago now, but I can remember coming home for the hols quite often, when father was at sea and mother was here on her own. Teresa and I have always got along together very well, and we had a very happy childhood."

"What do you do in the Navy?" Emily asked him curiously.

"Well, I'm in a branch of the service known as the Fleet Air Arm. I fly aeroplanes on and off the deck of an aircraft carrier. But tell me more about yourself. What do you like doing particularly?"

They spent the rest of the evening in each others company, dancing together for most of the time, occasionally sitting down to talk, when their conversation flowed easily and naturally amid a good deal of laughter, as they shared a joke together, or recounted some amusing incident.

Once, during the evening, she said to him, "Hugh, hadn't you better dance with somebody else for a change?"

"I reckon I've done my stuff as host," he replied. "I danced at least once with everybody earlier," adding, with his attractive boyish grin, "it was all part of my plan, so that I could have you to myself for the rest of the evening!"

As they motored home later, Peter remarked dryly, "You seemed to be getting on very well with Hugh."

Emily was miles away. She replied dreamily, "Yes. He's very easy to get on with, isn't he?"

Over the following months Hugh and Emily spent much of their time together, sometimes going to London for the evening to a theatre, or to dine and dance at the Berkeley, or the Savoy. On other occasions they would go for long walks together across the downs, or simply laze around talking, or listening to records. As she watched the two of them, Mary noticed how fond they were growing of each other, and wondered if they themselves realised it.

Mary liked Hugh and considered him to be a very suitable companion for her daughter, nevertheless she was concerned whether Emily should be seeing quite so much of him, to the exclusion of the many young men who used to flock around her, like moths drawn to a candle.

When she voiced her concern to Stephen, he gently reassured her. "I shouldn't worry too much, old thing. It isn't as though Emily hasn't had ample opportunity to meet other, equally eligible young men at all those various parties she used to go to. Hugh is certainly not the first young man in her life."

Mary said rather doubtfully, "But she seems so young Stephen, to start becoming serious about anyone . . . "

Laughing, Stephen reminded her, "She's about the same age as you were, my darling, when we first met!"

4

IT was the summer of 1939. Emily had completed her domestic science course and had planned to spend the next few months visiting James in Paris where, for the last two years, he had been attached to the British Embassy. During the time he had been there, he had witnessed, with growing concern, the gradual disintegration of Europe. German forces first occupied the Rhineland, then the Saar, followed by Austria and Czechoslovakia, and recently there had been the latest threat to Poland. Towards the end of August James wrote to Mary, strongly advising against Emily's proposed visit, saying bluntly that, in his opinion, war with Germany was now inevitable.

Throughout the long, hot summer, the impending threat of war hung like a pall over the whole of Europe, dark and ominous, until on Sunday, the third of September, the Prime Minister broadcast to an expectant nation the news that Britain was now at war with Germany.

It was a week after Emily's nineteenth birthday, and she was spending the weekend with the Mallorys. Hugh, on weekend leave, was immediately recalled to his ship, leaving Emily and Teresa to discuss their own plans. Both girls had already decided that, in the event of war, they would join the Women's Royal Naval Service. Emily's decision to do so was influenced, not altogether surprisingly, by the fact that Hugh was in the Navy. Returning home the next day, she talked to her mother about her proposed plan.

"Darling, don't you think it might be advisable to wait for a few months?" Mary said, rather doubtfully. "You are only just nineteen."

"But Mummy, everyone I know is either going into one of the services or becoming a nurse, or driving an ambulance," Emily remonstrated. "Doing something useful anyway, and I'd like to feel that I can contribute something towards the war effort too. After all," she reminded Mary, "you worked with the

Red Cross during the last war, didn't you? Please Mummy, do say it's alright."

Mary realised that she was fighting a losing battle and gave in without further argument. Although she was sad at the thought of Emily leaving home quite so soon, she understood how she felt.

Signing on at a recruiting centre, Emily and Teresa joined the WRNS as ratings, and were sent to HMS Arthur in Skegness. Here Emily found herself ensconced behind a typewriter, from whence she dealt with leave passes, daily orders and such like while Teresa was employed as a steward in the wardroom. A few months later they applied to go on an Officers' Training Course and were sent to Greenwich, where after six weeks' training, Teresa was posted to the north of England, and Emily joined the Royal Naval Establishment in Sheerness.

For the first few months of the war Hugh had been stationed at a naval base in Scotland. Emily had seen him on only two or three occasions, and then very briefly. During the time they had known each other, the happy and carefree relationship that there had always been between them had, with Emily, grown into something far deeper. She knew that she cared for him a great deal. She was also fairly sure that Hugh felt the same way as she did. She pieced together the fragments of conversation they had had, unimportant at the time, but significant in retrospect. She recalled how, on occasions when glancing up, she had caught him watching her with a look in his eyes that had made her heart leap. And then there were his letters . . . reading between the lines, they left her in little doubt about how he felt towards her. They were not love letters in the accepted sense, more letters of love, and Emily treasured them as the only tangible evidence of his feelings for her. She was unable to understand why he said nothing, and began to wonder if, like some of her friends, he had reservations about wartime marriages. Her moods alternated between happiness and bleak despair, and she longed to be able to talk to someone about how she felt, but she knew that this was something she could not discuss with anyone.

Matters finally resolved themselves,

when early in 1940, they were able to synchronise their leave, and Emily and Hugh went to Sussex for the weekend. Staying with their respective parents, they planned to spend the whole of the next day together. It was a cold, blustery March morning when Hugh collected Emily in his car and they drove off together in the direction of the coast. They parked the car and, hand in hand, climbed the steep path that led up on to the downs. After walking in silence for a while, for once neither of them having anything to say to the other, Hugh stopped abruptly in his tracks. He looked down at the sweet, innocent young face that gazed up at him from under its red woolly cap. He noticed with a feeling of anguish, her strained expression, and the troubled look in her eyes.

Firmly resisting the impulse to gather her in his arms and once and for all dispel her doubts and fears, he said instead, simply and honestly, in the only way he knew how, "I love you Emily. I want to marry you more than anything I've ever wanted in my life. Will you marry me?"

Her eyes brimmed with tears. "Oh Hugh, my darling, darling Hugh. If only you knew how much I've wanted to hear you say that."

He folded her in his arms and drew her towards him and standing on the bare, open downland, while all around them the wind blew in great gusts, and the gulls screeched overhead, they kissed for the first time. Gently, tenderly, his lips lingering on hers . . . and for one brief moment in their lives, time stood still.

★ ★ ★

Hugh and Emily decided on a short engagement, but their plans were overtaken by events of far greater importance. In May 1940, France was invaded by the Germans. The British Expeditionary Force was driven back towards the French coast, and in a massive operation, involving not only ships of the Royal Navy, but a veritable fleet of every imaginable type of sea-going craft, thousands of allied troops were evacuated from the bombed and blasted beaches of Dunkirk. All leave was cancelled while the army was reformed and the country waited expectantly for Hitler's forces to invade its shores. It was July when Hugh and Emily were finally married in the small church in Applefold, with just their immediate family and a few close friends present.

After a brief honeymoon, Hugh rejoined his ship and Emily returned to Sheerness.

By then the Battle of Britain had begun. All through that beautiful summer, the cloudless blue skies were criss-crossed with ribbons of white as, in an all-out offensive on the United Kingdom, German bombers flew in their hundreds across the coastline of Britain, their main objective to demolish and obliterate our airfields. But relentlessly intercepted and pursued by RAF fighter planes, the Germans suffered heavy losses, and gradually the tide began to turn, until a few months later the Battle of Britain was finally won, although at a tremendous cost.

Hugh's ship, the aircraft carrier HMS Formidable, was on operations in the Mediterranean. Towards the end of 1941 Emily was posted to the Admiralty.

Working in the operations room, she had access to information concerning the movement of ships, and knew at any given time the whereabouts of Hugh's ship, and of the dangers to which he was exposed.

Tense and anxious, she went about her work calmly and professionally, but her mind was in a constant turmoil of fear and apprehension. At sea, the convoys of merchant ships and their naval escorts, made easy targets for the German U-boats as they plied their way across the Atlantic, and the toll on both men and ships was enormous. Emily knew that Peter's ship, the destroyer Vehement, was engaged on escort duty, and this only helped increase her anxiety.

At home, the air raids on London and other big cities, continued unceasingly. The incendiary and high explosive bombs dropped by the Germans, not only devastated vast areas of what had once been shops and offices, privates houses, historic buildings, and even churches and hospitals, but caused untold hardship and suffering to the people of Britain. Thousands of families spent each night in London's underground stations, not knowing whether their homes would still be standing the following morning, or be nothing more than a pile of rubble. Yet up and down the country, the mood that prevailed was one of courage and fortitude, humour and cheerfulness, and a great sense of camaraderie between total strangers, drawn together by mutual suffering and misfortune.

The only person to whom Emily could turn during those anxious and difficult days, was James.

★ ★ ★

James had been recalled to London from the Embassy in Paris, shortly after the Germans had marched into France, and was now working in the Foreign Office. Soon after his return, he moved back into his old flat in Marlborough Court, gave Emily a key, and suggested that she used the flat whenever she wished. Emily found the peace and quiet of his comfortable home a welcome change from the rather austere surroundings of her own quarters. Understanding her anxiety over Hugh, James did his best to take her mind off her problems; sometimes taking her to the theatre, or out to dinner in a restaurant. On other occasions, they would have a quiet supper together in his flat, Emily cooking them a meal from whatever was available in the larder.

James often pondered on the strange way in which things had worked out in his itinerant and varied life. It was now over twenty years since Victoria's death and the time, when after much soul-searching, he had taken the momentous decision that was to affect Emily's whole future. In arranging for Stephen and Mary to adopt his small, motherless baby, he had automatically given up all claim to the child that had been the fruit of his and Victoria's love. Yet, in the end, fate had smiled kindly on him. Now, all these years later, there was a deep affection between the young woman, who reminded James so poignantly of her mother, and the ageing yet still distinguished looking man, who was her father.

Apart from spending quite a bit of the

time when she was off duty with James, Emily also had the occasional glimpse of Peter, usually when he was on his way home for a few days leave in between convoys. She derived great comfort and pleasure from their meetings. He was the one dependable link with her old life, and they spent many happy hours in each other's company, talking over old times, and laughing together as they recalled various childhood memories. But there had been a period before her marriage, when, on the few occasions on which they had met, Emily had been conscious of a slight change in Peter's manner towards her.

At the time she had been puzzled and somewhat curious as to what had initiated this change in their once easy and companionable relationship, and had mentioned the matter to Teresa, who, raising her eyebrows, had looked at her friend a little quizzically.

"It's not altogether surprising Emmy, the man's in love with you."

With a look of astonishment on her face, Emily exclaimed, "Whatever do you mean?"

71

Teresa saw from Emily's expression that she was obviously unaware of Peter's feeling towards her. She said gently, "Didn't you know?"

Shaking her head, Emily replied in a bewildered voice, "He can't be Teresa, you must be imagining it."

"But he is, darling," Teresa insisted. "You can take it from me, and with you and Hugh seeing quite so much of each other, it's bound to have altered things between you."

Emily was still unconvinced. "How do you know he's in love with me? Has he said anything to you?"

"No," replied Teresa. "He hasn't actually said anything, but it is quite obvious to anyone how he feels about you."

The conversation had left Emily feeling thoroughly disconcerted, and not a little saddened to realise that by being so engrossed in her own affairs, she had failed to understand the reason for Peter's change of manner. Looking back, she realised it had all begun with the party at the Mallory's house the Christmas before the war. Emily had known at the time that she had hurt and upset Peter by having spent so much of the evening with Hugh. Then, as she began to see more and more of Hugh in the ensuing months, Peter had gradually faded into the background without her realising it. For as long as she could remember, Emily had always looked upon Peter as a much loved, older brother, taking it for granted that he felt much the same way about her. It had never occurred to her that either of them could feel differently towards the other. But Peter had cared for Emily from the time she was a child. He had watched her grow into a beautiful young woman, and without realising it, had fallen deeply in love with her.

Peter had been through a difficult time during the months that followed that fateful Christmas party. He had stood by helplessly as he watched Hugh and Emily grow more and more fond of each other, in what he felt could only be a prelude to falling in love. It had taken Hugh's arrival on the scene for Peter to realise how much he loved her, by which time it was too late. Emily, caught up in her own affairs, appeared to have forgotten his very existence; but since her marriage, Peter had gradually begun to accept the fact that there was now no hope for him. He had put aside his own feelings, determined not to let his love for her interfere with their friendship, and gradually their slightly strained relations had returned to normal.

★ ★ ★

Emily was coming out of her office one morning, when a familiar voice hailed her from down the corridor.

"Em?"

Swinging round on her heels, she exclaimed delightedly, "Peter!"

"I thought it was you," said Peter, "but you girls all seem to look alike from behind in your uniform!"

Emily laughed happily, "How lovely to see you but why didn't you let me know you were coming? We might have missed each other, I was just on my way out to lunch."

"It's only the briefest of visits," Peter replied, "I had to make a quick dash up to London this morning, and I have to

74

get back right away. But I've got time for a quick lunch and was on my way to your office to see if you were free."

They lunched together at a nearby restaurant, and afterwards took a taxi to Waterloo, where Emily saw him off on a train for Portsmouth. For the last few weeks he had been on a course at HMS Dryad, the naval school of navigation. Emily was thankful that he was no longer engaged in escort duty and felt that it was one less thing she had to worry about.

★ ★ ★

America had now been in the war for eighteen months and London particularly was full of GIs. Fresh faced young men who, with their plentiful pay packets and generous gifts of chocolate and nylon stockings, quickly won their way into the affections of many of the wives and sweethearts of British servicemen. By the middle of 1943 the war situation had began to change for the better. The navy had achieved supremacy at sea. The bombing raids on Germany had caused extensive damage to war production lines, as well as to many of the bigger cities. Following a successful campaign in North Africa, the British and American armies had landed in Europe, and after heavy fighting at Anzio, were making their way through Italy. But on the home front there was still more to come. Later that year Hitler disclosed his 'secret weapon'. The V1s or doodle bugs, as they became known, were followed later by the considerably more formidable V2 rockets, which, launched from the Dutch coast, were aimed at London in a further attempt to undermine the morale of the British people. But, with no aiming device on board, they often fell wide of their target, and landed indiscriminately, killing thousands of civilians, as well as causing further damage and destruction. Daily life was disrupted for everyone by the constant bombing and the strict rationing of food, clothing and many of the other day to day commodities that had once been taken for granted.

Towards the end of that year Hugh had three weeks leave, and he and Emily returned to the small hotel in the Cotswolds where they had spent their brief honeymoon. It was late autumn. The trees had almost lost their leaves and each morning the ground was covered with a light layer of frost. But the days were warm and bright, with clear blue skies and brilliant sunshine as hand-in-hand they wandered across the bracken-covered hill sides, blissfully happy in each others company, the war forgotten.

And Emily became pregnant.

5

JAMES was in his office one morning when his secretary announced over the intercom, "Mrs. Mallory on the telephone, Sir, shall I put her through?"

"Please," he replied, and on hearing the connection said, "Is that you Emmy?"

"Yes, James." There was an underlying note of excitement in Emily's voice as she continued. "Sorry to disturb you, but I wondered if we could have dinner together this evening, if you are not doing anything else?"

"Of course we can," James answered, "I will pick you up and we will go straight out to dinner. What time are you off duty?"

Emily hesitated, "Would you mind awfully, if we had something to eat at your flat? I've got something I want to tell you and it's easier to talk there."

"Whatever you like, darling," he replied, "but I can still collect you on my way back."

"Thank you James, that would be lovely, I'm off duty at six o'clock, if that's all right?"

After they had finished supper James leant back in his chair and lit his pipe. "Now, what's so important that I have to put up with reconstituted scrambled eggs for supper, instead of being allowed to take you out to some exclusive restaurant?" He drew on his pipe. With a twinkle in his eye he went on, "You know I enjoy being the envy of every other man in the room, with such an elegant and beautiful young woman on my arm!"

Emily threw back her head and laughed. "James you really are an awful old flatterer!" But unable to keep the news to herself any longer she announced delightedly, "I'm going to have a baby! Is that sufficiently important?"

James was taken aback for a moment. His reaction was one of surprise and disbelief. "Good grief, are you really?"

"Yes, darling," she laughed, "I am, really, isn't it wonderful? Hugh is exactly like a puppy with two tails at the thought of becoming a father!"

Emily looked so happy that all James could find to say was "I think it's splendid news, Emmy. I'm so glad for you both. How did Stephen and Mary react to the prospect of becoming grandparents?"

"I've only spoken to them over the 'phone so far," Emily replied, "but they sounded terribly thrilled." Then, in a more serious tone she continued, "James, I want this baby so badly. If something should happen to Hugh . . . " James heard a choke in her voice. He gave her a quick glance. He saw her hand go up to her face as if to brush away a tear. His heart went out to her. For all her smart uniform and confident appearance, he thought fondly, she looked absurdly young and vulnerable as she sat curled up in a corner of the sofa, in exactly the same way as Victoria had liked to sit.

His voice was gentle as he replied, "I understand how you feel, Emmy, but you mustn't allow yourself to dwell on such morbid possibilities. After all, the losses at sea have been negligible over the past months. It is only a matter of time now before this bloody war is over and you'll have Hugh home again safe and sound," he ended with forced cheerfulness.

Emily smiled tremulously. "You always seem to say the right thing, James. I suppose that's the diplomat in you! You are quite right, of course, I'm being an idiot."

"Nonsense," he replied, with a good natured laugh. "Your anxiety is perfectly understandable. Now put your coat on. I'm taking you home. I heard the all clear sound five minutes ago."

* * *

The baby was not expected until the following July, but towards the end of April Emily received her discharge from the WRNS. In many ways she was sad at the thought of leaving for she knew that she was going to miss the friends she had made, as well as the way of life to which she had grown accustomed. She had also found the work interesting and it had kept her in close touch with what was going on in the war. She had been aware for some time of the preparations that were being made for a second front. Suddenly she was without any information as to how things were progressing. She also discovered to her dismay that she was now no longer able to check on Hugh's whereabouts.

When she arrived home, Mary greeted her fondly, telling her how well she looked, but she noticed at the same time, the dark shadows under her eyes and the strain that showed on her face. Stephen held her in his arms and hugged her and Mrs. Soames, now in her mid-sixties, came bustling forward, her arms outstretched in welcome. Happy and contented to be back in the peaceful and familiar surroundings of her old home, Emily submitted gratefully to being spoiled and fussed over by both Mary and Mrs. Soames.

It took Emily a week or two to settle into her new life. She soon found that everything had changed very considerably since the start of the war. Mrs. Soames was still in charge in the kitchen, although the meals she produced, based largely on rather strange Ministry of Food recipes, were very different from the appetising and extravagant dishes she had been used to preparing in pre-war days. After living in the mess, where food rationing as such was barely noticeable, Emily was shocked by the small amount of food obtainable on a civilian ration book. Going down to the butcher's shop for Mary one morning, she returned home with a small lump of meat, which apparently was the week's ration for four people.

When she asked Mrs. Soames how she managed for the rest of the week, she replied in a cheerful voice, "We do all right, Miss Emily. There's always a bit of corned beef to fall back on and Mr. Robinson always lets us have a bit of offal when he's got it to spare."

Lily had long since departed and was working in a munitions factory, where she was paid a wage that was considerably more than she had ever dreamed of earning in her days as a house-parlour maid. Nowadays Mary did all the housework and Stephen, in between his office work and organising the air raid precautions in Hurstborough, gave Jessop a hand in the garden, doing most of the hard work himself, as the old man was almost beyond it.

Several changes had been made about

the house since Emily was a child. Mains electricity had replaced the warm glow of oil lamps, and instead of the cheerful log fires that used to burn in all the downstairs rooms, a central heating system had been installed. Now, with insufficient fuel to keep the central heating boiler functioning, the house was often bitterly cold in winter, relying on electric fires to keep the chill off. In the kitchen, Mrs. Soames' coal range had been replaced by an electric cooker and since then she had never stopped complaining of how much she missed her old range, in spite of the hours of hard work she had had to spend on keeping it black-leaded and polished.

It distressed Emily to see her parents working quite so hard — Mary, as well as running the house, did voluntary work several days a week — but Emily soon began to realise that that was how things were in civilian life these days. Most people were doing jobs of one sort or another, and her respect for the uncomplaining way in which everyone went about their particular task, increased by the day, and made her feel that during the four years she had been in the Wrens, she had had it easy by comparison.

Emily had been at home for over a month, and some of the signs of tension were beginning to leave her face, although at seven months pregnant she was starting to find the extra weight she was carrying a little irksome. She felt like a huge porpoise as she waddled about the place, slow and ungainly. She did what she could to help in the house, preparing the vegetables for Mrs. Soames, assisting with the washing up and helping Mary with the housework, as well as giving Stephen a hand in the garden, dead-heading the flowers and cutting the edges.

Emily was upstairs in her bedroom one morning, sorting out her baby clothes and delighting in the tiny garments that she had knitted: little matinee coats, bootees and mittens, beautiful crocheted shawls, and long, soft Irish linen night-dresses, that she herself had worn as a baby.

There was a tap on the door, and Mary called out, "Emily?"

"Yes Mummy. Come in."

As Mary opened the door, Emily held up a little smocked tunic that she had been given by Teresa, "Isn't it sweet, Mummy," she exclaimed, "I can't wait to see him wearing it."

From the start, Emily had always referred to her expected baby as a boy, quite convinced that that was what it would be.

Mary stood silently in the doorway. Her face looked pinched and drawn. Then walking towards Emily, she put her arm around her shoulders, and said to her in a quiet, controlled voice, "Come and sit down for a moment, darling. I want to talk to you."

She led Emily towards a small armchair that stood by the window. She drew up the dressing stool and sat down opposite her. Holding both Emily's hands in her own, she said, "I'm afraid I have some bad news for you. A Captain Lewis from the Admiralty has just rung up. He thought you would rather hear from him than by telegram. He asked me to tell you that Hugh . . . " She took a deep breath. "Emily, darling, there is no way I can say this that will make it any easier for you . . . I'm afraid Hugh has been killed in a plane accident."

Ashen faced, Emily said slowly, "What happened?" As Mary hesitated, she insisted, "Tell me, Mummy. I want to know."

Mary replied in a faltering voice, "It seems that after landing on the deck of the aircraft carrier, his plane skidded and went over the side."

6

EMILY lay in the narrow, white hospital bed. The shock of Hugh's death had brought on a premature birth, and the baby, a boy, weighing under four pounds, had lived for only a few days before giving up the unequal struggle for existence. The child had spent its brief life in an incubator and Emily had never so much as held him in her arms.

Her mind was still unable to absorb anything other than the fact that she had lost Hugh. She returned home at the end of a fortnight in hospital, looking pale and drawn, but outwardly calm and composed. Within a week of coming home, she resumed her jobs about the house, explaining to Mary when she remonstrated with her to take things easily for a little while longer, that she would prefer to keep busy. Mary felt a sense of bleak despair as she watched Emily go through each day as though the double tragedy of losing both her husband and her child had never happened. She knew that if only Emily could give way to her grief, instead of keeping such a tight rein on herself, it would help to release some of her pent up emotions and act as a safety valve.

Concerned and anxious about her daughter, Mary spoke to Andrew Stuart, who had been keeping an eye on Emily since her return from hospital.

Andrew sympathetically reassured her. "She's still in a state of shock, Mary. Give her time. We all deal with tragedy in our lives in a different way. Perhaps Emily finds it easier to block out of her mind what has happened, until she feels she can cope with it. Let her play it in her own way for a little while longer. She's young and resilient and she's got a lot of courage. She'll pull through. Time is a great healer," he added, giving Mary an affectionate smile. "You know, Mary, I've known Emily since she was a few weeks old, and I love her almost as much as if she were my own daughter. Between you and me, I must admit to having once entertained hopes that she and Peter might have married." He smiled reminiscently, then, returning to his professional manner he continued, "But besides being the little girl that I've known all her life, she is also my patient, and my advice to you is to give her time, plenty of time, and a great deal of love and understanding." He added as a practical afterthought,"You might also try giving her a glass of stout each day. It's a good tonic and helps the appetite. She needs to put on a bit of weight."

As Andrew made his way to the door, he said kindly, "Try not to worry too much, Mary my dear, otherwise I shall soon be including you on my visiting list!" Comforted by what he had said, Mary took his advice. She was more than prepared to give Emily all the time she needed to come to terms with the situation in her own way.

Then, early one morning, as Mary crossed the landing outside Emily's bedroom, she heard loud, tormented sobs coming from the room. Shocked at first by the intensity of Emily's grief, she then experienced an enormous sense of relief that the flood gates had finally opened and that Emily was at last able to give way to her feelings. Mary waited for the weeping to subside a little before quietly opening the door and going inside. Emily lay in her bed, her body racked by sobs, her eyes red and swollen. Mary sat down beside her and gently stroked the long, fair hair that lay on the pillow in a tangled mass.

The weeping gradually ceased and before long Emily sat up. She threw herself into her mother's arms and said in a pitiful voice, "Oh Mummy, what am I going to do? I can't go on without Hugh. I know I can't."

Mary held her in her arms, and replied, comfortingly and reassuringly, "Yes you can, darling, and you will, because you know that that is what Hugh would want you to do."

★ ★ ★

Early in August Teresa took a few days leave and went to visit her sister-in-law. Worried by Emily's withdrawn and listless manner, she was at a loss to know how to help her friend, until she learnt from Mary how Emily had refused to leave the house, other than going into the village. Teresa decided that perhaps what was needed more than anything was a complete change of scene, to take Emily out of herself and to help to stimulate her mind.

One morning over breakfast she said cheerfully, "Emmy, what do you think about a day out in Eastbourne as an idea? I haven't been there for ages and I don't suppose you have either."

She watched Emily's face for any sign or reaction. "I know! Why don't we go to buy you a new dress. I can remember you wearing the one you've got on at the moment when we were at college. It must be years old! I've got plenty of clothing coupons to spare," she added, "so that's no problem!"

Mary noticed Emily's reluctance to agree to Teresa's suggestion. She quickly intervened, saying, "I agree with Teresa, darling. It's high time you had something new." Then, as if suddenly struck by an idea, she went on. "Well, if you two girls are going to Eastbourne, perhaps you would be kind enough to take a clock that needs repairing to the jewellers for me?"

"Yes, of course we will, Mrs. Larby," Teresa replied, adding after a quick glance at Emily, "That is if Emmy would like to go?"

Emily finally agreed, albeit a trifle reluctantly. "We'll take the clock with us, Mummy, but I really don't want a new dress."

"Oh yes you do," Teresa insisted, "and what's more, we're going to buy you one." Then, tucking her arm through Emily's, she said cheerfully, "It will be like old times, going shopping together, won't it?"

They bought a pretty, suitable everyday dress, with the usual 'Utility' label inside and before lunching at Bobby's, they deposited the clock for repair. Then they went for a walk along the sea front, noticing with dismay, the concrete blocks and barbed wire entanglements all along the beach.

The day out did Emily good. She returned home with colour in her cheeks and a more lively expression on her face, and that night she slept better than she had done for a long time. It was her first step back into the world.

★ ★ ★

Although Emily had been married to Hugh for nearly four years, the time they had actually spent together under the same roof, totalled little more than a year. They had once rented a small flat in London for a short time while Hugh was working at Greenwich. But apart from that, there had been no more than a few brief intervals when, managing to get leave at the same time, they had usually spent what time they had together with one or other of their respective parents. She had loved Hugh deeply and passionately and now, several weeks after his death, she was only just beginning to come to terms with the fact that the one bright shining moment that had been her life with Hugh, was now over, gone forever. Gradually, she began to realise just how much the tragedy of Hugh's death, as well as that of their baby, had also affected the people around her. Hugh's parents had lost their only son and Teresa her beloved brother. Then there were her own parents, who had given her so much love and support throughout the last few difficult weeks. With a troubled conscience she sought out her mother.

Mary had just returned from a morning's shopping in Hurstborough. She had queued patiently for some foodstuffs, only to discover that by the time she had reached the head of the queue the shop had sold out. As Mary sank wearily into a chair, Emily was filled with compassion to see how tired she looked.

"Mummy," she began. "I've only just realised how selfish I have been all these weeks. I've thought only of myself and how Hugh's death affected me." She paused briefly, unable to bring herself to refer to the loss of the tiny baby who had lived for so short a time. She took a deep breath and continued.

"I know how fond you were of Hugh and how much you and Daddy were looking forward to becoming grandparents. It has only just dawned on me how awful all this must be for you too."

Mary opened her mouth to say

something, but Emily went on, with a trace of urgency in her voice, "I must get in touch with Admiral and Lady Mallory. Do you think it would be a good idea if I invited myself to stay with them for a few days?"

"I think it is an excellent idea if you feel confident that it won't put too great a strain on you, darling." Mary replied, "I'm sure they would love to have you and would enormously appreciate a visit from you."

Accordingly plans were made for Emily to spend a few nights at Dykes Manor. But, despite the kindness and understanding shown to her by the Mallorys, Emily found the visit a considerable ordeal. The familiar surroundings, so closely connected with Hugh; the nostalgic memories; the wedding photographs of them both in uniform and the constant references to Hugh by his parents, was almost more than she could bear. Back at home, she broke down in Mary's comforting arms and sobbed her heart out.

Eventually, wiping her eyes and blowing her nose, she said in a strained voice,

"It's no good, Mummy. I've got to get away. Right away from everything that is associated with Hugh. I've been thinking about it for a while now, and I would like to find some sort of a job — anything to keep my mind occupied."

Mary was concerned yet understanding. "I dare say you're right, darling. Perhaps that would be the best thing for you. Have you anything special in mind?"

"My only training is secretarial, so I suppose that is what it will have to be, although I don't particularly want to spend the rest of my life sitting behind a typewriter," Emily replied.

Mary was anxious to be helpful. "Well, it's a good idea. We'll talk to Daddy about it this evening and see if he can suggest anything."

In the end it was James who came up with a solution to Emily's problems. A few days later he came to stay for the weekend. He was thankful to see Emily looking slightly better than the last time he had seen her, soon after her return from hospital. Emily told him of her decision to find some kind of job.

After a moment's deliberation, he said

"I think perhaps I may be able to help, if it's secretarial work you want. A colleague of mine in the Foreign Office is about to lose his present secretary — she's getting married, I believe — and I know he's having a bit of difficulty in replacing her. Leave it to me and I'll see what I can do when I get back to the office on Monday."

Emily, looked cheerful for the first time in weeks. "James you're wonderful! Thank you so much. It sounds exactly what I want."

He laughed, "Don't count your chickens just yet!"

Privately, James was relieved to hear of Emily's decision. He had felt for some time that she ought to get away from the slightly claustrophobic atmosphere of village life, where not only did she lack the companionship of people of her own age, but where also there was singularly little to stimulate her mind. He felt the time had come when she needed to stand on her own feet again and start planning a new life for herself. His first job on returning to London was to get in touch with his friend Gerald Masters. Using all his powers of persuasion he finally got him to agree to employ Emily. A short time later Emily started work at the Foreign Office. Gerald, a contemporary of James, was a quiet, kindly man, with a grown up family of his own and treated Emily in much the same way as he did his own daughter.

Emily spent the week days in James' flat and the weekends in Applefold. Her life began to fall into a routine. She found that concentrating on her work helped her to put her personal problems to the back of her mind. Encouraged by James, she contacted some of her old friends, until, very gradually, she began to discover a returning interest in life.

On the 6th June 1944, the day that was to become known in history as D Day, Operation Overlord began with the landing of more than 160,000 Allied troops on the French coast in Normandy. The second front had begun. A year later the war in Europe was over and VE Day was celebrated up and down the country. Meanwhile, hostilities with Japan continued until, in a bid to end the war in the Pacific, American planes dropped atomic bombs on the cities of Hiroshima and Nagasaki and finally brought to an end nearly six years of killing and bloodshed, devastation and ruin, as well as untold hardship and suffering to millions of people all over the world.

★ ★ ★

It was a swelteringly hot day towards the end of August. Emily, travelling home for the weekend as usual, was thankful to be able to escape from the stifling heat of London to the comparative cool of the country.

She arrived hot and exhausted and was met by Mary, who greeted her daughter fondly, saying, "How lovely to have you home again, darling."

Kissing her, Emily said, "It's good to be home, Mummy. London is very hot and sticky at the moment. How's Daddy?"

"He's well," Mary replied. "But I wish he would stop working quite so hard. He seems to get so tired these days. Oh! before I forget," she went on, "Peter rang up a short while ago to say he'll be round to see you later on this evening — he's home on leave I gather. I asked him if he'd like to come to supper — we're having one of Mrs. Soames' nice macaroni cheeses," she added inconsequentially, "but he said he would rather come round later, so I told him I would let you know as soon as you got home."

"Thank you Mummy," Emily replied, "I'll just pop up and change out of these clothes and I'll be down in a moment."

Emily rummaged through her wardrobe for the coolest thing she could find to wear. She unearthed an old, faded, blue sleeveless cotton frock — a remnant of her teenage days. She combed her hair, powdered her nose and after a quick glance at her reflection in the mirror, she ran down the stairs, and crossing the hall, pushed open the green baize door that led to the kitchen.

She poked her head inside and said cheerfully, "Hello, Mrs. Soames."

Mrs. Soames, looked hot and flushed. She replied in a weary voice, "Good evening, Miss Emily." She was about to pick up a heavily laden tray, when Emily stepped forward.

"Here let me carry that for you, Mrs. Soames."

Gratefully she let Emily take the heavy wooden tray from her, murmuring "It's this hot weather, Miss Emily, that's what it is."

Supper over, Emily cleared away and did the washing up and then disappeared into the garden where she sat rocking herself slowly backwards and forwards on the swing lounge while she waited for Peter. Dusk was beginning to fall by the time he arrived.

She heard his footsteps on the gravel drive and called out, "Hello Peter. I'm in the garden." She watched his tall, slim figure walk towards her with an easy, swinging gait. Over the years his fair hair had darkened slightly and his once lanky frame had filled out and matured. As he greeted her, Emily noticed that his usual cheerful smile was absent from his face. Almost abruptly he said, "Let's walk. I want to talk to you."

He seemed unusually quiet and preoccupied as they strolled down the garden towards the orchard, their arms linked companionably.

Pulling an apple off a tree as he went by, Peter began, "Em. I'm being sent out to Washington in a few weeks time, as an instructor on naval control of shipping."

Emily stopped in her tracks. She exclaimed excitedly, "Peter, that's wonderful news. Does it mean promotion? How long will you be there?"

"It's a two year appointment," Peter replied with a smile, "and yes, it does mean promotion."

"I am so glad for you," Emily said, "I'm sure you'll have a wonderful time out there. Oh, but I'm going to miss you! You will keep in touch won't you?"

"Yes, of course I will."

He stood there staring into the distance, apparently absorbed in his own thoughts. Emily realised that there was more on his mind than he had told her.

She asked gently, "Peter, what is it? What's worrying you?"

Facing her, he said in a low, subdued voice, "Emily, I wouldn't be saying this to you if this posting hadn't come up. I've never told you before, but I love you very

103

much." Searching for the right words, he continued, "This is not something new, I've loved you for as long as I can remember . . . I realise it's early days yet as far as you're concerned, but do you think that in say, a year or two you might consider getting married again?"

He looked at her entreatingly, as he went on, "We know each other so well Em, and we've always got on so well together, will you at least think about it?"

Surprised and deeply touched, in a voice full of compassion, she replied gently, "Darling Peter. I wish I could say yes, but I don't think I will ever want to get married again. I love you too, but not in the way you would want me to if we were married." She looked into his eyes. "I look upon you as the best friend I have ever had and apart from the short time I had with Hugh, the happiest moments in my life have been the ones we've spent together."

She saw the hurt and sadness in his face, "Peter, I haven't meant to hurt you. I've known for years that you were once in love with me — although I must admit

I thought that you had got over it — but I'm too fond of you to let you go off to America, believing that in a couple of years time I might have changed my mind, because I really mean it — I don't think I shall every marry again."

From the house Mary had watched the two of them walking down the garden together, arm in arm.

Twenty minutes later she saw them return, walking separately, a world apart, and she knew that any hope she may have had of Emily and Peter finding happiness together was no more than an over indulgence of wishful thinking on her part.

Part Two

1945 – 1950

Part Two

1945 – 1950

7

IT was now over a year since Hugh's death. With the resilience of youth, Emily's natural zest for life had begun to return. The war finally at an end, she had started to consider seriously what she was going to do with the rest of her life. Her present job, for which she knew she would always be grateful to Gerald Masters, had served its purpose, but it was now time to move on. Lately she had become conscious of a growing desire to find a home of her own in which to live; somewhere in which she could let her roots down and establish her own way of life. Consulting her bank balance, she decided she could afford to leave her present job and concentrate on looking for a small flat.

Now that she had reached a decision, she felt that she owed it to James to at least talk things over with him. Accordingly she waited until he had lit his pipe and settled himself comfortably in his chair one evening before broaching the subject.

"James," she began, a little diffidently, "would you understand if I told you I've decided to try and find a place of my own in which to live?"

James drew on his pipe, "Of course I would understand," he replied calmly. "It's perfectly natural to want to be independent and if you want my opinion, I think it's a very sensible decision!"

"Thank you for being so understanding about it," she said gratefully, "I would hate to have upset you in any way. You've been so marvellous putting up with me all these months as it is, and I really am tremendously grateful."

"Nonsense," he replied brusquely, "you know perfectly well how much I've enjoyed having you, even if you do bully the life out of me from time to time!" Then in a more serious tone he asked, "What were you thinking of, a small flat?"

"That's what I had in mind", she replied. "I've been looking through the advertising columns in the papers and there seem to be quite a few flats going.

I rather thought I would like to live in the Kensington area, what do you think?"

"It's certainly central," he replied, "and a nice part of London in which to live. There are several blocks of flats in that area that went up just before the war, which might be suitable. I should feel inclined to get in touch with an estate agent if I were you."

"Yes, perhaps I will," Emily answered. There was a note of concern in her voice, as she went on, "James, do you think that it will upset Mummy and Daddy if I stop going home every weekend as I'm doing at present? The last thing I want to do is to hurt them, but when I get my own home, I don't think I shall want to keep dashing off to the country every weekend."

"Oh, they'll understand alright," James said reassuringly, "they will soon get used to the idea of not seeing quite so much of you. But Emmy, you won't want to be on your own the whole time, you know, you must get away now and again."

He noticed the anxious expression on her face. "I shouldn't worry about it too

111

much, these things have a way of sorting themselves out."

★ ★ ★

Early in September, Emily left the Foreign Office. With time now to concentrate on looking for somewhere to live, she sought advice from a firm of estate agents whom James had recommended. Within a few weeks she had found an unfurnished, second floor flat in Milford Court, a small, unpretentious block of flats in a quiet road, not far from Kensington High Street. The flat faced west and consisted of a small entrance hall, a sitting room, a bedroom, a bathroom and a tiny kitchen. And to Emily it was paradise.

Once Mary had grown accustomed to the idea that Emily had decided to set up house on her own, she was full of helpful and practical suggestions. She offered Emily the contents of one of the large spare bedrooms at Wisteria House, saying laughingly that it would be one less room for her to have to dust and a short time later, a small van arrived outside Milford

Court containing everything that Emily required to furnish her new home. As she looked around she reflected, not for the first time, how very fortunate she was in having such understanding parents. She knew how disappointed they were that they would no longer have her weekend visits to look forward to, but having accepted her decision, like James, they had given her their full support.

Mary though, had enquired with a note of anxiety in her voice, "Darling, how are you going to manage financially with only your widow's pension?" She glanced towards Stephen as she went on, "We would so like to help, wouldn't we Stephen?"

"Thank you, Mummy," Emily said gratefully, "but I've saved up quite a lot while I've been living in James' flat with no expenses and James has been terribly kind. He has given me a very generous cheque, which he says is to celebrate the fact that he has managed to get rid of me at last! But thank you both all the same. I promise I'll let you know if I get into difficulties. Once I find a job, I'm sure I'll be all right," she ended cheerfully.

Emily was walking along Kensington High Street one morning when she came to a halt outside a small shop called the Picture Gallery. Peering through the window at a painting she had noticed several time recently as she had passed by, she decided to go in and have a closer look. As she opened the door a young man came forward from the back of the shop.

"Good morning, Madam, can I help you?"

Emily smiled at him. "I would really like to browse around for a bit if I may?"

"Certainly, Madam," the young man replied civilly. "Please let me know if I can be of any assistance."

Emily walked over to where the picture rested on a stand. It was a painting of a small village, built high on a mountainside, in what she imagined to be a Mediterranean country — Southern France, or Spain, perhaps. The small, white-washed houses reflected the brilliance of the sunshine. The lower hills, green and verdant, gave way to barren rock as the mountain rose steeply from the valley, from where a blue haze drifted across the landscape like a soft veil. In the foreground, a narrow road, bleached by the sun, wound its tortuous way up the mountainside, disappearing from view as it reached its final destination. The picture reminded her vividly of a holiday she had spent with her parents in the South of France, when she was in her teens. It stirred many nostalgic memories.

Her thoughts were interrupted by a voice behind her saying, "You seem to be particularly interested in that picture?"

With a half glance over a shoulder, Emily replied, "I think it's lovely. The colours are so beautiful. It has a tremendous atmosphere about it."

Then turning round she gave an apologetic laugh and with a slightly sheepish grin on her face, she said, "I'm so sorry. I'm afraid I got a little carried away! Actually, I'm looking for something to hang over the mantelpiece in my flat. I've noticed this picture each time I've gone past the shop and I couldn't resist having a closer look at it, although," she ended a little disconsolately, "I'm afraid it's rather beyond my means."

The man she addressed whom she assumed to be a customer like herself, looked about fifty. He was short, with a ruddy complexion, immaculately dressed and spoke in an attractive, cultured voice.

"Perhaps I could show you something similar that is not quite as expensive," he said.

Startled for a moment Emily began, "Oh, I'm so sorry, I thought . . . "

He smiled at her disarmingly, "Let me introduce myself, I am Joshua Frere, the owner of The Picture Gallery and incidentally the artist of the painting you've been so kind about. Come with me, if you will," he continued "and I will show you something that I think you may like." He led the way towards the back of the shop, saying as he went, "The picture I have in mind is very alike in colouring. It's another French landscape and it has the same atmosphere of warmth and sunshine about it, that seems to appeal to you." He stopped in front of a pile of pictures. Carefully lifting one out, he held it up for her to see.

"This is the one." His eyes twinkled at her as he asked, "How do you think this would look over your mantelpiece?"

Emily liked it immediately. She replied with enthusiasm, "It's lovely, I see what you mean, it does have the same sort of colouring. Did you paint this one too?"

He shook his head, "No, it was painted by a young artist I know. But let me show you a few more paintings before you make up your mind."

He led her round the shop commenting on the various water colours and oil paintings as he went. As a girl, Emily had done a certain amount of painting herself. Her interest was genuine as he showed her around the small gallery. But, feeling that perhaps she was taking up too much of his time, she said firmly, "I'd like to have another look at the first one you showed me, if I may."

After studying the picture closely for a few moments, she turned towards him with a smile.

"I think I would definitely like to take this one. I like the painting very much indeed and it's at a price that I feel I can afford."

"Are you quite sure you wouldn't like to think it over for a few days? I could put it to one side for you."

"Yes, I'm quite sure, thank you. It's exactly the sort of thing I was looking for." Her eyes lit up with merriment, as she added "And what's more, I think it will look very nice over my mantelpiece!"

A few minutes later, after she had handed him a cheque, he said, "Thank you very much Mrs. Mallory. Now if you would let me have your address, I will arrange for the picture to be delivered to your flat."

"I think I can probably manage to carry it," Emily began, a little doubtfully.

"I wouldn't hear of it," he replied, "it's far too heavy for you."

"Well, it's very kind of you . . . My address is 23 Milford Court, Bramley Street, SW7."

Writing it down, he said, "Ah yes, it's only just round the corner from here. I know Bramley Street quite well, my sister lives a short distance away in Maddox Street. In fact, I am going round to have supper with her this evening and I could drop off the painting on my way. If I left it with the hall porter, would that do?"

Emily laughed, "I'm afraid we don't run to a hall porter, but if it's no trouble for you to bring it up to my flat, I'd be most grateful."

Later that evening he arrived on Emily's doorstep carrying the carefully wrapped picture under his arm.

As she opened the door to him she said appreciatively, "This is kind of you." She hesitated for a moment before she asked, "Would you like to come in? After all the trouble you have been to, I think you at least deserve to see where the painting is going to live!"

Ten minutes later the picture was unpacked and in position over the mantelpiece.

He stood back and looked at it with a critical eye. "Are you pleased with it now that it's hung?"

"Yes I'm very pleased." Emily replied, "It looks just right and makes all the difference to the room. I shall enjoy looking up at it and imagining that I'm basking in the sunshine somewhere in the

South of France!"

She turned towards him with a grateful smile, "Thank you so much for your help in hanging the picture." After a slight pause she went on, "Can I offer you a glass of sherry? That's about all I've got I'm afraid."

"That's very kind of you," he replied, "I should enjoy a glass of sherry very much, if I'm not keeping you."

"Do sit down, I won't be a minute." Emily disappeared into the kitchen. A moment later she returned with two glasses and a bottle of sherry.

"How charmingly you have furnished your flat," he remarked.

Gratified that he should have noticed, Emily explained that most of the furniture had come from her parents home.

"Where do your parents live?" he enquired.

"In Sussex," she replied, "in a small village called Applefold."

Drawing her out he encouraged her to talk about herself. Twenty minutes later he had learnt that she was a widow, that she had been in the WRNS during the war, that she had worked in the Foreign

Office for a short time and that she had only recently moved into her flat and was now about to start looking for a job.

"What sort of job had you in mind?" he asked.

Emily laughed, "More or less anything, provided that I don't have to sit behind a typewriter. I would really like a job that has some connection with people."

There was a pause in the conversation while he took out his cigarette case. "May I smoke?" he asked.

"Yes, of course," Emily replied. She shook her head as he offered her his case. "I don't smoke actually — at least I haven't done since my school days!"

He lit his cigarette and slowly, weighing his words, he began, "My sister, whom I mentioned earlier, runs a hat shop, although," he added with an amused glint in his eye, "I think she would probably describe it as a milliners. Her name is Christobel Blair and the shop itself is called Christobel's. I know she wants to spend less time in the shop and is looking for an assistant." There was another pause before he enquired, "Would you be interested at all?"

★ ★ ★

Thus it happened that a few days later Emily found herself walking in the direction of Maddox Street. She had no difficulty in finding the little hat shop. The decorative, gaily coloured awning that she had been told to look out for, made it instantly recognisable. Her appointment was for six o'clock and the shop was closed by the time she arrived. The door was opened to her by a woman in her late forties. Like her brother, Christobel Blair was short in stature, as well as being a little on the plump side. Her iron grey hair was beautifully coiffeured, her clothes expensive and carefully chosen. She had her brother's same attractive voice, low and resonant and the same humorous expression in her eyes. She led Emily through to the far end of the shop, where she sat down behind a delicately carved rosewood table and motioned Emily to a chair opposite her. A quick glance round showed a long narrow room, carpeted in pale grey. Against one wall stood a large, comfortable looking sofa. Dotted around the room were two or three small tables, each with its winged mirror and gilt framed chair. The decor and furnishings had been chosen with obvious care and discernment, and the general effect was one of elegance and style.

Christobel Blair was business like and to the point. She asked Emily one or two pertinent questions then explained what would be required of her. She ended by saying, "My brother seems to think that you could do the job. What do you think?"

In a confident tone, Emily replied, "I could certainly do everything you have outlined and I have, in fact, done a bit of millinery work at the domestic science college where I was before the war." She went on with an engaging smile, "I would really like the job. It's exactly the sort of thing I had in mind."

Christobel Blair leaned back in her chair and looked thoughtfully at the young woman seated opposite her. She had to agree with her brother that she was undoubtedly an extremely attractive young woman, if a trifle unsophisticated, but perhaps, Christobel mused, that was part of her charm. She was also presentable, nicely dressed, well spoken and polite, with as far as she could judge, a friendly and cheerful disposition.

Finally she said, "Well, Mrs. Mallory, supposing we give it a month's trial? I shall have to ask you for a reference naturally."

"Of course," Emily replied. "I can give you the name of my employer at the Foreign Office, and I'm sure that Captain Lewis — who was my boss when I worked at the Admiralty — would give me a reference."

After writing down the details, Mrs. Blair said, "When would you want to start?"

Emily replied, "I would really like to start as soon as possible, if that would suit you?"

Christobel Blair smiled, "Well, subject to your references being satisfactory, shall we say next Monday then? Eight thirty sharp."

Emily walked home feeling well pleased with herself. She was fairly confident from the way the interview had gone that she would get the job. She liked Christobel

Blair, the little she had seen of her, and decided that she would be happy working for her. The shop itself was an added attraction, with its pleasant, almost homely atmosphere. It was within walking distance of her flat and that was yet another bonus. The salary she had been offered was a good deal more than she had anticipated and the hours of nine to five, Mondays to Fridays left her the weekends free.

When she reflected on the chain of events that had led up to her interview with Christobel Blair, Emily wondered if it was all a coincidence, or whether fate had decided to take a hand in shaping her future. She concluded that either way, she was fortunate to have found the sort of job that she wanted, and one that she felt she would enjoy doing.

8

AFTER a final glance round the shop to see that everything was in order before she locked up, Emily opened the door and walked out onto the pavement. It was a mild spring evening. There was still warmth in the late evening sunshine as she set out to walk the short distance home. All around her were signs that heralded the arrival of spring. The early flowering prunus trees that lined the street like rows of sentinels, were already in leaf; cocky little sparrows chirped merrily as they darted to and fro among the branches, and clumps of yellow daffodils showed their heads in window boxes, and in the pocket-handkerchief-size front gardens that bordered the pavements. Emily was suddenly filled with a sense of contentment and well being. Spring had come at last and with it, hope for the future flowed through her veins once more.

At the age of twenty seven Emily had matured into a poised and elegant young woman. She had recently taken to wearing her hair up. The new style gave her appearance a slight air of sophistication, which if anything enhanced her beauty and emphasised the delicate bone structure of her face. Dressed neatly in a dark grey, tailored coat and skirt, a stylish little hat of her own design and a pair of smart high heeled shoes, she exuded confidence and self assurance, as she cheerfully wended her way home.

It was now nearly two years since she had first started working at Christobel's. It had not taken her long to discover that her employer was a hard task master, who demanded perfection in every detail, but she also found her kind, considerate and patient. Christobel in turn found Emily to be a quick and intelligent pupil as well as showing a considerable aptitude for millinery work. Emily, in fact, took to the job like a duck to water. She soon came to know Christobel's regular clients by name, treating them with the right amount of deference and learning to handle one or two of her more difficult customers with tact and discretion. After a while, satisfied that Emily was now able to deal with the day to day running of the shop, Christobel left her in sole charge. She appointed her to the position of manageress, and increased her salary accordingly. Though Christobel herself continued to do most of the millinery work, Emily was full of fresh ideas when it came to re-modelling clients' hats — an important part of her business. Over the time she had been with her, Christobel had grown fond of Emily, treating her more as a friend than an employee. Emily in turn had a considerable liking and respect for her employer and had thought to herself more than once how providentially every thing had worked out for her.

★ ★ ★

Christobel Blair had had a hard life. Soon after the end of the first world war she had married an impecunious young airforce officer by the name of Ian Blair. It had been a very happy marriage until, a few years later, he had been killed in a flying accident, leaving Christobel to bring up a two year old son on a widow's pension and not much else. She had invested everything she possessed in her hat shop, and had managed to eke out a living for herself and her son by dint of sheer hard work, a lot of initiative, and a good head for business. Twenty years later she had established for herself a well earned reputation and her clientele varied from wealthy society women to casual passers-by.

Early on in the war tragedy had nearly wrecked her life for a second time when her son Jeremy was killed at Dunkirk. It had taken her a while to get over the shock of his death, but Christobel Blair came of fighting stock. She immersed herself in her work and struggled on, determined that although the war had taken her son, she would not let it destroy all she had worked for over the years. With the war now over, she realised that there was no longer the necessity to work the long hours she had been used to and she had recently begun to think about taking on an assistant. She was a keen bridge player, and felt that she would like to have more time to indulge in her favourite pastime. So when Joshua arrived for supper one evening and told her about the young widow he had just met, to please her brother, to whom she was devoted, she had rather reluctantly agreed to interview the girl. Since when she had had no cause to regret her somewhat impulsive decision to take on as her assistant, a young woman about whom she knew next to nothing.

★ ★ ★

Much had happened in Emily's life during the past two years. Soon after Peter's departure for Washington, Teresa had announced her engagement to Robert McNeil, a captain of the United States Army, whom she had first met in London early on in the war. Robert hailed from Norfolk, Virginia. When she met him for the first time, Emily immediately took to the tall, nice looking, young American, with his quiet, unassuming manner, and slow, attractive southern drawl. Teresa and he were obviously blissfully happy and content in each other's company. Emily could only feel glad for Teresa, although she knew how much she would miss her sister-in-law when eventually she and Robert left for the States. Robert had been stationed in Germany since the end of the war and was expecting to be posted home in the near future. After a brief engagement, during which time Teresa proudly introduced him to both her family and her friends, they were married quietly in a registry office and shortly afterwards set sail for America.

Emily, already missed Peter a good deal more than she had imagined she would. She was feeling at a particularly low ebb without her two closest friends, when she was invited to a small drinks party with Anthea and Fred Bradley — a young couple who lived in the flat opposite. There she had met Nicholas Frensham — a man a good bit older than herself, whom she guessed to be in his late forties.

Emily had noticed him as soon as he entered the room. There was a style and elegance about him that made him immediately noticeable. He was a tall, distinguished looking man, with dark, mocking eyes that surveyed the world with an air of cool detachment. After they had been introduced, they had spent much of the evening in conversation together. She had found him easy and interesting to talk to, while he had made no attempt to disguise the fact that he considered her to be a very charming and attractive companion. At the time Emily had been mildly flattered by the attentions of the older man, but later she had given their chance encounter no further thought, except to wonder vaguely who the tall, good looking stranger might be, until some days later the phone bell rang.

As she lifted the receiver Emily heard an unfamiliar voice say, "This is Nicholas Frensham. We met last week at the Bradley's party, if you remember . . . ?"

Mildly surprised, Emily replied in a friendly voice, "Yes, of course I do. How nice to hear from you."

"I hope you won't be too offended at my having asked Anthea for your phone number," he went on, "I am entertaining a few friends for dinner at my club next

Thursday evening — Anthea and Fred are both coming — and I would be delighted if you were free to come too."

Emily had accepted his invitation, albeit with a few doubts in her mind. She felt that she hardly knew the Bradleys and had only met Nicholas for a short time. Nevertheless she had enjoyed the evening considerably more than she had anticipated, and over the next few weeks had gone out with him on two or three other occasions.

After the first evening when there had been several other people in the party, it had always been a quiet dinner *à deux* in some small rather select restaurant, where Nicholas appeared to be well known by the head waiter and was clearly regarded as an esteemed and favoured patron. He chose both the food and wine with the expertise of a connoisseur and proved himself to be an excellent host as well as an accomplished and entertaining companion.

Not only did Emily enjoy being entertained in such style and luxury but she soon learnt to appreciate his humorous, intelligent conversation, his dry, sometimes caustic wit, and his fund of amusing and interesting stories. As she got to know him better, she began to look forward to their meetings with genuine pleasure. The evenings she spent in his company were in complete contrast to the informal, often impromptu parties that she was used to attending among her own circle of friends. The conversation on these occasions was usually in much lighter vein, and the venue considerably more modest than the exclusive restaurant to which Nicholas took her.

As their friendship developed, it had occurred to her more than once, that she knew singularly little about him. He seemed strangely reticent to talk about himself and turned the conversation adroitly if it became too personal. Curious to learn more about him she had turned to Anthea in the hope that she would be able to enlighten her further. But Anthea had replied a little vaguely, "I really don't know anything about him at all I'm afraid, bar the fact that he's something fairly influential in the city. He's a business colleague of Fred's actually and I've only met him on two or three occasions."

One evening a few months after they had first met, Nicholas had greeted her by saying, "I've booked a table at the Mirabelle this evening. I thought perhaps you might enjoy to go dancing for a change."

Emily's eyes sparkled with delight, "Oh Nicholas how lovely, that will be fun. I've not been dancing for ages, but are you sure that you wouldn't rather dine quietly as we usually do?"

With an amused expression on his face he replied, "Emily, my dear, I'm not quite as decrepit as you appear to imagine, I can still manage to make my way around a dance floor!"

The evening had gone particularly well. As she danced with him, in the dimly-lit, intimate atmosphere of the night club, it had stirred strange, almost forgotten emotions in her. She was suddenly aware that not only was she becoming very fond of him, but that she also found him very attractive. It was the first time there had been any sort of physical contact between them, other than a formal handshake, and it came as something of a shock to her to discover the slightly hedonistic sensation she felt at being held in his arms while he guided her expertly around the dance floor.

Escorting her home later that evening, instead of telling the taxi driver to wait for him while he saw her to the door of her flat, Nicholas paid the taxi driver, saying to Emily, "May I come in for a few minutes?"

Emily, buoyed up by the success of the evening, as well as having consumed a fair amount of champagne, had thrown caution to the winds. She replied cheerfully, "Yes of course you can. I'll make some coffee." She unlocked the front door and led him inside.

He cast an appraising glance around the small flat, and remarked admiringly, "How very delightful."

"I'm glad you like it," Emily replied. "It's fairly modest, but it's home and it suits me very well. Now, how about a cup of coffee, or is there something else you would rather have?"

A slight smile hovered around the corners of his mouth as he replied, "There is indeed." He reached out and took both her hands in his. Then drawing her towards him he bent and kissed her lightly on the lips. Taken by surprise, Emily half pulled away from him, but his arm was already around her waist. Almost before she knew it, she was in his arms, her whole body trembling as she leaned against him and felt his lips seeking hers. This time insistent and demanding.

A short while later, in the privacy of the bedroom, he had made love to her. Gently, unhurriedly, with consummate skill; and with all the natural desires and instincts of a healthy young woman, Emily had responded to his love making with ardour and passion.

It was several days before she had heard from him again, during which time she had tried to sort out her feelings towards him, without coming to any real conclusion. She imagined herself to be half in love with him and all she could think of was that she needed to talk to him, to find out how he felt about her. Several times she had picked up the receiver to phone him, quickly replacing it, her pride preventing her from making the first move. At the end of the week he had phoned her to suggest that they met for lunch the following day. It was a Saturday. Emily had planned on going down to Sussex over the weekend, but in her relief at hearing from him, she immediately put the idea out of her mind. She replied happily, "That would be lovely." Suddenly it occurred to her that it would be easier to talk in the privacy of her flat, rather than in a public place. She went on quickly, "Would you like to have something to eat here? I could easily rustle up an omelette and there's a bottle of wine."

He arrived the next day with a large bunch of flowers in his hand and greeted her affably, with no sign of the slight tension that Emily was feeling. Opening the bottle of wine, he poured out two glasses and handed one to Emily. He then sat down opposite her, talking generalities in his usual easy, relaxed manner, until Emily, nervous and on edge said, "I'll go and make the omelette, it won't take a minute."

As she walked towards the door, he said, "Emily, my dear . . . before you go,

I have something I want to say to you." She stood in the doorway expectantly. "This may come as a slight surprise," he went on, "but I think perhaps the time has come that I should tell you that I am married." Emily stared at him, an expression of shocked disbelief on her face. He continued calmly, "I have a wife of whom I am very fond and two teenage children."

Her immediate reaction was one of anger that she had known him all these months, yet only now had he seen fit to tell her that not only was he married but that he also had a family.

After a moment her anger subsided a little. She said coldly, "What made you decide to tell me this now, after all this time?"

"Simply that after the other evening, you must obviously be wondering what the next step in our relationship will be. I thought it was only fair to tell you that I was married, so that you understood the situation before we got any further involved." He paused for a moment before continuing in a more conciliatory tone of voice, "Emily, I'm very fond of you, you know, and there's no reason whatsoever why we shouldn't enjoy a discreet affair, without anyone getting hurt."

Angry and indignant, Emily said, "How can you possibly say that — what about your wife?"

He shrugged his shoulders, "My wife appreciates that my work keeps me in London during the week and that not unnaturally, I have my own circle of friends. When I go home at the weekend, she is sufficiently intelligent not to enquire as to how I spend my spare time. That way, no one gets hurt."

In a curt, abrupt voice she said, "I see. So I take it there have been other women in your life?"

With a slightly cynical expression on his face, he replied "You flatter yourself, my dear if you imagine that you are the only woman that I have dined and wined . . . ."

"And made love to?"

"Occasionally — yes," he admitted calmly. "But while I enjoy the company of beautiful women, I am not quite the philanderer that you appear to imagine.

I am genuinely fond of you."

He walked towards her and placed his hands lightly on her shoulders. "Be honest Emily. Would it really have made all that difference if I had told you earlier on that I was married?"

She pulled angrily away from him. "If I had known you were married I wouldn't have got so involved with you in the first place and I certainly wouldn't have gone to bed with you."

"Oh, come now Emily," he said, exasperation beginning to sound in his voice. "I can understand that it may have come as a bit of a shock to you, but there's no need to get quite so upset about it."

"What do you expect me to be," she retorted, "when you've deliberately misled me all these months?"

"Emily, Emily," he soothed, "believe me, I've not set out to deliberately mislead you, but I do think you have been a little naive in taking it for granted that I was . . . 'unattached'."

Suddenly, in her anger and distress, Emily could only see him for what her fraught imagination conceived him to be;

vain, conceited, selfish and arrogant, for all his outward charm and attraction.

Her pride coming to her rescue, she said icily, "I admit that I may have been somewhat naive in not having considered the possibility that you might be married, but if I may say so, you are being even more so if you imagine for one moment that I would consider having, what you choose to call, 'a discreet affair', with someone who is already married. It's not the sort of relationship I am looking for, or the kind I want to get involved in. And now, I think I would prefer it if you were to leave, for there is really nothing more we have to say to each other." Avoiding his eyes, she turned away from him and walked towards the door, determined to keep her feelings under control until he had left, and so was unaware of the hurt and bewildered expression on his face as he picked up his hat and walked past her.

★ ★ ★

At work the following Monday morning, Emily had looked tired and strained.

Christobel, dropping in towards closing time, had taken one look at her and had enquired anxiously, "Emily, is anything the matter? You don't look awfully well."

After a miserable weekend Emily was just about at the end of her tether, and the sympathy and kindness in Christobel's voice was all that was required to make her dissolve into tears.

Christobel was somewhat taken aback by this unexpected display of emotion. She put a comforting arm around Emily's shoulders and said kindly, "Let me just lock up, then we'll go upstairs and have a cup of tea, and you can tell me all about it."

Five minutes later they were sitting in her small comfortable flat above the shop and after blowing her nose, Emily, was recounting her troubles to a sympathetic and understanding ear.

Finally Christobel asked, "Were you in love with him, do you think?"

Emily replied a little uncertainly, "No . . . at least I don't think so. I was very attracted to him, but I think it was probably more an infatuation than anything else." She gave a rueful smile,

143

"I suppose it was my pride that was hurt as much as anything. It came as a bit of a shock to discover that I was just another woman in his life! Looking back, I think I may possibly have reacted somewhat over dramatically, but the whole thing made me feel as if I'd been used by him, manipulated for his own ends." She shrugged her shoulders, "I realise now that I was an absolute prize idiot not to have considered the possibility that he could have been married. It really and truly never entered my head. I just took it for granted that he was a bachelor — like Joshua — and was stupid enough to imagine that his intentions were honourable!"

"Well I can quite understand that," Christobel said sympathetically, "particularly as he appears to have said nothing to make you think otherwise. Although with someone as attractive as Nicholas appears to be, the likelihood of him remaining single all these years is somewhat improbable. Unless, of course," she shrugged, "there is some other reason for him not marrying, such as there is in Joshua's case." A slightly sour note crept into her voice as she continued, "My beloved brother for all he's a bachelor, in the sense that he's not actually married, shares not only his flat, but his life, with another man. The young artist whose painting hangs over your mantelpiece."

Astonished, Emily gasped, "Joshua . . . ?"

"Did you not realise that he was that way inclined?"

"Not for one moment," Emily replied, "I simply can't believe it."

Christobel gave a wry smile. "Perhaps I shouldn't have told you, but I'm surprised that knowing him as well as you do, you hadn't already guessed." Then getting up from her chair, she said in a more cheerful voice, "I think it's time we had a drink, don't you?"

As she went home by taxi later that evening, Emily was aware that she felt a good deal better having talked things over with Christobel. She had stayed for supper, and by the end of the evening found that her troubles had, to some extent, receded into the background. Nevertheless, several weeks elapsed before the spring returned to her step and she was able to completely dismiss Nicholas from her mind, and put the whole rather sordid affair down to experience. She knew then that she had never really been in love with him, but considerably attracted to him and not a little flattered by the intentions of an older man, she had mistakenly confused love with passion and desire.

★ ★ ★

About a year after Peter had left to take up his appointment in Washington, Emily had received a letter from him, in which he told her that he had met an American girl by the name of Myra Fingleton, and that they were planning to get married in a few months time. His letter had gone on to describe in some detail Myra's various attributes and qualities, and had ended by saying that he was confident that both girls would get on well together when eventually they met.

Emily was shattered by the news. For some reason she had never considered the possibility that Peter might one day decide to marry. He had had several *affairs de coeur* she knew, but none of them had amounted to anything serious and their own particular relationship had continued as before.

Recently she had found herself thinking about him a great deal. She cast her mind back to the hot summers evening, just over a year ago, when he had asked her to marry him, and when, foolishly and mistakenly, she had told him with such certainty, that she would never marry again. Over the last few months she had decided quite definitely that if he still felt the same way towards her when he came home again, she would marry him gladly, without any doubts or reservations. Since Hugh's death, now over three years ago, she had been in the habit of seeing Peter fairly frequently before he had left for the States and had come to rely on him more than she knew. It had taken his prolonged absence for her to realise just how important he had become in her life. She pictured him as she had always known him. Loyal, high principled, dependable; sensitive and warm; funny and endearing and she knew that she loved him deeply, not only as a friend whom she trusted and respected, but as a man, who aroused in her all her natural instincts and emotions.

Writing to congratulate him on his engagement had been a hard task, but after several attempts she had finally managed to pen him a loving and generous letter in which she expressed her happiness for him, and wished him every success in his marriage.

9

ARLY in the spring of 1948, at the relatively young age of sixty two, James suffered a massive heart attack and died a few days later without regaining consciousness. Shocked by the suddenness of his death, Emily knew that his demise would leave a big gap in her life. She had always had a deep affection and respect for him, and though she had never regarded him as her father — in so many words — she was nonetheless conscious of the blood tie that had existed between them.

The following week, Emily attended the funeral service with Stephen and Mary. As they entered the church Emily caught a glimpse of Peter's familiar figure amongst the congregation. After the service she saw him make his way to where she was standing outside the church exchanging a few words with the Vicar.

He gave her an affectionate kiss. "Em,

I'm so sorry about James. It must have been an awful shock for you. Are you all right?"

Pale but composed, Emily gave him a brief smile, "Yes, thank you Peter. It was good of you to come. How are you?"

It was the first time they had met since his return from Washington a few weeks previously, although they had spoken briefly over the phone, when he had explained that he was at present on leave, before taking over his new appointment at the Admiralty. He had gone on to say that he and Myra were busy trying to find a suitable house somewhere in the Portsmouth area and that once they had settled in she must come down for a weekend and meet Myra.

It seemed to Emily that he had changed quite a bit since she last saw him. He appeared quieter and more serious than she remembered him and for a brief moment she almost felt as if she was talking to a stranger.

From the time that Peter had first told her that he was engaged to be married, she had looked forward to this first meeting with mixed feelings. The pleasure she felt at the thought of seeing him again, mingled disquietingly with the knowledge that her relationship with him could now only ever be one of friendship.

But the moment she had dreaded passed more easily than she had anticipated although her voice sounded strained and unnatural as she asked, "How's the house-hunting going? Have you found anywhere to live yet?"

Peter's voice was equally strained as he replied, "I think we probably have. Myra is seeing the agent today. The house is a good deal larger than we're ever likely to need, but she seems to have set her heart on it." His tone softened as he went on, "Em, we simply must get together soon. There's such a lot to catch up on. As soon as I start work at the Admiralty in a couple of weeks time, I'll give you a ring and perhaps we could meet?"

★ ★ ★

Shortly after the funeral, Emily received a formal letter from James' solicitors, asking her to call at their office in connection with the late Mr. Frobisher's Will. She made an appointment and was received by a Mr. Wakeham, the senior partner in the firm, who offered her his condolences and went on to explain that according to the Will she was the principal beneficiary of James' not inconsiderable estate. Once probate had been granted, he added, she would find herself fairly comfortably off.

He smiled at her benignly across the wide, leather-topped desk. "However," he continued, placing the tips of his fingers together, "apart from one or two small bequests, about which I won't bother you, there is a fairly considerable sum of money that has been left to a Mrs. Elsie Stokes." He broke off to refer to the document that lay in front of him, "Of 14 Bay's Road, Streatham."

Emily enquired with a puzzled frown, "Who is Mrs. Stokes?"

With a discreet cough he replied, "Mrs. Stokes is a lady with whom Mr. Frobisher had a long standing relationship, and for whom, I understand, he had a high regard." He allowed Emily a moment in which to digest the significance of his remark before he continued. "The sum of money to which I have just referred is in fact in the form of a trust. Mrs. Stokes is to receive the income from it during her life time, and on her death the money will pass to her daughter."

By now Emily was thoroughly confused, "I don't quite understand — how does Mrs. Stokes' daughter come into it?"

He cleared his throat before replying. "Mr. Frobisher was the girl's natural father."

Emily said slowly, "I see." She tried desperately to muster her bewildered thoughts into some semblance of order, and asked, "How old is the girl?"

"She's seventeen," he replied. "I believe she's due to leave her boarding school where she is at present, at the end of the year, by which time she will be eighteen."

"Do you know what her name is . . . ?"

"Yes," he replied, "It's Margaret. Margaret Stokes, although I believe she's known as Meg."

After a moment's thought, Emily remarked, "I suppose Mrs. Stokes knows about James . . . ?"

"Oh yes indeed," he replied. "I had specific instructions that she was to be notified of his death immediately."

Emily looked surprised. "It sounds almost as though he had a sort of . . . premonition that he was going to die."

He looked at her kindly over the rim of his spectacles. "Mr. Frobisher informed me when I last saw him a few months ago, that he had recently consulted a heart specialist, and in the light of what he had been told, I gather that he had decided to put his affairs in order."

Before she left, Mr. Wakeham said in a sympathetic voice, "I'm afraid this has been very difficult for you, Mrs. Mallory, but it was necessary for you to know the details in order that you should be able to fully comprehend the contents of the Will."

Emily's mind was in a turmoil as she made her way home. It had come as something of a shock to learn that James had had a mistress all these years, although on reflection she realised that like any normal man, he would have had certain physical needs and requirements and this was something she was able to understand and accept. But it had come as an even greater shock to discover that as a result of his liaison there was a seventeen year old daughter to bear witness to the fact — a girl whom Emily supposed would be her half-sister.

Prompted by a certain amount of concern, as well as a faint curiosity to meet this woman with whom James had not only sought comfort over a considerable period of time, but for whom — apparently — he had had a high regard, she decided to phone Mr. Wakeham. She explained her predicament and asked him, a trifle apprehensively whether he thought Mrs. Stokes would be willing to meet her.

"I see no reason why not," he replied, "would you like me to get in touch with her? If she agrees, I could make an appointment for you both to meet."

Emily thanked him and hung up the receiver with a sense of relief at having set the ball in motion.

The following Saturday morning Emily caught a bus bound for Streatham that deposited her within a short distance of

Bay's Road. Mrs. Stokes lived in a small, unpretentious, semi-detached house in a row of similar houses, each with their lace curtains and unmistakeable air of respectability.

As Emily rang the bell, she noticed a sign in the window which said 'Dressmaker'. A moment later the door was opened to her by a pleasant looking woman in her early forties. She was neatly dressed in a blouse and skirt over which she sported a rather worn looking cardigan. Her homely looks and quiet, unassuming manner were not in the least what Emily had expected, and for a brief moment she felt slightly confused as she confronted her on the doorstep.

"Mrs. Stokes . . . ?" she began.

With a faint smile, the woman replied, "Yes. Please come in." There was an air of polite deference about her as she led the way along a narrow passage into a small room at the far end of the house, saying as she went, "I live at the back I'm afraid as I have to use the front room for my dressmaking. I'm a dressmaker you see," she added by way of explanation. Nervously she continued, "Perhaps you would like to sit in this chair — it's the more comfortable of the two." She hurried on, "Would you like a cup of tea perhaps?"

Thinking that it might help to break the ice, Emily replied, "If it's not too much trouble, I'd love one."

While Mrs. Stokes was in the kitchen, Emily took a quick look around the room. There were two arm chairs, both of which had clearly seen better days, placed one either side of a small gas fire. A plain wooden desk stood in one corner and in the window, was a circular table covered by a red chenille cloth, on which reposed a freshly arranged vase of daffodils. The room though sparsely furnished, was clean and tidy and Emily formed the impression that Mrs. Stokes was probably a fairly house proud woman. She returned a few minutes later carrying a tray on which was a delicately fashioned bone china tea service.

She set the tray on the table, and asked politely, "Do you like milk and sugar?"

Emily replied, "Just milk thank you." They sat in silence for a few moments, until feeling that the next move was up to her, Emily said quietly, "I'm afraid that James' death must have come as a great shock to you — as it did to us all — and I was wondering if there was anything I could do to help."

Elsie Stokes raised her head and over her tea cup looked across at Emily before replying with the same polite smile, "It's very kind of you, but there's really nothing, thank you."

After another long pause, Emily said cheerfully, "Tell me about Margaret, or is it Meg? I gather she's at boarding school?"

Mrs. Stokes replied, "Yes, that's right. She comes home for the Easter holidays next week. James — er, Mr. Frobisher that is — was very good to her, he sent her to an expensive boarding school and paid for all her school fees, which I couldn't possibly have afforded."

"I should so like to meet Meg when she comes home," Emily said warmly. "Do you think we could fix up something during the holidays?"

Mrs. Stokes' voice sounded apprehensive and uncertain. "Well, I really don't know what to say — I don't know what she has planned." Then, changing the subject abruptly, she said, "If you don't mind me asking, why exactly are you here and what is it you want from me?"

Slightly taken aback, Emily began, "I thought perhaps it might help if we were to get to know each other."

Suddenly, and without warning, the woman broke down. All at once the events of the last few weeks became too much for her. Covering her face with her hands, she sobbed as though her heart would break. But just as quickly she regained control of herself. She looked uncomfortable and embarrassed as she pulled out a handkerchief from the pocket of her cardigan and dabbed her eyes, murmuring in a low voice, "I'm very sorry . . . whatever must you think."

All at once, Emily felt a great surge of pity for her. She got up from her chair, and kneeling down beside Mrs. Stokes, put a comforting arm around the woman's thin shoulders. "Please don't apologise," she said quietly, "It's a good thing to let go sometimes and there's nothing to be ashamed of in grieving for someone you cared for."

It was an hour or more before Emily finally took her leave. During that time she learnt a good deal about Elsie Stokes' past life. After years of having had to keep her emotions under strict control, the words came pouring forth like a flood tide in her relief at being able to unburden herself to Emily's sympathetic ear.

She began by describing how, as a young girl, she had lived with her widowed mother in a two bedroomed house in Wandsworth. She had left school at the age of fifteen and had worked, first, as a waitress in a Lyons Corner House, then in a small dress shop, where she was employed in the workroom as a seamstress. Later on she got a job as an assistant librarian in a lending library in the Strand, where the pay was better and she was able to see a bit more of life.

It was here that she first met James. He had come into the library one day and sought her assistance in locating a particular book he was looking for. Elsie was nineteen at the time and as she modestly described herself, 'quite pretty then, with a nice figure'. Attracted by the tall, good looking man with his innate charm and impeccable manners, she went out of her way to acquaint herself with the kind of books he liked to read — mostly biographies and travel books she discovered. Very gradually an unusual and somewhat bizarre friendship began to blossom between them. A short while later her mother died, leaving her the house and its contents. Elsie decided to stay on in the only home she had ever known, and continued to live there on her own. It was about this time that James began visiting her. By the time she discovered that she was pregnant, James had gone abroad once more.

★ ★ ★

It was then that she took the decision to move to somewhere where she was not known. She gave up her job, sold the house in Wandsworth and bought the one in Bay's Road. Changing her name to Mrs. Stokes, she let it be known that she had recently been widowed and quickly made a new life for herself in her new surroundings. She earned her living dressmaking and after a short time — painstaking and competent in her work — she managed to establish quite a good clientele, although she admitted to Emily with a wry smile, there was always a shortage of pennies.

After leaving Wandsworth Elsie lost touch with James, until one day while she was waiting at a bus stop in Piccadilly, she suddenly saw him walking along the pavement in her direction. He recognised her immediately and appeared pleased to see her. He explained how he had tried to contact her at her old address and asked her where she was now living. At first she had prevaricated, not wanting him to know about Meg, who by then was nearly four years old. Unconvinced by her feeble excuses he continued to press her, until gradually the truth came out. Distressed at the hand to mouth existence she was living, as well as feeling a certain responsibility towards the child, James arranged with his solicitors for a sum of money to be paid into her bank account each month after which things became a good deal easier for her.

James continued to visit her at regular

intervals, although there were long periods while he was abroad, when she did not see him for several years at a time. But on his return home, he always got in touch with her and over a period of twenty years, the relationship that had begun as an almost entirely physical one, gradually grew into a warm and companionable friendship.

Elsie Stokes explained, "He was never in love with me, you understand. I filled certain . . . gaps in his life, that was all. And although I was very fond of him, I always knew that there was no place in his life for me. But he was a good, kind man, was James, and often a very lonely one."

Emily was conscious of a growing feeling of admiration and respect for this stoic, matter-of-fact woman, who seemed to accept everything in life both philosophically and without complaint. Demanding little, she gave herself wholeheartedly to those she cared for, and as Emily listened to her she began to glimpse some of the same qualities that James had admired and respected.

When she had finished speaking, Emily asked, "Does Meg know that James was her father?"

"No, I've never told her, although I've sometimes wondered if the thought had perhaps occurred to her."

Emily vividly remembered her own overwhelming curiosity to find who her natural father had been. "Perhaps she instinctively felt some connection with James?" she suggested.

"It's possible, I suppose, but she never really showed much interest in the matter."

There was a long, drawn out silence, then with a deep sigh, and an almost imperceptible shrug of her shoulders Elsie went on in a resigned voice, "Perhaps you had better know . . . the truth of the matter is that Meg is ashamed of me, and embarrassed by her background. It's been like this ever since she first went to this rather grand boarding school in Bexhill. You see," she went on, "not satisfied with her own home and family, she has 'invented' one to suit her own purposes. She tells her school friends that her father is a rich and influential

164

business man, a widower, who owns a large house in the country. She explains his absence from attending any of the school functions, by saying that he is abroad for much of the time, leaving her in the charge of his housekeeper." She paused for a moment and looked out the window. "On the only occasion on which I attended the school speech day, she introduced me to her friends as her father's housekeeper."

Emily was horrified at what she was hearing. She could only begin to imagine the hurt and humiliation that Mrs. Stokes must have felt at her daughter's rejection of her. All at once it became clear why she had shown such reluctance for Emily to meet Meg.

Not knowing what she could say that would be of any help, she murmured quietly, "I am so sorry. How awful it must have been for you." A moment or two later she went on thoughtfully, "This background that Meg invented for herself, do you think perhaps that not knowing who her father was or anything about him, she is subconsciously associating herself with James? The 'rich influential business man' could well be James and the 'large country house' might be where she imagined he lived?" She looked questioningly as Mrs. Stokes, but receiving no reply she went on, "I'm not making any excuses for Meg's behaviour, but maybe she feels insecure, uncertain of herself. Knowing who her father was, might help her to relate to the reality of the situation, as well as reassure her . . . What do you think?"

"I dare say you're right," Elsie replied, somewhat doubtfully, "it might be best to tell her. She has a right to know I suppose. I must admit I have often thought about it, but that's as far as I ever got." She gave a rueful smile.

"Did you ever discuss the matter with James?" Emily asked gently.

"I didn't want to worry him. I felt it was my problem, not his."

It was sometime later before Mrs. Stokes finally showed Emily to the front door. With a warm smile she held out her hand. "Thank you for coming. I am glad we have met." On impulse Emily bent forward and kissed her lightly on the cheek. They had met as strangers, but parted as friends — two women drawn together by the loss of someone for whom, each in their own way, they had both cared deeply.

167

10

A WEEK or two after her meeting with Elsie Stokes, Emily received a letter inviting her to tea the following Sunday. Written in a neat hand on pale pink, lined note paper, the letter went on to say that she had taken Emily's advice, and had spoken to Meg concerning her relationship with James. Emily noticed though that she made no mention of how Meg had received the news.

On arrival, Emily caught a glimpse of a slight movement behind the lace curtains in the window as she stopped in front of the house. After she had rung the bell, the door was opened to her almost immediately by a tall, dark haired girl, who stood framed in the doorway. She stared at Emily with a look on her face that was a strange mixture of curiosity and indifference. For a moment Emily stared back, startled by the girl's quite extraordinary likeness to James. That she

168

was James' daughter there could be no doubt. She had the same dark eyes — deep, limpid pools, fringed by long curling eye lashes; the same colouring and the same distinctive features.

Emily held out her hand towards her. "Hello, I'm Emily, you must be Meg?" she began with a friendly smile.

The girl limply returned her handshake. Her expression was cold, almost hostile, as she replied in an abrupt, singularly ungracious tone of voice, "You'd better come in. My mother is in the kitchen." At that moment Elsie Stokes appeared. Her face showed clearly the pleasure she felt at seeing Emily again.

She greeted Emily warmly and led the way into the sitting room where the table was already laid for tea.

"Meg has been so looking forward to meeting you, haven't you, dear?" she remarked cheerfully. But Meg had disappeared. With an apologetic laugh, Elsie went on "I expect she's gone up stairs. She'll be down in a minute. Do sit down, and I'll put the kettle on." She returned a moment later. But there was still no sign of Meg.

As she closed the door behind her, Elsie said in a bewildered voice, "I can't understand Meg sometimes, she seemed so eager to meet you."

"Don't worry please," Emily replied, "I expect she's feeling a bit nervous." She hesitated for a moment before she asked, "How did she take the news about James being her father?"

Elsie looked down at the floor, her eyes focused on a threadbare patch of the worn carpet. "I explained matters to her as gently as I could, not wanting to upset her any more than was necessary. When I had finished, she just laughed, and said that she had always known that he must have been her father, because of her close resemblance to him." She went on with a small, bitter laugh, "I got the impression that she was just surprised that I had taken so long in getting round to telling her."

Some ten minutes later their conversation was interrupted by Meg's arrival. She threw open the door and announced in the same abrupt, almost insolent manner that Emily had noticed previously, "The kettle's been boiling for hours. Do you want me to make the tea?"

Over tea, Emily watched Meg covertly as she sat staring out of the window, taking little interest in the conversation. Emily perceived a tall, slender, potentially beautiful young girl, with dark eyes and pale skin. Her thick, ebony-black hair was shaped in a long bob with a straight fringe: a style, Emily decided that suited her well. But her general appearance was spoilt by the short, tight fitting, black satin dress that she wore with a somewhat ostentatious display of cheap jewellery. Besides being entirely inappropriate for the occasion the dress made her look considerably older than her seventeen years, and gave her an altogether too bold and provocative an appearance.

The girl sat morose and silent for most of the meal and Emily's endeavours to draw Meg out and get her to talk about herself, were met with such a casual response that Emily was at a loss to understand what it was that prompted Meg to act in a manner that lacked any sort of civility or normal politeness.

Changing her tactics Emily suggested that Meg might be interested to see the hat shop where she worked. She went on a little tentatively, "If you would like to come in one morning and have a look around, we could have lunch together afterwards perhaps."

Meg's reply was brief, "Thanks, but I'm going to stay with a school friend in Norfolk next week so there won't be any time." Her manner was so off-hand that Emily decided not to pursue the matter and turned to talk to Elsie who, for the most part, had sat quietly throughout the meal, looking uncomfortable and embarrassed by her daughter's surly behaviour.

Later, as she made her way home, Emily came to the reluctant conclusion that her first meeting with Meg could hardly be chalked up as a great success. She was also aware of a slight feeling of disappointment that her effort to be friends with Meg had evoked so little response. While there was no denying the fact, that to look at — Meg certainly bore a close resemblance to James — there the likeness ended for she appeared to have inherited none of his charm and courtesy, nor any of the warmth and kindliness that had been so much part of his makeup.

During the short time Emily had known Elsie Stokes, she had grown to both like and respect the quiet, composed, agreeable woman. It was clear that Elsie was in need of a friend and ally and Emily decided that — in spite of, rather than because of Meg — she would continue to keep in touch with her and hope that in time, Meg would begin to show a slightly more friendly attitude towards her.

* * *

Emily had just shown out one of Christobel's more valued clients one morning, when she received an unexpected phone call from Peter. She recognised his voice immediately and exclaimed delightedly, "Peter, how lovely to hear from you. Where are you speaking from?"

"The office," he replied cheerfully. "I only started work last week and I'm still trying to find my way around! I know it's short notice, Em, but would you be free to have dinner with me this evening? I'm staying at the club and I thought that we might have a quiet dinner together there."

It was a wet and windy evening in March and Emily took a taxi to his club in Pall Mall. The sense of elation that had been with her since his phone call that morning, had suddenly left her. All at once she was beset by doubts and misgivings at the thought of seeing him again. She paid the taxi driver and as she crossed the threshold of the club, she felt nervous and apprehensive. She was about to enquire at the desk for Commander Stuart when she saw Peter walking towards her. He gave her a friendly kiss and said warmly, "I'm so glad you could come, Em, it's good to see you again." He led the way towards a small table in a secluded corner of the room. "What would you like to drink — your usual glass of sherry?" He smiled at her questioningly, while his eyes appraised her poised and elegant appearance.

She smiled back at him. "Please, that would be lovely." For a long moment there was an uncomfortable silence while both of them searched for words to break the sudden tension between them. Then, as of one accord they began to talk at the same time and in so doing, broke into spontaneous laughter. And the moment passed. By the time they went into dinner, they had slipped effortlessly into their old, companionable relationship, relaxed and completely at ease with one another.

Over dinner Emily recounted the events of the last few weeks. She described at length, first her meeting with Elsie Stokes, then her subsequent, somewhat unfriendly encounter with Meg. Peter listened to her intently as she talked. His eyes scanned her face, noticing a new maturity about her, a poise and seriousness that she had previously lacked. He thought poignantly that she was more beautiful than ever. It was not until they were drinking their coffee that Emily realised that she had monopolised the conversation for most of the meal.

She laughed at him across the table and said half apologetically, "Peter, I've done all the talking! It's your turn now. I want to hear all about your new home and how Myra is settling down over here. It must be very strange for her after New York." But Peter seemed disinclined to go into any great detail, saying briefly that Myra was busy moving in. Later he explained that as his job necessitated working fairly late hours, they had decided that for the moment, he should stay in London for two or three nights a week, in order to save Myra the inconvenience of having to turn out late at night to meet him.

As they reminisced over old times, the evening sped by, until looking at her watch Emily announced that it was time she went home.

She rose, turned to Peter and said, "It's been a wonderful evening, thank you so much." Loathe to let her go, he replied, "It has been wonderful, hasn't it. But there's still so much to talk about . . . Can we meet again — soon?"

After a moment's hesitation she replied cautiously, "Yes of course, Peter, but next time, perhaps Myra would be able to come too? I do so want to meet her."

"I'll see what I can fix up," Peter promised.

While they waited for a taxi, he asked

tentatively, "Am I going to be allowed to see your flat sometime? I'd also very much like to meet your friend Christobel — she sounds an absolute winner from your description of her. And then there's that artist chap? What's his name, Joshua? I'd like to meet him too."

Emily laughed. "I don't quite know what you'd make of Joshua, but I'm sure you'd like Christobel." On a sudden impulse she continued, "What about coming to supper one evening next week and I'll try and get Christobel and Joshua to come too. Then you could see the flat and meet them both at the same time."

Peter brightened visibly. "That would be marvellous, but I probably shouldn't be able to make it much before eight o'clock. Will that be all right?"

"Of course," she replied.

On her way home she found herself wondering about Peter's marriage. It was a little hard to understand the rather strange arrangement that Peter should spend three nights a week in London, while Myra stayed at home on her own, particularly when they had only been married for barely two years. She recalled how at James' funeral she had sensed his apparent need for her friendship in spite of his marriage. Now, after spending the evening with him, when he had appeared so reluctant to talk about either Myra, or his life at home, she began to wonder if all was not quite as it should be. Conscious of her own feelings towards him, she knew full well that she could not afford to allow herself to get too involved in Peter's life.

★ ★ ★

The supper party went particularly well. Peter arrived earlier than Emily expected and by the time Christobel and Joshua appeared, he had inspected the tiny flat in every detail and had given it his full approval. He remarked especially on the elegant rosewood desk that stood in one corner. "It's lovely, isn't it," Emily agreed. "It was a house warming present from Mummy and Daddy."

The next morning as Christobel breezed into the shop, she remarked enthusiastically, "What a simply lovely party it was last night, Emily my dear, I'd no idea you were such an excellent cook. I like your young man tremendously," she continued cheerfully, "I think you should seriously consider marrying him before he gets snapped up by somebody else. He's obviously extremely fond of you, judging by the way he hardly took his eyes off you the whole evening. In fact," she rambled on in her usual forthright way, "I'd almost go as far as to say that he might even be in love with you."

The colour flooded Emily's cheeks. "He's already been 'snapped up' as you put it. He's married to an American. As for being in love with me, you've got it all wrong Christobel. We're just very old friends. That's absolutely all there is to it." She coldly turned her back and busied herself with re-arranging a hat display.

Feeling contrite, Christobel said, "Forgive me Emily, I shouldn't have said that. I didn't mean to upset you."

Emily saw the look on Christobel's face and immediately regretted having been quite so brusque with her. In a gentler tone she replied, "That's all right, but now can we just forget it please."

Mildly surprised at Emily's prickly, dismissive manner, Christobel was nevertheless pretty sure that she was right about Peter's feelings towards her, in spite of Emily's flat denial. She was now beginning to consider the possibility that Emily might feel the same way about him. All at once Christobel was aware of a feeling of deep concern for this girl of whom she had grown inordinately fond. She wanted desperately to help her, but knew there was little she could do unless at some stage Emily chose to confide in her.

11

PETER was as good as his word. Shortly after Emily's supper party, he phoned to say that Myra was hoping to come to London one day during the following week. Would Emily be free to have lunch with them at his club?

Intrigued at the prospect of meeting Peter's wife at last, Emily nevertheless viewed the whole thing with somewhat mixed feelings, as she speculated on what the chances were of Myra and herself getting along together.

She arrived at his club punctually, where she was met by Peter. He apologised for Myra not being there to greet her and explained that Myra had intended doing some shopping and had presumably been delayed. He ordered two glasses of sherry and they sat and talked for a while, until across the room, Emily noticed a tall, strikingly attractive woman poised elegantly in the doorway.

Instinctively she knew it to be Myra.

Peter caught sight of her at the same moment. His voice held a note of relief as he exclaimed, "Ah, there's Myra at last."

She stood there for a moment — her eyes leisurely scanning the crowded room. Then, with consummate ease and grace, she slowly made her way across the room to where they were sitting.

In a rare moment of spite Emily could not help but feel that Myra was well aware of the glances of undisguised admiration that followed her progress. Her cool, detached manner suggested that she was well used to being the focus of attention, and indeed, relished every moment of it.

Emily's first impression of Peter's wife was of a very beautiful, sensuous woman, with small, delicate features and a dazzling smile. But her light, pale blue eyes were hard as steel and beneath the smile, her expression was cold and indifferent.

Her appearance was difficult to fault. She was tall and willowy, with long slender legs and beautifully shaped ankles. Her taste was impeccable from the smart designer outfit that she wore, to the expensive and exquisite jewellery that adorned her person. Her short fair hair was fashionably coiffeured, her long painted finger nails were perfectly manicured and her make up applied with the expertise of an artist.

She casually offered her cheek to Peter, then moved towards Emily, her hand outstretched in an elegant gesture.

There was a faint note of condescension in her voice as she said, "So, you're Emily. I guess I'd have recognised you from Peter's description, though he sure didn't tell me you were quite such a good looker." She sank languidly into a chair and lit a cigarette before she continued in the same slightly patronising tone, "I gather you've known each other for quite some time?" All at once Emily felt strangely uncomfortable and ill at ease with this poised, sophisticated woman, only a year or two older than herself. She knew instinctively that they would have little in common.

In a dry, constrained voice she replied,

"Yes, we have indeed. We grew up together."

Myra gave a polite, indifferent smile, "Is that a fact?" Then turning to Peter she said almost petulantly, "Order me a drink will you Peter, I'm quite exhausted after shopping all the morning."

As Emily toyed with her second glass of sherry, she watched Myra knock back a couple of dry martinis in fairly quick succession before they eventually made their way into the dining room. Over lunch the conversation became more relaxed, but as the meal progressed, Myra's mood changed. The martinis began to take effect. She became aggressively talkative, taking complete charge of the conversation and for the rest of the meal, regaled them with an account of her life as a New York socialite. As Emily listened, she formed the opinion that Peter's wife was a spoilt, self centred woman, with pronounced narcissistic tendencies. She seemed to have little interest in anyone other than herself, and was apparently only happy when she was the centre of attention.

Suddenly Myra was aware that her wine glass was empty. She drew breath for a moment to complain irritably, "For God's sake, Peter, let's have another bottle of wine."

Peter replied firmly, "I don't really think we need another bottle, Myra. I doubt that Emily will want any more and I think you've already had enough, old thing. Besides," he added lightly, "I've got to work this afternoon!" Myra gave him an infuriated look. She lit a cigarette and elaborately exhaled a spiral of smoke into the air, in an attempt to disguise her anger at Peter's rebuke.

Peter looked at his watch as he ordered coffee. "I'm afraid I'll have to be going in a few minutes," he said, with an apologetic glance in Emily's direction.

She took the hint and replied lightly, "So will I in fact. Christobel is very kindly holding the fort for me, so I really ought to get back fairly soon."

Some minutes later as she took her leave, Emily said formally, "It's been so nice meeting you Myra, I do so hope we shall meet again soon." She knew as she said it, that besides being far from the truth, her remark must have sounded both trite and banal.

Accompanying Emily to the front entrance, Peter said shortly, "I'll be in touch," then turned and went back inside.

There was now no longer any doubt in Emily's mind that Peter's marriage was in trouble. From the cool, off hand manner in which Myra greeted him on arrival, to the total lack of any warmth or affection in her attitude towards him. Now that she had met Myra, Emily could well understand how Peter had fallen for her many and considerable physical charms, though she seriously doubted whether he had anything in common with her on a more intellectual level.

Some days elapsed before she heard from him again. When he eventually got in touch it was to suggest that they met for dinner in a restaurant, where on occasions they had dined together during the war. On arrival Emily was informed that Commander Stuart had left a message to say that he had been slightly delayed. As she waited for him in the foyer, she noticed a young couple walk in through the revolving doors.

She recognised the man immediately. "Anthony?" she exclaimed in surprise. "Anthony Foster?"

The man spun round. "Emily . . . My goodness, fancy running into you. It must be years . . . I don't think you've met my wife?" He put his arm round the girl's shoulders and drew her forward. "Pat, this is Emily Mallory — You remember Hugh?" Embarrassed, he went on quickly, "Pat was in the Wrens during the war and knew Hugh quite well, didn't you darling?" Talkative as always, he continued, "We were both terribly sorry to hear about what happened to him. It was damn bad luck. He was such a decent chap."

They chatted together for a few minutes until Emily said, "Don't let me hold you up, please. Actually I'm waiting for someone who seems to have got bogged down at the office, but he should be here any moment now."

Anthony replied cheerfully, "Well, let's all go and have a drink and we can leave a message to say where you are."

Emily had first met Anthony Foster

early on in the war and though they had never been at all close, they had several friends and acquaintances in common. He appeared to be remarkably up to date and well informed on bits of gossip and information concerning people they both knew and prattled on in his usual rather garrulous, verbose manner.

"Then there was that nice chap Peter Stuart." He paused to ask, "You knew him slightly, didn't you Emily?" Without waiting for an answer he continued. "Poor old Peter. On the rebound from some girl or other, he got caught hook, line and bloody sinker by a ghastly American girl. Absolutely stunning to look at, but a complete . . . " Seeing the expression on Emily's face he stopped. "Oh I say," he stammered, "have I said something I shouldn't?"

Emily smiled sweetly. "No Anthony, it's all right. It just happens to be Peter Stuart that I'm meeting this evening. We are very old friends in fact."

The chance meeting with the Fosters, and Anthony's rash, slightly unguarded remark concerning Myra, merely added to Emily's suspicion about the Stuart's marriage. She had taken what she knew to be a quite unreasonable dislike to Myra from the moment she had met her. Yet in the light of what Anthony had said, she began to wonder if after all there might be a logical reason for her instinctive feeling of antagonism towards her.

Peter arrived shortly and after he had spent a few minutes talking to the Fosters, they made their way to their own table. He appeared tired and strained and Emily noticed that during the course of the evening, he made no mention of the lunch party the previous week, so taking her cue from him, she too remained silent on the subject. Later in the evening he took her home by taxi and after they had arranged to meet during the following week, he dropped her off and took the taxi on.

★ ★ ★

Spring became summer. Summer turned into Autumn. And Emily and Peter continued to see each other. Their weekly meetings had become an essential part of both their lives, although at first Emily had questioned the wisdom of them seeing each other on quite such a regular basis.

Occasionally they would dine out together in some small restaurant, but more often than not they supped in the privacy of Emily's flat where, after conjuring up a simple meal for themselves amid a good deal of happy laughter, they would linger over a candlelight supper, sipping their wine and talking companionably, an easy relaxed intimacy between them. The conversation was usually on a light-hearted, cheerful note, but there were times when Peter would lapse into a more serious mood and would talk about his troubled marriage. He had long ago given up any pretence that all was well between him and Myra, yet it was obvious from the way in which he excused and defended her behaviour that he still felt a strong sense of loyalty towards her.

In a calm, emotionless voice he would describe the empty, often stormy relationship that existed between him and Myra. As she listened to him, Emily began to learn something of what his life had been over the past two years and, in doing so, was finally able to understand the reason for the strained expression in his eyes, the deeply etched lines around his mouth, and his frequent moods of despondency.

★ ★ ★

Myra, she learnt, was the only daughter of Cyrus B. Fingleton, the wealthy owner of a large department store in New York. The apple of his eye, he indulged her every whim. From a pampered, spoilt child, she grew into a strong willed, recalcitrant young woman, determined to get her own way, regardless of the cost to those around her. There had been an endless succession of men in her life, of whom, after a brief period, she had inevitably tired, discarding them like play things for which she no longer had any use.

She was twenty nine when, on a visit to some friends in Washington, she first met Peter, shortly after his arrival in the United States. She found him refreshingly different from the men she was accustomed to dating, and immediately set her cap at the tall, nice looking young British naval officer, determined at all costs to win his heart.

Peter was an easy catch. Sad and dejected after Emily had turned down his proposal of marriage, he was quickly captivated by Myra's beauty and lively, vivacious personality. Almost before he knew it, they had become engaged.

Thankful that his daughter had finally decided to settle down, Cyrus Fingleton urged them into a swift marriage. He knew his daughter's whims and vagaries all too well and feared that Myra might have a change of heart if they waited too long. At first all had gone well, although Peter soon discovered Myra to be headstrong and determined, brooking no interference as to how she conducted her life.

Their first row had taken place following his discovery that she had written to her father to ask him to increase her already considerable allowance, explaining that she could not possibly manage to run the house on the meagre amount of money that Peter allowed her. Peter had reacted angrily, his pride wounded by the implication that he was unable to provide adequately for his wife. Reminding her coldly, that she had been fully aware of his financial situation when she married him, he pointed out that other married couples managed to live on their husband's pay and suggested that she should learn to do likewise.

That was the first time that he learnt of her dependency upon alcohol when under any kind of stress. When he returned home from the office that evening he found her in his own words — 'four sheets in the wind', an almost empty bottle of vodka at her elbow. She immediately became so verbally abusive that Peter, fairly used to barrack room bawdiness, was deeply shocked by her crude, obscene language. As he tried to calm her, her mood altered to one of violence. She began smashing up their home with whatever object came to hand, until physically exhausted she collapsed into a semi comatose state, when Peter carried her upstairs and put her to bed.

He quickly learnt to handle her with

velvet gloves, giving in to her tantrums and learning to live with her whims and extravagances, to avoid the drinking bouts that inevitably followed if she was thwarted in any way. By the time they had been married for a year, their marriage was little more than a charade. Tiring of Peter and what she considered to be his pompous, goody-goody manner, she began to play around with other men, pouring scorn and contempt on Peter's head when he remonstrated with her. Little by little she killed any feelings for her that might have remained in Peter's heart, other perhaps than those of loyalty. She was still his wife, and as such, he was both supportive and protective towards her, knowing that beneath the poised, self-confident exterior was a woman of complex character, confused and insecure. Without her realising it, he had become a requisite part of her life, acting as her sheet anchor and whipping boy all in one.

Once during their conversation, Emily had asked him, albeit with a certain amount of hesitation, whether they had ever thought of starting a family.

In a toneless voice, Peter replied, "Myra made it abundantly clear soon after we were married that she had no intention of having children. She argued that besides spoiling her figure, she was not the maternal type."

Without warning, all the animosity and resentment that Emily had harboured towards Myra for so long, finally erupted. Peter's voice — drained and empty of any emotion — tore at her heartstrings. All at once, her love for him and her overwhelming desire to comfort and protect him became too much. In an attempt to hide her feelings she quickly got up from her chair and disappeared into the kitchen, on the pretext of making some more coffee.

Some minutes later, mildly surprised at her sudden departure, Peter slowly got to his feet and followed her into the kitchen. "Can I help?" he asked.

Emily stood with her back towards him. Fighting to gain control of her emotions, she said abruptly, "No thanks. I can manage." She filled up the kettle from the tap and placed it on the gas cooker. With trembling hands she picked up a box of matches and in the process of extracting one, dropped the contents on the floor. She muttered under her breath, "Oh damn," and was about to bend down to pick them up when she felt Peter's hands on her shoulders. He spun her round so that she faced him and looked at her long and searchingly. As their eyes met, he saw reflected in hers all the love and longing that he felt towards her and knew in one blinding, bittersweet moment, that Emily loved him in the same way that he had never ceased to love her.

★ ★ ★

One wet November evening Peter caught an earlier train home than usual. He took a taxi from the station and as the taxi drove in through the wrought iron gates, he noticed Myra's car standing in the drive.

He let himself in through the front door and closing it behind him, called out, "Myra, I'm home." Receiving no reply, he hung up his hat and coat and after placing his brief case on the table, walked across the hall and opened the door that led into the comfortably furnished drawing room. Myra stood by the mantelpiece, a drink in one hand, a cigarette in the other.

"You're home early," she observed indifferently. "I was just on my way out to have a drink with the Phillip's." One look at her told Peter that she had already been drinking for some time. He hid his annoyance and replied quietly, "I don't think you're in a fit state to drive Myra. Give me a minute and I'll drive you there myself."

Suddenly she lost all control. "You goddamned son of a bitch," she spat at him. "Who the hell do you think you are to tell me what to do. I'm perfectly capable of driving myself." With which she flounced out of the room and slammed the door behind her. Peter in the middle of pouring himself a whisky, turned round sharply. He quickly put down his glass and hastened after her. By the time he reached the front door, Myra was already in the car.

He caught a glimpse of her face — distorted with fury — as she threw him a contemptuous glance over her shoulder. The car jerked forward as she let in the clutch. Without looking to either left or right, she drove at speed through the open iron gates, out into the busy Portsmouth road, and straight into the path of a fast moving, articulated lorry.

There was a squeal of tyres as the lorry skidded on the wet, oily surface of the road before it ploughed into Myra's car, reducing the small vehicle to a mass of broken metal and debris.

An eerie silence followed, disturbed only by the gentle hiss of the rain as it continued to fall unremittingly on the scene of the accident.

Part Three

1950 – 1962

12

IN the summer of 1950, some eighteen months after Myra's tragic death, Peter and Emily were married. Peter was stationed in Plymouth at the time, and they started their married life in a small furnished cottage on the edge of Dartmoor.

Just over a year later, Martin was born. Within a few months of his arrival, Peter was given command of a destroyer and sailed for the Far East, where the war in Korea was still in progress.

From the beginning Martin was a happy, placid, and contented baby. Emily doted on the little boy as he lay gurgling in his cot, her joy marred only by the fact that Peter had known him for such a short time before, in the line of duty, he had to leave his wife and child.

Martin was six months old when Emily decided to take him on a visit to his grandparents. On arriving home she was distressed to see how pale and thin her mother was looking. Although Mary greeted her with her usual warmth and cheerfulness, it was clear that she was far from well.

A few days later, leaving Mary to coo over her small grandson, Emily went in search of Stephen. She found him in the garden, listlessly hoeing a flower bed.

He straightened up as he saw her approach. Leaning on his hoe he said cheerfully, "Hello Emmy, come to give me a hand?"

Emily disregarded his question. She said abruptly, "Daddy, I'm worried about Mummy. She doesn't look at all well. Has she seen the doctor lately?"

Taken by surprise at the directness of Emily's question, Stephen replied evasively, "Well, yes she has. She saw the new GP in the village, Doctor Thomas, quite recently."

"What did he think was wrong with her?" she asked.

Unable to avoid the issue any longer he replied unhappily, "As a matter of fact he sent her to see a specialist."

Alarmed, Emily said. "A specialist? What sort of a specialist?"

Suddenly his face crumpled pathetically. "Emmy, I really don't know how to tell you this, I'm afraid it's serious. She's got a malignant tumour. One that is unfortunately, inoperable."

Emily looked deeply shocked. "But why ever didn't you tell me?"

"She didn't want you to know. She felt you had enough on your plate with looking after Martin, and Peter abroad . . . "

"How much longer has she got?" she asked, quietly, "Have they told you?"

"Not more than a few months. She saw the specialist soon after Martin's christening. He gave her six months then, and that was three months ago." He bent down and pulled out a root of groundsel, "I know what a shock this must be for you, Emmy. I wish I could have prepared you for it more gently, but your mother was so insistent that you were not to know." He looked at her appealingly. "She'll never forgive me if she finds out that I've told you."

Emily realised that sooner or later she was going to be needed at home, certainly by Mary, and very possibly by

Stephen. She made a quick decision. "She need never know Daddy," she said firmly. "All we need to tell her is that I'm . . . missing Peter, and want to come home for a while." She slipped her arm through his, and trying to make her voice sound cheerful, she went on, "So that's settled then. Martin and I will be moving in right away."

They walked back to the house together, where they found Mary sitting contentedly in an armchair, with Martin asleep in his carry-cot beside her.

Beaming down fondly at his wife, Stephen announced with a forced brightness.

"What do you think, old girl, Emmy wants to come home for a bit. Says she's missing Peter. So I told her it would be all right."

Mary looked up at them both. For a moment tears glistened in her eyes. "Oh Emily, how perfectly lovely. It will be a wonderful opportunity to get to know our grandson. And think how delighted Andrew and Elaine will be too."

A few days later Emily returned to Devon to pack up their belongings, and to give a months notice on the cottage. By the end of April, she and Martin were comfortably installed at Wisteria House. She had spent so much of her life there that in some ways she felt that it was almost as though she had never left. The only difference was that Mrs. Soames was no longer there. Soon after the end of the war, Mrs. Soames, well into her seventies by then, had left the family she had served so loyally for over forty years, to live with her younger sister in the West Country, from whence she had originally hailed.

Since her departure Mary had run the house with what little help she could get from the village. Never having had to do any cooking in the whole of her life, she had not taken kindly to coping with the preparation of meals and all else it entailed. She felt that she had little aptitude when it came to culinary matters. Consequently she was more than thankful to be able to hand over to Emily the responsibility of running the kitchen, while she assisted the daily help with the housework.

As the weeks passed Mary grew

noticeably more frail. One hot afternoon in July, having gone upstairs for her usual after lunch nap, she failed to awake, slipping away quietly and peacefully as she slept.

Overnight Stephen became an old man. Emily had been amazed at how cheerful he had managed to keep throughout Mary's illness. He was attentive to her every need, sometimes reading to her, at others content to sit quietly by her side, holding her hand in his. He was there without fail whenever she needed him, his manner comforting and reassuring.

On her death he lost all interest in life. He wandered aimlessly about the house, looking lost and bewildered. He turned to Emily for comfort and reassurance, and relied on her to make any necessary arrangements or decisions. As the months passed and he continued to show no sign of picking up the threads of his life again, Emily sought advice from her father-in-law.

Andrew Stuart had recently sold his practice. Approaching retirement age, he felt that he was too old to adapt to the newly formed National Health Service, which had been introduced by the labour government soon after the end of the war. He had sold his house with its adjoining surgery, and he and Elaine had moved into a pretty little thatched cottage on the outskirts of the village.

Emily frequently put Martin in his pram and wheeled him round to see his other grandparents, so there was nothing unusual about it when she said to Stephen over lunch one day, "I thought I would take Martin to see Andrew and Elaine this afternoon."

He looked up at her across the table, immediately apprehensive at the thought of being left on his own. "You won't be away for too long, will you?" She gently reassured him, then washed up the lunch things before getting Martin ready for his afternoon walk.

It was a raw November day. Warmly wrapping him up in his pram, she smiled to herself as she thought how adorable he looked in his little red woollen bonnet and matching mittens — lovingly knitted for him by Mary — and wished with all her heart that Peter could see him at this moment. At just over a year old, Martin was a sturdy little boy. Fair-haired like his mother, with rosy cheeks and bright blue eyes, he was the epitome of a healthy happy child, and Emily's pride in her small son knew no bounds.

She had just turned out of the drive when she saw Elaine walking towards her. Elaine had not seen Emily for some days, and had set out with the idea of accompanying her daughter-in-law and grandson on their afternoon walk. But a glance at Emily's face quickly made her change her plans.

"Emily my dear, you look worn out . . . Why don't I take Martin for his walk while you go up to the cottage and put your feet up in front of the fire for a short time. You'll probably find Andrew snoring his head off, but he'll be delighted to see you."

Emily said thankfully, "Oh what a wonderful granny you are. There's nothing I would rather do at this particular moment! Besides, I did rather want to have a word with Andrew. I'm a little anxious about Daddy."

"Well, you go and have a good pow-wow with Andrew while I look after

Martin, then we'll all have a cup of tea."

Emily had always considered her relationship with her parents-in-law to be unique. She had known them both all her life, and had adored Andrew from the time she was a child, though she had never felt quite so relaxed with Elaine. There was a reserve about her mother-in-law that, when Emily was young, she had found a little disconcerting. Recently however, she had got to know her better and now felt a genuine warmth and affection for Peter's mother.

She found Andrew dozing in front of the fire, an open newspaper on his lap. He looked up as he heard the door open. She planted an affectionate kiss on his cheek, "I hope I'm not disturbing you?"

"Of course you're not, child. Come and sit down and warm yourself up."

He got up and put a log on the fire. "Have you seen Elaine? She was on her way to join you for a walk."

"Yes I met her just as we were leaving. She's taking Martin for a walk for me so that I could come and talk to you. Andrew, I'm worried about Daddy and

I want your advice."

"What's worrying you particularly?" he asked, as he settled himself back into his armchair.

"Well, it's now nearly four months since Mummy died, and he's still showing no signs whatsoever of being able to come to terms with her death. I can't get him to take an interest in anything. He hardly ever reads, or listens to the wireless. He just sits, staring into space, immersed in his own thoughts. Any decisions that have to be made he leaves to me — which is so unlike him. Each day that goes by he seems to become more and more reliant upon me." She paused for a moment while Andrew waited silently for her to continue. "I'm wondering among other things what is going to happen when Peter comes home," she went on. "I can't leave Daddy on his own as he is at present . . . "

Andrew, being the wise and shrewd person that he was, replied gently, "I know it's very difficult for you, Emmy, but you must try to remember that Stephen worshipped your mother. She was always the dominant character of the two, and now that she's gone, he is, quite understandably, lost without her. This is why he relies on you so much. Try to be patient with him. It's bound to take him a bit of time to adjust, although I must admit that I would have expected him to be taking a little more interest in life by now." There was moment's silence before he asked, "Has he seen the doctor lately?"

"Not since just after Mummy died. Why? Do you think that there might be something wrong?"

"Not necessarily, but it wouldn't do any harm for him to have a check up. He may possibly have a slight problem with any number of things, such as his blood pressure, or even a touch of indigestion. If there is something not quite right, it's not going to help him to get back on his feet again if he's feeling a bit under the weather. See if you can persuade him to go and see Doctor Thomas. He might be able to prescribe something that would help him." As Elaine came in through the gate with the pram, he said, "We'll talk about this again Emmy, but meanwhile, try not to worry about what's going to happen when Peter comes home. Let's deal with one thing at a time, eh?"

Comforted by her talk with Andrew, Emily arrived home to find Stephen standing in the hall, looking confused and upset. In an agitated voice he said, "Where have you been? You said you wouldn't be long."

Emily lifted Martin out of his pram, then put an arm around her father's shoulders. "We've only been out to tea with Andrew and Elaine, Daddy," she said soothingly. "I told you at lunch time that we were going. Remember?" But he appeared to have forgotten. Worried by his absentmindedness and confused state of mind, Emily made a mental note to go and talk to the doctor herself the next day. She knew full well that she would never get her father to agree to go on his own.

But the next morning Martin awoke with a feverish cold. Not anxious to leave him, Emily postponed her visit to the surgery. A few days later, Stephen complained of not feeling well, and shortly afterwards collapsed unconscious on the floor.

After a spell in hospital Stephen returned home. He had suffered a slight stroke which had left him partially paralysed on one side of his body.

Emily soon realised that she was going to need some extra help in looking after him, and immediately set about making a few enquiries for someone suitable. She eventually found a pleasant, capable woman of around fifty who lived in Hurstborough and came in for a few hours each morning to get Stephen bathed and dressed.

Mrs. Potter's advent proved to be an unqualified success. A retired nurse, she was excellent with Stephen. She encouraged him to do things for himself, and gradually managed to persuade him to take more of an interest in life. Over the next few months he made steady progress, and quickly regained the use of his limbs, until, with the aid of a stick, he was eventually able to walk by himself. But his speech remained slurred, his words a little confused, and he sometimes had difficulty in making himself understood.

Martin adored Mrs. Potter, and as soon as Stephen was comfortably ensconced in his chair each morning, she would take charge of the little boy. This allowed Emily a good deal more freedom and gave her a brief respite from the constant pressure she was under. Mrs. Potter's brisk, cheerful manner was a tonic to them all, and by degrees Emily's life began to take on some sort of normality after the disruption of the last few months.

★ ★ ★

That summer, after nearly a year and a half's absence abroad, Peter returned home, and was subsequently posted to the Admiralty for a second tour of duty.

He quickly sized up the situations at home, and agreed with Emily that they had little option but to continue to make their home at Wisteria House. It was clear that Stephen could not be left on his own, and Peter knew that Emily would never agree happily to leaving her father to be looked after by a housekeeper. There was plenty of room in the rambling old house for them all. Martin had his own nursery, a garden in which to play, and loving grandparents within a stone's throw. Stephen, apart from joining them for meals, spent much of his time in what had once been his study, so that to all intents and purposes they had the house to themselves.

Stephen was both delighted and relieved at their decision to stay on. He reminded Emily constantly that the house would eventually belong to her, and told them that meanwhile they must do whatever they wished to make themselves comfortable and at home.

13

MARTIN was nearly four years old by the time that Cara was born. Unlike her brother she was a difficult baby from the moment she made her appearance into the world. For the first few weeks of her life she yelled non stop. A shrill, piercing scream that not only denied anyone within earshot any peace or quiet, but drove the entire household to distraction.

While Emily attempted to breast feed Cara, she was near to tears as the child — red in the face from screaming — kicked out and struggled, and refused to feed properly. She fought her mother every inch of the way, until on the doctor's advice Emily put her onto a bottle. Things then began to improve. The screams subsided to some extent, although she was still fretfull and restless.

Throughout her pregnancy Emily had not felt well in the same way as she had done with Martin. The birth had been long and exhausting for both mother and child, and to the dismay of her parents, Cara was born with a birthmark on her forehead. About an inch in diameter, the strawberry coloured mark stood out prominently against the child's fair skin.

Despite the doctor's assurance that the blemish would fade with time, Emily was nevertheless devastated that such a cruel blow should have befallen her baby.

Suffering from post-natal depression, she began to imagine that the child was somehow aware of her disfigurement, and holding her mother responsible, resented any kind of physical contact with her as a result.

While Cara would allow herself to be bathed and dressed without undue protest, if Emily so much as picked her up for a cuddle, the simple, natural act of cradling the baby in her arms would invariably provoke a fresh outburst of ear-piercing shrieks. At her wits end, Emily would return the child to her cot, when the screaming would cease almost immediately.

With Peter, things were slightly better. But not at his best with small babies, he was inclined to handle her awkwardly. The baby, sensed his lack of confidence, and was rigid and unrelaxed in his arms, although she at least remained silent. The only person whom Cara permitted to hold her without any real objection was her grandmother. Elaine, though not a particularly maternal person, would firmly but gently gather the baby into her arms where she would lie contentedly, until, for no apparent reason, she would suddenly become restless and fidgety. A sign that invariably heralded a fresh outburst of screaming.

Emily had long since recognised that this child of hers was a law unto herself. Cara bore no resemblance to the happy, contented baby that Martin had been at the same age. She was none the less deeply worried and concerned by Cara's apparent rejection of her, and decided to seek advice on the matter from Doctor Thomas, the young doctor who had taken over Andrew's practice soon after the end of the war.

After he had carefully examined Cara, he assured Emily that he could find nothing wrong with the baby's physical condition that would account for her objection to being handled. He advised her to be patient, adding kindly that given time, these sort of problems usually cleared up of their own accord. But Emily derived little comfort from her visit. She returned home unconvinced wishing — not for the first time — that it had been Andrew's calm, reassuring figure in the chair opposite her, rather than that of the well meaning, but somewhat inexperienced young National Health Service doctor.

As she wheeled the pram up the drive, she saw Martin waiting for her by the front door. He rushed headlong towards hers, and flung his arms around his mother hugging her tightly. His rapturous, ecstatic welcome helped to revive her spirits. She returned his hug, and taking his small hand in hers they all went into the house together.

★ ★ ★

Soon after Cara was born Emily received a letter from Elsie Stokes. She had seen little of her since her marriage, although she had kept in touch by letter. Elsie wrote with the disturbing news that Meg was pregnant. It appeared that there was no question of her getting married. Meg could not, or would not, say who the father was.

Emily had seen Meg on a few occasions only since the first time they had met. Sadly, their relationship had never progressed. Meg had continued to show nothing but resentment and antagonism towards her. Elsie had once tried to explain that deep down, Meg was jealous of Emily, and harboured a resentment and bitterness that was now too securely rooted to do anything about. While Emily was disappointed that things had not worked out better between Meg and herself, she philosophically accepted Elsie's explanation and had given up any further attempt to win Meg's friendship.

After leaving school at the age of eighteen, Meg had gone to secretarial college. Mixing with a wider and more varied strata of society she had soon lost some of her rather ill-conceived and grandiose ideas that she had acquired at school. She had done one or two temporary jobs before joining a large firm of accountants, where, according to Elsie, Meg had settled down happily, and was doing quite well for herself.

But Meg soon became bored with her rather humdrum social life, and began to seek greener pastures. She gradually abandoned the friends she had made, and started to cultivate new acquaintances. However, she was not too discriminating in her choice of companions, and before long she was associating with a crowd of young people with a somewhat unsavoury reputation. She began arriving home at all hours, often in large, expensive cars. Her sometimes rowdy arrival not only disturbed the neighbourhood, but caused a certain amount of gossip, much to Elsie's shame and embarrassment.

For some time Elsie had suspected that her daughter was rather too free with her favours, but Meg was over twenty one and Elsie no longer had any jurisdiction over her. Nevertheless she was deeply shocked and upset when Meg boldly announced that she was four months pregnant.

In due course Meg's baby was born.

A little girl whom she named Maisie.

By the time the child was just over two months old, Meg had returned to her old job, leaving Elsie to look after the baby. In a letter to Emily, Elsie explained that with the money that Meg earned, added to what she made from her dressmaking jobs, they were managing quite well.

The letter went on to say that greatly to Elsie's surprise, since Maisie's birth, Meg had become a different person. She returned straight home from work each evening, and immediately took charge of Maisie, bathing her and putting her to bed. She cared for her lovingly, and watched with delight as her baby grew from a tiny helpless object into a beautiful little girl who lay gurgling happily in her cot. The letter ended on something of a poignant note. Elsie wrote that recently Meg's manner towards her had been much more thoughtful and considerate, and that their once strained and uneasy relationship was gradually beginning to improve.

Emily felt pleased and happy for Elsie that finally, things were working out better for her. She even warmed to Meg as she decided that perhaps at last Meg was beginning to grow up and get her life into better perspective.

Then without warning, tragedy struck. A few days before the Christmas of 1956 Meg was on her way home from an office party. It was the season of good will, and the wine had flowed fairly freely. Earlier there had been a slight fall of snow. The pavements were wet and slippery, the road slushy from the traffic.

Meg had left the office block in the company of several of her friends — all laughing and joking merrily as they congregated on the wet pavement. There was a certain amount of good natured jostling and pushing going on, and in the melee, Meg suddenly found herself propelled towards the edge of the pavement. From then on everything happened with a frightening suddenness. Inadvertently stepping backwards off the pavement, she missed her footing, lost her balance and fell headlong into the direct line of an approaching car. Before she could get to her feet the car — swerving to avoid her — skidded on the wet road, spun round and ran straight into Meg's prostrate body, killing her instantly.

Meg's simple funeral had taken place before Emily knew anything about what had happened. Not wanting to spoil the holiday for them, Elsie had withheld the news until the Christmas festivities were over.

A brief, unhappy note told Emily what had transpired. Filled with sadness for Elsie, Emily was also stunned and shocked to learn of the tragic accident that had ended Meg's short life so abruptly.

Leaving Mrs. Potter in charge, Emily immediately drove up to London. She parked her car outside the small house in Bay's Road, and rang the bell. She waited for several minutes, and was about to ring again when the door was slowly opened. Elsie stood there looking tired and ill.

Surprise showed in her face as she faintly remonstrated, "You really shouldn't have bothered to come, but do please come in."

Noticing how flushed she looked, Emily asked anxiously, "Are you all right?"

"I think I may have got a touch of flu,"

Elsie replied as she led the way into the sitting room, "there's a lot of it about." She sat down abruptly and put her hand to her head.

It was obvious that Elsie was far from well. Practical and matter of fact, Emily took charge of the situation. The sitting room was bitterly cold. She quickly lit the gas fire and said in a firm, cheerful voice, "Right, I'm going to make us both a cup of coffee, then we're going to pack up a few things for you and Maisie, and you're both coming back with me to Wisteria House, until you're quite well again." She broke off. "Where is Maisie by the way?"

"She's asleep in her cot upstairs," Elsie replied. "It's the bedroom at the top of the stairs, if you would like to go up and see her." Her voice trailed off. She rested her head against the back of the chair, a great weariness showing in her face.

Emily put on the kettle, and went upstairs. As she quietly opened the door of the bedroom that had so recently belonged to Meg, the child stirred and opened her eyes. Emily saw a tiny, dainty little girl with her mother's dark hair and beautiful eyes. Maisie stared up at Emily, wide-eyed, curious. Then her face slowly broke into a broad grin. As she smiled back at her, Emily was suddenly aware of a strange rapport with this small, dark-haired child. She reached out toward her and took Maisie's hand in hers. "Hello Maisie," she said softly. "I'm Emily." The child grasped hold of her hand, her fingers playing with Emily's rings as she continued to stare up at her, her eyes friendly and trusting. Emily suddenly remembered she had put the kettle on.

"Now, be a good girl Maisie and I'll come back in a minute or two." She ran downstairs, aware of a strange feeling of excitement and exhilaration. There was something about Maisie that conjured up a great warmth and tenderness in her, an odd feeling that somehow she had always known her, although until this moment, they had been strangers to one another. Then she understood. This child bore the same likeness to James that Meg had done. Maisie was no stranger, just a small chip off the old family block.

Emily made the coffee and handed a cup to Elsie.

"I'm afraid I woke Maisie, but I left her lying quite happily in her cot. What a beautiful little girl she is."

Elsie replied listlessly, "She's a very good little girl, no trouble at all." Then rousing herself she went on, "Perhaps you could give her a cup of milk and a biscuit before we leave?"

Emily had noticed that Elsie had not demurred at being told that she and Maisie were being taken to Sussex. She decided that with the shock of Meg's death and flu on the top of it, the poor woman was about at the end of her tether.

On the way home Emily drew up outside a convenient call box to phone Mrs. Potter. She explained what had happened, and asked her to get the spare room ready. It was early afternoon by the time they arrived home. Elsie was put straight to bed and the doctor sent for. Doctor Thomas confirmed that she had a bad attack of influenza, and prescribed warmth and rest, and plenty of good food once she began to feel better. He added that besides suffering from flu, Elsie was in a very low state mentally.

Introducing the children to each other proved easier than Emily had anticipated. For a few seconds Martin stared curiously at the little girl. Then coming over to where Maisie was sitting on Emily's lap, he picked up one of his toys and held it out towards her. Maisie took it in her hand, solemnly returning his stare. Then a slow, shy smile spread across her face. Martin grinned back. And the ice was broken.

While Emily had had few worries over Martin's reaction, she was nevertheless apprehensive and uncertain as to how Cara would welcome this small visitor into her home. But Cara, unpredictable as always, toddled across the room towards her, and examined Maisie warily. Then to Emily's immense surprise she put a motherly, possessive arm around Maisie, and smacked a large wet kiss on her cheek.

As she recounted the day's events to Peter later that evening, Emily's voice was full of suppressed laughter. "I do so wish you could have seen Cara, Peter. She was really sweet with Maisie. She fussed around her like an old mother hen! It was the first time I can remember her showing any real sign of affection towards anyone before."

"She probably thought that Maisie was some sort of new toy for her to play with." Peter remarked dryly.

"Darling," Emily chided him. "You shouldn't say things like that, even in fun."

Peter was somewhat prejudiced regarding his small daughter, knowing how much unhappiness she caused her mother, by the apparent lack of any filial affection towards her.

He realised at once that he had upset Emily by his remark, and put an arm around her shoulders. "Sorry, darling, perhaps I shouldn't have said that. Let's go to bed. You must be exhausted after your day."

On their way upstairs Emily quietly opened the door of the night nursery.

"Come and have a peep at Maisie."

Peter peered down at the sleeping child. "Good God!" he exclaimed. "She's exactly like James."

Emily laughed softly. "I know. It's extraordinary isn't it."

Maisie quickly adapted to her new surroundings, and within a week of their arrival she celebrated her first birthday. To mark the occasion Emily made a birthday cake, with one solitary pink candle placed in the middle of it, which Cara helpfully assisted Maisie to extinguish. Elsie was just well enough to join them for nursery tea, and with Stephen putting in a brief appearance, the party was an undoubted success.

Cara's reaction to Maisie's arrival caused something of a stir among her family. At eighteen months old Cara was still obsessed with a strong sense of aversion to any demonstration of affection, drawing away in dissent if she was pampered or fussed over. Self contained and independent from the start, she would play with her toys in some quiet corner of the room, and seemed to prefer her own company to that of her fellow human beings. A remote, solemn little girl, she was the complete antithesis of Martin with his friendly, happy nature, and extrovert personality.

There were times when Emily wondered to herself how it was that she had managed to conceive a child so entirely unlike Peter or herself. Not only in character, but in appearance as well. Cara was dark-haired, with brown eyes and a pale complexion, and took more after her grandmother, Elaine, than either of her parents. As she looked at the two little half cousins, Emily felt they could almost be mistaken for sisters.

Cara soon began to show an interest in Maisie that was quite out of character. She watched intently as Emily bathed and dressed Maisie and even proffered a certain amount of help. Careful to avoid giving any cause for feelings of jealousy, Emily encouraged Cara's assistance, finding her to her great surprise, helpful and responsive.

Maisie appeared to have awakened some deep down maternal instinct in Cara. While she remained detached and indifferent towards the rest of the family, she softened noticeably in her response to Maisie, anxious to share her toys with her, and clearly enjoying her companionship.

Elsie's convalescence had been a slow process. Though she had fully recovered from her bout of flu, beneath her cheerful exterior, she was still suffering from the shock and pain of Meg's death. But once up and about again, she soon began to busy herself about the place, blending into the daily routine of the household quietly and unobtrusively. She was always ready to lend a hand where it was most needed, whether it was keeping an eye on the children, or assisting in the kitchen. She was also frequently to be found talking to Stephen, while she occupied herself with some sewing or mending. They seemed to have formed a gentle, companionable alliance. Stephen welcomed her visits, and gradually regained his confidence as he found she was able to understand his slow, hesitant way of talking, without undue difficulty. Elsie had a happy knack of getting on with whomsoever she came into contact. Peter appreciated her gentle, unassuming manner, her quiet efficiency, and unfailing cheerfulness, and quickly discovered that she also possessed a dry, often droll, sense of humour. She was soon on friendly terms with Mrs. Potter, and Martin had taken to her from the start.

Each morning Martin would accompany his mother upstairs as she carried up Elsie's breakfast tray. Knocking politely on the bedroom door he would wait impatiently for her to say, "You can come in Martin," before jumping on to the end of the bed where he would sit cross-legged, until Emily, taking him firmly by the hand, dragged him downstairs for breakfast in the kitchen.

Even Cara gradually came round to accepting her. Initially, she had viewed Elsie with grave suspicion. But it was not long before she was clambering up onto the sofa to sit beside her, albeit at a safe distance, as with Maisie on her knee, Elsie would turn the pages of a picture book, while they listened enrapt as she read to them. Cara would edge closer and closer so that she could see the pictures, until she eventually ended up in immediate contact with Elsie. Satisfied that no advantage would be taken of her, she quickly gained sufficient confidence automatically to take up her position next to Elsie as soon as she sat down with a book in her hand.

Elsie was endlessly patient with Cara. She spent a lot of time with the little girl, playing with her, gaining her confidence and drawing her out, until Cara slowly began to show signs of wanting to become part of the family circle, instead of isolating herself in some far off corner of the room.

Emily was amazed at the difference in her daughter in a few short weeks. One half of her was overjoyed to see Cara beginning to join in their family life, while the other half was filled with a great sense of inadequacy, as she realised that where she herself had failed to break through Cara's reserve and restraint, Elsie had managed to succeed.

One day she asked, "Where did I go wrong?"

Else replied with a shrug of her shoulders, "I don't think you did go wrong. Some children are just more difficult than others. Take Meg for instance . . . " She gave Emily a comforting smile before going on, "It's always easier for an outsider. One isn't quite so vulnerable."

By now Elsie had been at Wisteria House for several weeks. Once or twice she had mentioned that it was time she was getting back to London, but on each occasion Emily persuaded her to stay a little longer. Somewhat to her surprise she found that she had grown exceptionally fond of Elsie over the last few weeks, as she came to know her in a way she had never done before. She soon discovered that there was considerably more depth to Elsie's character than she had at first imagined, and was more than ever aware of what James had seen to appreciate and admire in this practical, down to earth, warm, kindly woman. Emily had also grown to love Maisie with an intensity that was both tender and protective. The little girl returned her love with a warmth equalling that of Martin and Emily knew she was going to miss her sorely when the time came for them to go.

★ ★ ★

Towards the end of March Peter returned home one evening with the news that he was soon to be posted to a shore establishment at Portland in Dorset. When he explained with a somewhat rueful look, that this would of course mean that he would only be able to get home at the weekends, Emily's face fell.

Although by now she was fairly used to the inevitable partings and separations of service life, she was nonetheless unable to disguise her disappointment as she replied in a dejected voice, "Oh Peter, I shall miss you not coming home each night." All at once she felt unaccountably depressed and sorry for herself as she continued, "With you away during the week and Elsie and Maisie about to return to London, I shall be completely lost . . ."

Peter gave her a scrutinising look. "I suppose you've never thought about asking Elsie to stay on?"

Emily looked surprised. "Well, no I haven't. Do you think she would?"

"You'd have to ask her of course, but personally I think she might. She seems happy enough here, and over the last few weeks she has made herself practically indispensable. Let's face it darling, she'd be a tremendous help to you, not only with the children, but with Stephen too."

"But if she moved in here, it would mean her having to give up her own home . . . "

"To be honest, I can't see how she thinks she is ever going to manage financially, with only the few hundred a year she gets from the trust that James set up for her — plus what little she is able to earn from her dressmaking. If she were to sell her house and move in here," he continued, warming to his theme, "in whatever capacity you like to call it — general factotum perhaps — she'd be a lot better off and she would be independent at the same time."

Emily laughed with sheer delight, "Peter, you are absolutely super! Only you could have come up with such a wonderful solution to all our problems. But are you quite sure you wouldn't mind her living with us?"

"Darling, as long as you are happy, and if it means that I can have you to myself a bit more, then of course I don't mind. Besides," he added with a twinkle in his eye, "I'm very fond of Elsie. Nevertheless I think you'll have to draw up a few ground rules. For instance, could you perhaps offer her her own sitting room?"

"Yes of course I could. But I've got an even better idea. Why don't we convert what used to be the servants' quarters into a flat for Elsie? There are three rooms in all. That would give her a bedroom and a sitting room, and if Daddy agreed, which I'm sure he would, we could make the third room into a bathroom for her."

It took little persuasion for Elsie to agree to the suggestion that she and Maisie should make their home at Wisteria House. Not only had Elsie been dreading the time when she would have to return to the lonely, empty house in Bay's Road, but she had also been greatly concerned about how she would manage financially. She remembered all too well the uphill battle it had been when Meg was small. And when, she reminded herself painfully, she had been twenty five years younger.

Since Elsie had been living at Wisteria House, she had discovered for the first time in her life, what it meant to be part of a happy family. She had grown to love this particular family. Also, she was filled with a deep sense of gratitude towards Peter and Emily, not only for all they had done for her during her illness and subsequent convalescence, but their offer to give her her own self-contained flat meant that her days of struggling to make two ends meet, were now at an end.

Once the alterations had been carried out and the rooms redecorated, Elsie was able to move into her new home. Peter had arranged for her house to be put on the market, and shortly afterwards, a small van arrived outside Wisteria House containing all her worldly possessions. Surrounded once more by her own furniture and all her familiar belongings, Elsie was more than content.

★ ★ ★

Peter had almost completed his two year appointment in Portland, and was waiting to hear with some interest what his next assignment was to be. Returning home one weekend, he was met by Elsie as he walked through the front door.

She gave him a cheerful smile as she took his suitcase from him. "Good evening Commander. I hope you had a good run home?"

"Yes thanks Elsie. How is everybody?"

"Everyone is fine. Your wife is upstairs saying goodnight to the children. She was hoping you would be back before they went to sleep."

"Right. I'll pop up straight away. By the way Elsie — what's for dinner?"

"Chops," she replied.

"Good, I'll open a bottle of red wine. Tonight we're going to celebrate, and what's more, you are having dinner with us too." Elsie was in the habit of leaving Peter and Emily to have dinner on their own at the weekends, while she would have hers on a tray with Stephen who, these days, preferred to have his evening meal served in his study. Tonight, however, appeared to be something of a special occasion.

As she watched Peter bound up the

stairs, two at a time, it seemed to her that he was in particularly good spirits. She smiled indulgently, aware that she had a very soft spot for this warm-hearted, kind and considerate man, who always made her feel so welcome in his home.

During the two years that Elsie had lived at Wisteria House, she had taken over much of the cooking, in addition to helping Emily with the children. Emily frequently remonstrated with her, telling her that she was doing too much, but Elsie merely smiled, saying that she preferred to keep busy. She appeared to have an inexhaustible supply of energy. When she was not occupied about the house, she was frequently to be found working in the garden. She also tended to many of Stephen's requirements, once Mrs. Potter had departed each morning. She did so much to help that Emily sometimes wondered how she had ever managed without her.

Whenever Peter and Emily had a dinner party, Elsie was in her element. She was an excellent cook and produced meals that were comparable only to those that Mrs. Soames had prepared in the days before the war. Emily had once asked her how she had learnt to cook so expertly.

Elsie replied modestly, "Once you've learnt the basics of cooking, you can do anything really, providing you stick to the cookery book!"

On this particular evening there was a sense of expectancy in the air as the three of them sat down to dinner.

Unable to contain her curiosity any longer, Emily leaned her elbows on the table and rested her chin on her hands. "Peter, for heavens sake, when are you going to put us out of our suspense and tell us what all this is about?"

There was a mischievous gleam in Peter's eyes as leaning back in his chair, he replied casually, "Well, first of all, I've just learned that I am to be promoted to Captain as from the end of next month."

Elsie was the first to speak. Pleasure and excitement sounded in her voice as she exclaimed delightedly, "Oh Commander! That is good news. I am so pleased for you. Many congratulations."

Emily was more cautious in her

response, dreading that his promotion might mean that he would be sent overseas. "Darling, that's wonderful," she began, "I'm so glad. Have you any idea of what your next appointment is going to be?"

"Yes," he replied cheerfully. "I'm to be in charge of the Naval dockyard in Hong Kong. However the really good news is that it is a three year appointment, and better still, there is a house that goes with the job. This means that we can all go out there. You, Elsie, and the children. It's a wonderful climate for young children, and they'll have a super time. And, Em darling, you'll have a staff of Chinese servants which will enable you to sit back and enjoy life, without any domestic problems to worry about."

He watched Emily's face anxiously for her reaction. After a long pause, she replied uncertainly, "Peter, it sounds absolutely marvellous, but what about Daddy?"

"I was coming to that. If we could find someone to live in and do the cooking, don't you think Stephen would be all right with Mrs. P. coming in each day to look after him?"

Emily said nothing.

Elsie glanced quickly from one to the other. Sizing up the situation she said quietly, "There's no need for you to worry about getting anybody else, Commander. I will look after Mr. Larby. It's very kind of you to suggest that I should go with you, but I've never been abroad before, and I am really too old to start thinking about going to foreign parts now. No. I will stay here," she continued firmly, "and with Mrs. Potter coming in each morning, we will manage easily between us."

Consternation showed in Emily's face, "But what about Maisie . . . ?"

Aware of how much Emily would hate leaving Maisie behind, Elsie made the ultimate sacrifice. In a cheerful, matter of fact voice she replied, "You must take Maisie with you of course. It would be quite wrong for her to stay with me. Just think how she would miss you all."

No amount of persuasion could change Elsie's mind. She had read correctly the thoughts that were racing through Emily's head, sensing her disquiet and concern at the thought of leaving her ailing father, yet at the same time she realised how desperately Emily wanted to accompany Peter. While Elsie knew that Emily would never agree to leave her father in the care of a stranger, she hoped that by offering to look after Stephen herself, it would relieve Emily's mind to some extent. Elsie was aware that she was giving up the chance of a lifetime — to travel had always been one of her ambitions — but she was nevertheless grateful for the opportunity to show some of her appreciation for the continual kindness she had received from this family.

Plans for the departure began almost immediately. A few weeks later Peter flew to Hong Kong to take up his new appointment, leaving Emily and the three children to follow by sea.

14

IN the early summer of 1959, Emily stood on the deck of the ship as it slowly entered the port of Hong Kong. After four hot and rather tedious weeks at sea, when the children all suffered from prickly heat as well as various other childhood malaises, they finally arrived at their destination.

For a moment Emily held her breath at the splendour of the scene that met her eyes. In the foreground lay the harbour. All around her the sea glistened and sparkled in the bright early morning sunlight, its calm water reflecting the intense blue of the sky. In the distance, steep hills formed a lush green background to the scene, and overhead a cloudless sky stretched as far as the eye could see.

The harbour was filled with craft of every description. Passenger liners, sailing under their national flag; gleaming white pleasure cruisers — their decks lined with eager sightseers clad in colourful Hawaiian shirts and sporting expensive cameras; giant freighters with their huge consignments of merchandise, and small cargo boats laden to capacity with a miscellaneous selection of goods, which ranged from oriental spices to delicate ivory carvings and bales of brightly coloured silks. On the outskirts of the bay a sleek, grey naval destroyer rode at anchor, watchful and vigilant, while a custom's launch sped hurriedly about its business as it patrolled the busy water of the harbour. Nearer the shore there were yachts of varied dimensions; launches draped with gaily coloured awnings, junks and fishing boats, and countless small sampans that bobbed merrily up and down on the shimmering water. Amid the vast array of assorted craft, a ferry boat laden with passengers threaded its way from one side of the bay to the other. Boldly emblazoned on its broad canopy Emily could read the words STAR FERRY COMPANY.

To one side of the harbour stood Kowloon, beyond which the New Territories stretched towards China.

Ahead lay the island of Hong Kong — a huge, green mountainside rising majestically from the sea towards its summit, nearly 2,000 feet above sea level. In the foreground was the city. Constructed on different levels, it appeared to be one enormous built-up area that extended both horizontally and vertically, relentlessly encroaching on the green hillsides as it rose ever higher. Concrete blocks of what appeared to be flats and offices, intermingled with solid, dignified, colonial style residences.

Dominating the scene were several giant skyscrapers that towered above the surrounding buildings, dwarfing them into comparative insignificance.

Higher up the hill side the landscape began to alter. The habitations became more sparse, until they finally gave way to thick, dense undergrowth, dotted with the occasional tall building and a number of imposing looking houses, that Emily imagined to be the homes of some of the wealthier citizens of the colony.

★ ★ ★

It took Emily a while to adapt to her new, more leisurely way of life. She was unaccustomed to having everything done for her, and at first she found it somewhat irksome. She had little to do other than order the meals, arrange the flowers, and generally supervise the running of the house. In addition to Ah Ling the number one boy, there was a number two boy and an amah. The amah, Mei Chi, not only looked after the children for much of the time, but also did the interminable washing and ironing for the entire family, under conditions that, compared with Western standards, Emily considered to be little short of archaic. Between them, her staff attended to the complete running of the house, including the household shopping. Peter had already explained to her that the marketing was one of the perks of the number one boy. She quickly learned to turn a blind eye to the odd dollar or two that was added to Ah Ling's weekly account, knowing that he had saved her at least twice that amount by bargaining over every item that he purchased on her behalf.

Though there were few naval wives in the colony, there were many army families. Emily soon made friends with some of the army wives, many of whom had children of the same age as Martin and the two girls.

At the weekends the whole family usually spent the afternoons with a picnic tea on one of the sandy beaches on the island, where the children played happily in and out of the water, and Emily and Peter lazed peacefully on the hot sand under the shade of an umbrella, while they watched the children's antics.

Emily was soon to discover that a great deal of entertainment took place in the colony. Apart from a certain amount of official entertainment, there were frequent luncheon and dinner parties with their friends, as well as an endless round of cocktail parties. Her rapidly increasing social life began to occupy much of her day, making her appreciate to the full how little she had to attend to at home.

She took up tennis and golf again, after an absence of nearly twenty years. She swam regularly, a pastime that had seldom appealed to her in the cold waters surrounding the English coast. She went sailing with friends who had a small yacht and soon became a useful member of the crew.

Sailing was something Emily especially enjoyed. As the wind filled the sails and the boat moved restlessly under her, she experienced a sensation of excitement and exhilaration that compared with none other she knew.

Then there was the occasional launch picnic. Long, lazy days when the launch would cruise leisurely amongst the surrounding islands, dropping anchor in deep water for those who wished to swim before lunch.

On one such occasion Emily and Peter were the guests of Robert Maitland, the managing director of Maitland Struthers, an export and import company based in Kowloon. It was late morning. Emily had already been swimming, and after changing into a sundress was reclining in a deckchair in the shade of an awning, a long refreshing drink in her hand. A light sea breeze kept the temperature on deck deliciously cool. Overhead, the awning, caught by the breeze, flapped up and down in a flurry of excitement, as it tugged to be free from its stays. Idly Emily watched Peter as he swam in the deep, clear water, reluctant to leave its cool depths.

She gave him a wave as he swam towards the side and called out, "Peter, come on in and have a drink. It's nearly lunch time and I'm absolutely famished after my swim."

He laughed. "Okay darling. I'll join you in a minute."

Moments later, hearing footsteps, Emily turned her head and saw a young man walking towards her along the deck. She had noticed him earlier, moving among the dozen or so guests in an easy, relaxed manner. There was something vaguely familiar about his appearance that puzzled her.

As he approached her he said, "Is there something I can get for you Mrs. Stuart? Another drink perhaps?"

"No thank you very much — not for the moment anyway," she replied, smiling up at him. She was perplexed, unable to make out what it was about him that was so familiar.

"Forgive me, but have we met before? I seem to know your face, but for the life of me, I can't recall your name!" He grinned back at her, a friendly disarming smile. Again Emily had that feeling of déja vu.

"I'm David Frensham," he replied. "I work for Bob Maitland. And no, we haven't actually met before Mrs. Stuart, so please don't distress yourself by imagining that you've forgotten my name. I have in fact met Captain Stuart once or twice, but unfortunately I've never had the opportunity of meeting you before, although of course, I've often seen you at various parties. Actually," he went on, "I get invited on these launch picnics as a sort of glorified aide to Bob Maitland — he's an old friend of my father's. My job is to go around seeing that everyone is happy!"

Emily had not properly taken in his name as he had introduced himself. She replied, "That sounds rather fun. One of the perks of the job I suppose. Tell me again, what did you say your name was?"

"David Frensham."

Suddenly the penny dropped. "Are you by any chance related to Nicholas Frensham?"

"He's my father. Do you know him?"

Emily hesitated. "I met him years ago when I was living in London just after the war."

"How extraordinary." After a short pause he asked, "Are you still in touch?"

Emily shook her head, "No."

"Well, you wouldn't know then that my mother died a few months ago?"

"Oh, I am so sorry. I didn't know your mother of course." After a moment she asked curiously, "Haven't you got a brother or a sister?"

"Yes. A sister, Catherine. She's two years younger than I am, and has recently become engaged. I'm just thankful she was there to look after father when my mother died. Catherine said he was pretty cut up about it at the time, but is gradually beginning to perk up. In fact," he continued more cheerfully, "we're trying to get him to come out here for a few weeks at Christmas. I'm sure if he knew that you were here," he continued with an admiring glance in Emily's direction, "we'd have no difficulty in persuading him to come."

Emily vividly recalled the time nearly twelve years ago when, perhaps over-reacting a little, she had told Nicholas Frensham never to darken her doors again. It all seemed such a long time ago now, nevertheless, she was not sure she particularly relished the thought of meeting him again. She turned towards David and carefully inspected the young man. He was of medium height with light coloured hair and gentle, hazel brown eyes. He was clean shaven with an open, honest face and a wide generous mouth. She judged him to be in his late twenties, though his friendly, boyish grin and shy, sensitive expression made him appear younger. He possessed a natural, easy manner and before long they were conversing like old friends.

They were shortly joined by Peter, who had changed into an open-necked shirt and a pair of white shorts. David quickly jumped to his feet as he saw Peter approach.

"Good morning, Sir," he said politely,

"did you enjoy your swim?"

Peter gave him a friendly smile as he sat down beside Emily, "Very much, thanks."

David went on, "While I was talking to your wife, Sir, we discovered that she used to know my father. Did you ever meet him?"

Peter glanced towards Emily and raised his eyebrows enquiringly, "I don't recall doing so . . ."

Emily quickly interjected, "It was while you were in Washington darling. When I was living in the flat."

Slightly puzzled, Peter gave a noncommittal "Oh," and the conversation changed.

Over the next few weeks Emily saw David on a couple of occasions. The first time was at a cocktail party. She saw him make his way across the room towards her. They had spoken only very briefly when they were joined by some friends of Emily's. Shortly after she had introduced David, he made his excuses and disappeared into the throng. The second time they met, Emily was returning home after a morning's shopping — laden with parcels. Hearing footsteps behind her she glanced over her shoulder and saw a hot and perspiring David in pursuit. As he approached her, he began breathlessly, "I saw you further back and was trying to catch up with you. I say, do let me carry some of those things for you." He relieved her of some of her parcels, and accompanied her the short distance home.

Emily thanked him with an engaging smile.

"Would you like to come in and have a drink if you are not in too much of a hurry?"

"I'd simply love to," he replied with alacrity. "Actually I've got the day off, so I'm in no rush."

When Peter returned at lunch time, David was still there. He rose to his feet as Peter entered the room, and murmured apologetically, "I'm terribly sorry, Mrs. Stuart, I'd no idea it was so late."

Peter said affably, "There's no need to dash off. Why don't you stay and have lunch with us and meet the family?"

"That would be absolutely super Sir, if

it's really all right?" He looked at Emily for confirmation.

The children appeared almost immediately. Their arrival was heralded by the clatter of running feet, accompanied by the sound of high pitched childish voices that echoed and reverberated around the marble tiled hall. As they caught sight of David through the open doorway, they came to an abrupt halt, their enthusiasm silenced for a brief moment. But as soon as they had politely shaken hands with him, they broke into an excited chatter, plying their visitor with an endless stream of questions to which David replied with cheerful good humour.

When they had all finished lunch and Peter had returned to the office, Emily and David sat out on the cool verandah drinking their coffee.

His face wore a far-away expression as he remarked wistfully, "It's so good to be among a family again Mrs. Stuart. Although it's a wonderful life out here from the social point of view, I do miss home life." After a pause he went on thoughtfully, "I suppose we were a fairly close knit family, as families go, although my father only managed to get home at weekends. But when he was home, we always had an absolutely super time. Yet it was my mother who sort of held the family together, if you know what I mean." His voice trailed off. For a moment he averted his eyes, and gazed reflectively into the distance.

As far as Emily could recall, it was only a few months since his mother had died. Apart from the fact that her death must have been a great shock to him, it was obvious from the way in which he spoke about her that he had a very deep affection for her. Intuitively Emily felt that he was in need of someone to talk to.

"Tell me about your family, David." she said quietly.

He required no further encouragement and immediately embarked on an account of how he had spent his childhood in a small village in Dorset where, before the war, he and his sister had been brought up in the family home, surrounded by all the trappings of country life, ponies, dogs, fishing rods, bicycles. He explained how, soon after the end of the war, he had gone to Harrow, and that, after completing his three years national service with the army, he had landed the job with Maitland Struthers. He had worked in London for a couple of years before being sent out to join the Hong Kong branch, and for the last eight or nine months had been living in a small flat in Kowloon.

He spoke of his father with immense pride and respect. But it was obvious that he had been a good deal closer to his mother. Emily suddenly felt very maternal towards this young man. There was something about him that she found very endearing. She quickly formed the opinion that while he had inherited much of his father's charm and personality, he probably took more after his mother in character.

When eventually he came to take his leave he said, slightly apologetically, "I do hope I haven't bored you too much, Mrs. Stuart. It's been wonderful being able to talk to you."

Emily smiled at him kindly. "Well, any time you want a chat, David, you know where we live." Then on a wild impulse she continued, "If you would like a bit of family life why don't you join us for a bathing picnic over the weekend? Peter and I always take the children to the beach every Saturday afternoon. It's what we call our 'family day'! If you've got nothing better to do, you could stay on for dinner afterwards." He accepted the invitation gratefully, leaving Emily feeling that beneath his cheerful exterior he was possibly still a bit homesick and lonely.

After the first beach picnic, David became a fairly frequent visitor to the Stuart's home at the weekends. He was completely at ease with the children, treating the eight year old Martin as an equal, whether he was playing cricket with him on the beach, or just chatting to him man-to-man.

He was equally at home with Cara and Maisie. With endless patience he would help them build enormous sand castles that quickly drew the attention of every other child on the beach. He kept them happy by the hour as he sent them to collect buckets of sea water with which to fill the surrounding moat, or organised a game to see who could find the largest number of sea shells. As Emily watched him surrounded not only by her own brood, but by many of their little friends, she laughingly came to the conclusion that David was one of a rare breed of men who was a complete 'natural' with children.

At first, Cara had maintained her usual dignified aloofness, until curiosity began to get the better of her. She gradually drew closer to the scene of action and before long was joining in the fun with the rest of the family, any doubts that she may have entertained toward this stranger apparently satisfied.

Towards the end of the year, David announced that his father was arriving by air early in December. He added that he had booked him a room in the Peninsular Hotel, since he felt that his own flat would be too small and uncomfortable to house them both.

Peter said, "Good idea. I'm glad you've managed to persuade him to come. Once he's settled in you must bring him over for dinner one evening."

Emily had never told Peter of her association with Nicholas. For a long while after it was over, she had still felt humiliated by the experience, and had wanted only to put the matter out of her mind. Peter had accepted her explanation that she had known Nicholas during the time he was in Washington without argument, and with Nicholas' arrival imminent, she deemed it wise to let the matter rest.

15

MEETING Nicholas again, Emily was mildly surprised to find that although he looked a little older, he had not changed a great deal. His figure was still lean and erect, and his now silvery grey hair lent an added air of distinction to his appearance.

When, a few days after his arrival, Nicholas and David dined with the Stuarts, Nicholas' manner was charming and courteous. He thanked them both for having been so good to his son, and complimented Emily on her appearance, adding with an admiring glance that married life clearly agreed with her. Confident and relaxed, he gave the impression that they had been no more than casual friends.

Peter found the older man interesting and easy to talk to. He also discovered him to be an amusing and entertaining guest. The evening had gone well.

After Nicholas and David had left,

Peter said, "What an extraordinarily nice chap. I can see now where young David gets his charm from! Where did you say you had met him, Em?"

"Oh, he was a friend of the people who lived in the flat opposite mine," Emily replied vaguely. She stifled a yawn, "I don't know about you darling, but I'm exhausted. Come on, let's go to bed."

At breakfast the following morning, Peter said, "If you're not too busy during the next day or two, why don't you offer to take Nicholas on a tour of the colony? He'll be bored stiff on his own with David working all day." Emily said nothing. He went on persuasively, "I think it would be a great kindness, Em, if you could find the time."

She finally agreed to show Nicholas one or two of the more interesting sights that the Colony had to offer, albeit with a certain amount of reluctance. This puzzled Peter, since it was out of character for her to be quite so reticent.

When, a day or two later, Emily collected Nicholas from his hotel, she made it unmistakeably clear to him, that it was entirely Peter's idea that she should act as his guide.

A small, amused smile played around the corners of his mouth. "Of course," he replied agreeably, "I quite understand. It was most kind of him to suggest it."

Emily decided to start by taking him on a tour of the New Territories. As she drove in the direction of Fanling, she explained in a brisk, matter-of-fact voice that Fanling was the last village this side of the border with China.

"When we get closer," she continued, "you'll be able to see the Chinese sentries in their look-out post on the other side of the border. I always think it's slightly menacing in a way," she ended with a nervous laugh.

They drove in silence for some miles while Nicholas observed with interest the spectacular country through which they passed; the small villages they came to — the car scattering pigs, chickens, and ducks in every direction — and the rows of paddy fields that stretched for miles around them.

Prompted by a feeling that she should say something to him concerning his wife's death, Emily eventually broke the silence.

"David told me of how you had recently lost your wife. I am so sorry. It must have been a great shock for you."

"Thank you, my dear," he replied, "it's kind of you to be concerned." After a moment or so he continued in a calm, matter-of-fact voice, "I was very fond of my wife, but it would be wrong to pretend that there was anything more between us than a mutual affection and respect. Sadly, we were entirely unsuited to each other, and should never have married in the first place. We agreed to stay together solely for the sake of the children."

Feeling slightly embarrassed, Emily quickly changed the subject, "There is a golf course out at Fanling as well as a country club, where people often come for the weekend. I thought perhaps you might like to stop and have lunch there before we go back?"

The day turned out to be an unqualified success. Nicholas was as charming and as companionable as she remembered him of old, and any doubts she had had about meeting him again were quickly dispelled.

After the first day, there were other expeditions. She took him on the Peak Tram to the highest point on the island from where they looked down at the magnificent view of the harbour far below. On another occasion they had lunch together on one of the floating restaurants in the small fishing village of Aberdeen, on the far side of the island.

She took him round the shops. Not only the larger ones in the main shopping area but she showed him small shops, tucked away up narrow alleyways, where overhead, the buildings on either side seemed as though they were leaning forward to touch each other. In the stifling heat of the narrow streets, the air was foul from the stench of open drains, rotting fruit and vegetables, and the close proximity of human bodies. Drifting through unshuttered windows, the odoriferous smell of Chinese cooking mingled with the pungent, aromatic fragrance of oriental herbs and spices. Rows of washing hung from the windows, cascading onto the stalls below, and in the background was the unmistakeable click-clack of mah-jong being played in upstairs rooms.

As well as the usual tourist sights and attractions, they visited the shanty town villages built on the steep hill sides, where after a storm, the villages were swallowed up in a landslide of mud and filth. Here, thousands upon thousands of Chinese lived under conditions more suited to beast than man. She showed him also the numerous sampans and junks that lined the water front, where thousands more Chinese eked out a hand-to-mouth existence; the bare pavements where the homeless slept out each night, and the beggars that squatted in their rags on street corners, their begging bowls outstretched to passers-by.

Emily had not been in the Colony for more than a few months, before she had discovered that Hong Kong was a city of great extremes.

By the time she had completed her tour, Nicholas had seen for himself the immense wealth and prosperity that lay side by side with the abject poverty and misery that affected the lives of the vast majority of the three and a half million people that were living in the colony at the time.

Emily's carefully planned tour of the island had started out innocently enough. But while Nicholas' manner towards her had never been anything more than that of a friend, as the days passed, she found herself being slowly but inexorably drawn towards him, falling once more under the spell of his innate charm and charismatic personality. She began to look forward to their outings with undue pleasure, spending more and more time with him, until their excursions became almost daily events.

She knew that she was playing with fire, but she knew also that she was unable to do anything about it without giving away her own feelings, and risk causing a certain amount of speculation. She consoled herself with the thought that in another week or two he would be gone from her life forever.

Christmas came and went. Peter and David both returned to work once the holiday was over, leaving Emily and

Nicholas free to resume their jaunts together.

Early in the new year, with only two days left before Nicholas was due to fly home, he came to lunch. Emily had planned a quiet lunch for the three of them, knowing that it would be their last chance to see Nicholas. He arrived with a magnificent bouquet of flowers for Emily, some carefully thought out presents for the children, and a box of Havana cigars for Peter.

After they had finished lunch, the two men shook hands warmly. Peter then returned to the office leaving Emily and Nicholas on their own. For a moment he stood opposite her, a whimsical smile on his face. Reaching out he took both her hands in his.

"So it's finally goodbye Emily. I'm going to miss you, my dear."

"I shall miss you too, Nicholas," she said quietly. "We've had a lot of fun together, haven't we?"

"We have indeed. I can certainly recommend you as being a most excellent courier!" In a more serious tone he went on, "As an old friend, may I be allowed

271

to kiss you goodbye?"

Emily smiled, "Of course you may." Still holding her hands, he drew her towards him and bent forward to kiss her gently on her cheek. Emily could scent his distinctive, masculine aroma, as his lips lightly brushed her face. She felt the warmth of his body as he leaned towards her. For a brief moment she battled with her emotions, fighting to control the same animal magnetism that had originally drawn her towards this man. Then without warning her control snapped. She leaned against him murmuring, "Oh Nicholas, don't go. Please don't go." Suddenly his lips were on hers. All her old fervour awakened, she returned his kisses with passion. As his hands moved gently over the curves of her body her whole being responded to his touch. Until suddenly, almost roughly, he thrust her away from him. Startled, Emily stared at him uncomprehendingly.

He adjusted his tie, and said abruptly, "Emily, I have an important appointment this afternoon. I am afraid I must leave you." His voice sounded troubled as he ended lamely, "Forgive me, my dear."

"But Nicholas . . . "

He saw the bewildered expression on her face and the hurt in her eyes. He hesitated before saying gravely, "Emily, will you come to my hotel tomorrow afternoon? I'll be waiting for you if you decide to come."

Avoiding her eyes, he crossed the room towards the door. Emily hastily pulled herself together, and followed him into the hall. As he reached the front door he turned to face her. She saw in his eyes an expression of immense tenderness and affection, as in a barely audible voice he murmured, "Goodbye Emily." He then walked quickly away without looking back.

Weak-kneed, Emily went upstairs to her room. As she lay on the bed that she shared with Peter, she stared up at the ceiling unconscious of the tears that coursed down her cheeks, as torn between her love for Peter and the strong attraction that she felt for Nicholas, she struggled with her overwrought emotions.

She was aware that her feelings for Nicholas were largely physical, just as she was aware that she would always be drawn to him in this way, until she was old and grey, and all passion spent. Yet, during the time they had had together, she had come to know him in a way she had never done before. In doing so she had discovered another side to his nature. He had changed over the years — mellowed.

There was a warmth and consideration about him, and a greater depth of sincerity than she had ever given him credit for, all of which only served to increase her liking and respect for him.

She thought how much she loved Peter and the children. And she knew that whatever her feelings for Nicholas, she could never bring herself to betray her family, in order to satisfy her own desires. Her mind began to ease, as, with a feeling of relief, she realised that she had no choice to make. She had already made her decision.

Later she put through a phone call to the Peninsular Hotel and asked for a message to be delivered to Mr. Nicholas Frensham as soon as he returned. The message read 'Bon voyage. Love Peter and Emily.'

The following morning Ah Ling came into the room with an envelope in his hand.

"Letter come by messenger from Kowloon side, Missy," he said in his pidgin English, as he handed her the letter. Emily knew without looking at it that the letter was from Nicholas. As she saw the fine, scholarly hand on the envelope, she realised with a pang that it was the first time she had ever seen his handwriting.

'*My dear Emily,*' the letter began. '*I could not leave without first explaining the reason for my abrupt departure yesterday afternoon.*

As perhaps you may have realised, I had no important appointment to keep. In using it as an excuse I was merely playing for time. I knew that you would never agree to come to my hotel if you had sufficient time in which to think the matter over, and to consider the possible consequences.

What happened between us yesterday was no more than the outcome of four very happy weeks in each other's

275

company, *during which time we got to know each other better than we had previously. But like all good things it had to end, and the sudden realisation that the time had finally come for us to say goodbye ended in us both getting a little carried away by our feelings. Farewells always tend to play havoc with one's emotions, Emily, my dear. It would have been so easy in the heat of the moment to have swept you off to some secluded spot, and made love to you in the way that I have wanted to, time and time again during the last few weeks. A few years ago perhaps I might have done so. However, I have a great liking and respect for Peter, and have grown too fond of you to risk hurting you, or to take advantage of you in anyway.*

I have to confess that to my discredit, I have not always considered the feelings of others, but in doing so now, I hope you will understand and accept my actions as a measure of my deep affection and regard for you.

Thank you for everything, dear Emily. You have made my visit a truly memorable one.'

The letter was signed with the initials N.F. There was a postscript.

'Keep an eye on David for me. He is very devoted to you.'

She folded the letter, returned it to its envelope and tucked it into the pocket of her cardigan. She walked slowly towards the window and stared out across the bay, her mind focused on the sobering thought that in another twenty four hours, Nicholas would be gone from her life forever.

★ ★ ★

It was a little while before Emily was able to come to terms with the fact that her brief encounter with Nicholas was over. She missed him greatly, but knew that for her own peace of mind she had to put him firmly out of her thoughts, and regard the last few weeks as nothing more than a happy and memorable interlude in her life.

To compensate for the gap his departure had left, she threw herself into various social activities with resolve and determination. Nevertheless, there were constant reminders of their time together, and for the first few weeks after he had left, she felt under a certain amount of strain. No sooner had she begun to get her life back onto an even keel than came the sad news of Stephen's death.

In her grief at losing her father, she quite irrationally blamed Peter for placing her in the position of having to choose between accompanying her husband, or staying at home to look after her father. Peter sensibly pointed out that it would have made little difference whether or not she had been there. Stephen had apparently suffered a massive stroke from which there was no hope of recovery, and had died in hospital a day or two later. In an effort to comfort her, Peter added that Stephen would have been the last person to have wished her to have stayed behind to look after him. But Emily was inconsolable. She withdrew into herself, and with each day that passed, began to shut Peter more and more out of her life.

She deliberately turned away from him in bed at night, refusing his attempts to take her into his arms, until Peter, aggrieved and perplexed by her rejection of him, asked with a certain bitterness in his voice, if she would prefer him to move into another room. Almost indifferently, she agreed that it might be best if he were to do so, at least for the time being.

As soon as she got over her initial grief, Emily realised that not only was she being totally unreasonable in her attitude towards Peter, but also grossly unfair. She was aware without having to be reminded, that her first loyalty was to her husband, and she knew how much she must have hurt him by her thoughtless and insensitive behaviour. She tried to talk to him, to seek his forgiveness, but the words froze on her lips. He had become a stranger to her. Polite, remote, distant.

In a few short weeks they grew further and further apart, meeting only at meal times, exchanging only the briefest of remarks, and attending social functions together solely for the sake of appearances.

The children soon became aware of the tension in the house. At meal times Martin looked from one parent to the other, his eyes troubled and bewildered. The little girls, younger than Martin and lacking his perception, appeared to accept the situation. Maisie though, instinctively sensed something amiss between the two people whom she had always regarded as her mother and father and she became noticeably more demonstrative in her affection towards Emily.

The weeks wore on. Emily had never felt lonelier or more isolated in all her life. She began to lose weight. Deep shadows under her eyes spoke of sleepless nights, and she became increasingly short tempered and on edge.

Then came an evening, when going upstairs to say goodnight to the children, she noticed immediately she entered Martin's room that something was wrong. He looked very flushed, and complained of feeling sick and of having a bad headache. When Emily took his temperature she found that it registered 104°.

In a panic she ran down the stairs, across the hall and into Peter's study. Peter, immersed in a book, looked up at her sudden entry.

"Peter," she began, "Martin's not well."

"What's wrong with him?" he enquired.

"I don't know. He's got a temperature of 104° and says he's got a bad headache and is feeling very sick."

Peter heard the note of alarm in her voice. His tone was calm as he replied, "You go back to Martin and I'll phone the M.O." An hour later the Medical Officer had been and gone, and Martin had been removed to hospital by ambulance, with suspected meningitis.

Later that evening, the doctor explained to Martin's anxious parents that his suspicions were incorrect and that Martin in fact had polio: an inflammation of the spinal cord, which in severe cases could cause permanent paralysis. However, he added encouragingly, the medical profession knew a great deal more about polio these days and with luck Martin could make a complete recovery.

At the end of six weeks in hospital Martin returned home. He was painfully thin, his muscles emaciated and weak, a shadow of the robust little boy he had been a few weeks previously. A year passed before he was sufficiently recovered to lead a normal life, and even then, he tired easily.

Throughout Martin's illness David was a source of great comfort and support to the whole family. Every weekend he came over from the mainland to spend several hours each day with the boy. Martin was noticeably more cheerful after his visits, and David's purposeful and encouraging attitude towards Martin's illness, did much to speed his recovery. Emily was immensely grateful to him as she watched her son's response to David's efforts, as well as deeply touched at the way in which he gave up so much of his time to being with Martin.

Ironically, it was Martin's illness that was responsible for healing the rift between Emily and Peter.

Their tense, emotional reconciliation had taken place the same evening that Martin had been rushed into hospital.

On their return home some hours later the sight of Emily's strained and anxious face was almost more than Peter could bear. In an instant all the bitterness and resentment of the past few weeks vanished from his mind. His only thought was to comfort her in her anxiety and distress. He resisted an overwhelming desire to take her in his arms, and instead laid a gentle hand on her shoulder. His voice was soft as he said, "Try not to worry too much, Em, I'm sure Martin will be alright. He's a tough little boy." Emily's frayed nerves were already stretched to the limit of her endurance by the traumatic events of the last few weeks. At his touch all restraint left her. Dry, muffled sobs shook her slender body in a paroxysm of despair and loneliness. Peter watched her with an aching heart. Unable to trust himself to speak, he silently reached out his arms towards her. As she raised her tear-stained face to his, she saw in his eyes an expression that confirmed beyond all doubt his deep and abiding love for her. She saw also with a pang of bitter remorse, the lines of worry and suffering on his tired and haggard features. Suddenly drained of all emotion, she hesitated momentarily then with a deep, tremulous sigh she stumbled blindly into his open arms. That night as once more she lay by his side, Emily knew for the first time, the full measure of her love for him.

Part Four

1962 – 1990

16

PETER'S tour of duty in Hong Kong had been extended by a few months and it was towards the end of 1962 before the family finally returned home.

England was attired in all its autumn glory as they set foot on its shores once more. The leaves had already turned, taking on a thousand shades of red, amber and gold. An early morning mist hung lightly on the air, shrouding the landscape with thin wisps of silvery grey. The moist, damp atmosphere and soft mellow colouring was a welcome change after three years of endless blue skies, blazing sunshine, and the hot, often humid climate.

As they drove through the familiar portals of Wisteria House, Emily felt a twinge of sadness that Stephen was no longer there to greet them, but in the excitement of being home once more, she quickly forgot her despondency. Elsie was standing in the open doorway waiting to welcome them. The broad smile on her face showed the pleasure and happiness that she felt at seeing them all again.

Within a short time of their arrival, Andrew and Elaine appeared. The children were overjoyed to see their grandparents. They all began to talk at once, each one eager to be the first to impart their news, and for a few minutes pandemonium reigned. At that moment, Elsie came into the room carrying a tray of coffee and biscuits. Hearing the clamour, she quickly gathered up the children, and they all disappeared in a tumult of excitement to inspect the house and garden, and rediscover all their old haunts and hiding places.

Peter and his father settled down in front of the fire with a cup of coffee in their hand. Andrew, now in his late seventies, looked a frail, white haired old gentleman, but his eyes still held their sparkle, and his quick mind was as alert as ever.

Emily and Elaine were ensconced in the window seat that looked out over the garden. Elaine's first question was to enquire after Martin. The brief glimpse she had had of her only grandson had left her with the impression that although he appeared to have lost much of his robustness, he nevertheless looked fit and well. His hair, bleached by the sun, was a pale shade of gold, and his skin still retained a slight tan.

At eleven years old, the boy reminded Elaine vividly of Peter at the same age.

"How is Martin now?" she asked. "We were dreadfully worried about him."

"He's made a wonderful recovery, and all the swimming he's done has helped to strengthen his muscles and get him fit, although he still tires easily. We have so much to thank David for. He was quite determined to get Martin fit and well."

Elaine raised her eyebrows, "Is that the young man that was so good to Martin when he was ill?"

"Yes, that's right. David Frensham."

"Tell me about Cara," Elaine asked. "Is she any more . . . " she searched for the right word, "affectionate than she used to be?"

Emily sighed. Her seven year old daughter still maintained her cool, detached attitude towards her mother. Cara appeared neither to need nor want affection from her, and Emily had learnt to accept her difficult, wayward child's somewhat bizarre attitude as one of the facts of life, however unpalatable.

In answer to Elaine's question she replied, "I think there's a slight improvement. She doesn't seem to have quite such a chip on her shoulder towards people as she used to have, although I can't say that our own relationship has improved. The only person she seems to care about is Maisie."

"I am sorry. I had hoped that she might have grown out of her rather disagreeable manner by now. She's such a pretty little girl to look at, it really does seem a shame."

Elaine paused for a minute before asking in a more cheerful voice, "And what about Maisie?"

Emily's face softened. "Maisie? Well I suppose Maisie is all I ever hoped for in a daughter. She's still the same warm, loving, cuddly little girl that she's always been. She's friendly and affectionate, and very extrovert. Everyone loves her."

"How old is she now?" Elaine asked, "Nearly eight?"

"She'll be eight in January," Elaine replied.

At this point in the conversation they were joined by Andrew and Peter.

Peter announced cheerfully, "I am now going to open a bottle of bubbly to celebrate our return home. Mother, why don't you and father stay for lunch? I'm sure Elsie will have enough food for us all . . . "

From the doorway Elsie's voice interrupted him. "Don't you worry Commander, I've got a casserole in the oven large enough to feed an army. I thought you would like a good, traditional English meal on your return home." Elsie had never accustomed herself to addressing Peter as anything other than 'Commander'. It was as a Commander that she had first known him, and she had continued not only to think of him, but to address him as such ever since. Only in years to come when Peter was made a Rear Admiral, and given the job of naval secretary did she bring herself to address him correctly.

The following weeks passed in a frenzy of excitement and preparation. Christmas was only six weeks off, and in the new year Martin was to start at his prep school.

Apart from the customary arrangements that Christmas entailed, there was Martin's school uniform to be bought, name tapes to be sewn on, a tuck box to be acquired and stocked, as well as a hundred and one other jobs to be attended to, all in a comparatively short space of time.

It was with a heavy heart that, early in January, Emily stood on the platform and waved good-bye to her small son as he joined his fellow pupils on the school train. Clad in his new school uniform, he looked very different from the little boy in shorts and an open neck shirt that she was used to seeing about the place. He looked so grown up, yet at the same time pathetically young and vulnerable. She missed his cheerful, buoyant presence about the house; the continual noise, and the constant state of untidiness that he left in his wake, but most of all she missed his warmth and affection, his many loving and endearing ways.

At the same time that Martin went to prep school, the two girls started to attend the village school in Applefold, and the house seemed strangely quiet.

Emily and Peter had decided some time ago that once the children had begun school, they would put into operation their plan to modernise the large and rambling old house. The builders moved in and for several weeks they lived in acute discomfort, surrounded by brick-dust, falling masonry and the ever present smell of fresh paint.

Their job completed, the army of brick layers, carpenters, plumbers, glaziers and decorators finally moved out and Emily and Peter had their home to themselves once more. After weeks of brewing endless cups of tea, dodging under ladders and being forced to endure the sound of the latest pop hits that blared forth deafeningly from transistor sets, it was a welcome relief to them all.

In the kitchen a gleaming white Aga had been installed. Part of a wall had been demolished to let in a large window which gave the dark, north facing kitchen considerably more light and sunshine. A new, oil fired central heating system replaced the antiquated one there had been previously, and a washing machine now stood in what had once been the pantry.

Upstairs, a small dressing room had been converted into another bathroom, and one of the larger bedrooms divided into two, so that Cara and Maisie could each have their own room. The thick, heavy curtains that had hung in the windows since old Matthew Larby's days, were taken down and replaced with colourful chintz ones. Drab, worn floor coverings were superseded by new fitted carpets throughout, and gradually the old house took on a fresh, rejuvenated appearance.

The next few years passed quickly. Emily's life was divided into holidays and term times. She balanced her life accordingly, joining Peter whenever it was possible, and leaving Elsie in charge during her absence.

At the same time that Martin had started at his public school, Cara and Maisie had gone away to boarding school. Cara's relationship with Maisie had recently given rise to some concern. She had developed an almost unhealthy possessiveness towards Maisie, and as a result it had been decided to send the girls to different schools.

In 1972, Peter had retired from the Navy. He had ended a fairly distinguished career by achieving flag rank as Rear Admiral, and had been made a Companion of the Bath in recognition of his thirty four years' service to Queen and country.

It was in the same year, that Andrew had died. He was eighty nine, and in full possession of his faculties up to the end of his life. Emily had mourned her father-in-law profoundly. She had known him all her life, and had deeply loved and respected the old man.

Elaine, remarkably spright for her seventy nine years, stayed on in the cottage and Emily or Peter visited her each day to keep an eye on her.

By this time Martin was in his second year at London University where he was studying medicine. He had never had any ambition to follow in his father's footsteps, and from an early age had been firm in his decision to become a doctor. At twenty two, he was very like his father in appearance. Tall, fair haired and slim, with the same easy, outward-going personality. He had his mother's sensitive and compassionate nature — qualities that later were to stand him in good stead as a doctor — as well as a well developed sense of humour, and a great zest for life.

By then Cara had reached the age of eighteen. At school she had shown considerable academic ability, and it was generally supposed that she would go on to university. But Cara had other plans. To the surprise of her family and school teachers alike, she announced that she wanted to take up acting as a profession. It took her a while to convince her parents that she was serious, but she finally managed to do so, and for the next two years she studied at the Royal Academy of Dramatic Art. She was still very much a loner. She had made few friends while at school, and seemed unable to sustain a friendship for any length of time. After a year at RADA, she had gained a good deal more confidence, and appeared to have adopted a more friendly attitude towards her fellow human beings.

From a pretty child, Cara had developed into a striking young woman. She had a tall, almost boyish figure, and was lithe and graceful in her movements. She wore her dark, silky hair in her own particular style, short and straight. A thick fringe covered her forehead to hide any trace of the birthmark of which she was still needlessly conscious. The slight blemish was hardly noticeable, although on occasions it became apparent if she was worried or emotionally upset.

Maisie had stayed on at school for a further year. Her end of term reports had shown that while she had plenty of intelligence, she was not particularly intellectual. It was with a feeling of distinct relief that after two attempts she finally managed to scrape through her exams. At school she had been generally liked by both the staff and pupils, and during the holidays, the house was invariably full of her friends, confirming her popularity among her contemporaries.

After she left school, Maisie had no real idea of what she wanted to do, and for the first few months she happily pottered around at home, helping about the house and enjoying herself socially. It was at Peter's insistence that she finally agreed to take a secretarial course. He remarked with his usual dry humour, that with that behind her, she would at least have some qualification to help her earn her own living, should the necessity arise.

After completing the course, she then took a job as assistant to an elderly gentleman who owned what Maisie described as an up market book shop in Piccadilly. She quickly became involved in the intricacies of selling books to a discerning public, and appeared to have found her particular niche in life. She got on well with the old gentleman who owned the shop, and found the leisurely hours suited her social life to perfection.

Maisie had always reminded Emily of a delicate piece of porcelain. She was small and dainty with a perfectly proportioned figure. Her dark, beautiful eyes were warm and expressive. She was fun-loving, and had a merry, irrepressible personality, a warm, generous nature, and an innate talent for making friends. She shared a flat with three other girls just off the King's Road in Chelsea, and went home at the weekends. She would often take her friends home with her as before, only nowadays the old Sussex house echoed to the laughter of young men as well as girls.

Cara had also opted to live in London, and had rented a two bedroomed flat in Fulham. This she shared with a succession of girls who came and went with considerable frequency. Unlike Maisie, Cara chose to spend her weekends in London and rarely went down to Sussex.

Martin was hard at his studies, and was only able to put in an occasional appearance at home. He had a string of girlfriends — mostly fellow students — whom he would sometimes take home with him for the weekend. But his maxim appeared to be safety in numbers, and he seldom brought the same girl home more than once.

For the first time in years, Emily found she had time on her hands. She became a keen gardener, re-designing the fairly extensive garden at Wisteria House — which had once boasted a full time gardener — making it easier to manage and less formal in appearance. She took up bee keeping, selling her honey in Hurstborough Market. She also had time to turn once more to her girlhood hobby of painting and spent many happy hours with her canvas and easel.

Peter, on his retirement, had taken up golf again, and kept himself occupied and fit by playing two or three rounds a week. He helped with the heavier work in the garden, but more under protest than out of any real love for gardening. He was also a prominent figure on several local committees, and pulled his weight in village activities.

Elsie was now in her seventieth year. She was still as active as ever, though Emily had noticed that in recent months, she had taken to having an afternoon nap. She continued to do the cooking, and regarded the kitchen very much as her own domain. Only when they had visitors would she accept any help, resolutely insisting that she could manage on her own. Over the years she had watched her granddaughter mature into a well-adjusted, young woman glowing with health and happiness, for whom she felt an immense pride and affection. For some time now she had been content to leave any decisions affecting Maisie's future to Emily and Peter, in the certain knowledge that they loved Maisie as their own, and unstintingly accepted responsibility for her well being. Maisie had recently changed her name by deed poll from Stokes to Stuart, leaving Elsie with no doubts in her mind about how her granddaughter felt towards the two people whom she had always looked upon as her parents.

Their lives passed peacefully and contentedly. There were the occasional holidays abroad when they went in search of warmth and sunshine; and rare visits to London, from which Emily could hardly wait to return to the peace and quiet of the Sussex countryside. Sometimes there were sudden influxes of family who would arrive with their respective friends for

Easter or bank holiday weekends. There were also frequent visits from friends who came to stay for varying lengths of time. One of these visitors was Nicholas Frensham.

Not long after the family's return from Hong Kong, Peter had come back from London one evening saying that he had unexpectedly run into Nicholas that afternoon, and had invited him down for the weekend. He handed her an envelope on which he had scribbled down Nicholas' phone number, adding that he felt that Nicholas might appreciate a phone call from her to confirm the invitation.

At first Emily had viewed the prospect of Nicholas' visit with some misgivings, but on seeing him again, she knew instinctively that her feelings towards him had changed. While she still found him as charming and as fascinating as before, the fire and passion that he had once aroused in her had died down to no more than a gently glowing ember. In its place she felt a warm and genuine affection for the now slightly ageing yet still attractive man. As soon as she realised that she no longer had to contend with the strong physical appeal that had always drawn her towards him, she was able to relax and feel at ease in his company, and their relationship gradually took on a new and deeper significance.

After his first visit, Nicholas had become a frequent weekend visitor to their home until in time, he came to be accepted almost as one of the family.

Another welcome, albeit rare, visitor to Wisteria House had been David Frensham. Soon after Emily and Peter had returned home from Hong Kong, David had taken off on a short holiday to Japan, where he had fallen wildly in love with a very beautiful Japanese girl. A few months later, they were married, and after a brief honeymoon set up house together in Kowloon.

The girl, whose name was Tomoko, came from a good family and had a university education, but their cultures were too different. Gradually their marriage began to disintegrate, until it finally ended up in the divorce court.

Several years later David had come home on leave and had met an old flame. Over the weeks their friendship developed, and by the time his leave was up he asked her to marry him. By then David was nearly forty. His new wife, Felicity, was four years younger and, like David, was divorced. Sadly that marriage too was destined to fail. Felicity soon found that she was unable to adapt to life in Hong Kong. She disliked the climate. She missed the English countryside, in which she had always been accustomed to living, and after a few years she returned to England where she set up house on her own in rural Berkshire. Here David joined her whenever he was on leave, until some years later she met someone else who she decided to marry and asked David for a divorce.

Fortunately, perhaps, there had been no children by either marriage, although Emily had often wondered if David and Felicity had had a family whether their marriage would have worked out more happily.

Over the years David had kept in fairly close touch with the Stuarts. He came to stay whenever he was on leave, and in between his visits he wrote lengthy letters from Hong Kong. His letters contained a wealth of interesting information on the changes as they took place in the colony. He described in detail the building of the Metro that ran beneath the harbour, linking the island with the mainland; the growth in the enormous number of skyscrapers that had been constructed both in Hong Kong and Kowloon; and the huge increase in the population, which, he informed them, had almost doubled since they lived there. He wrote interestingly about the amount of land around the coastline that had been reclaimed and built on and gave for example the extension of the airport at Kaitak. He also gave vivid and dramatic accounts of the riots and unrest there had been in the colony when the relatively minor incident of the Star Ferry Company increasing its fares by twenty five per cent, had sparked off riots that had terrorised the colony for two days and two nights. He told how the police and the army had been mobilised to quell the thousands of Chinese youths who, after marching in protest on Government House, had attacked cars and buses, set fire to hotels and public buildings; looted shops; caused indiscriminate and malicious damage to property, and had finally resorted to the use of firearms.

His most recent letter had contained news of how — at the time of writing — a large number of the wealthier Chinese families were already booking their flight out of Hong Kong for the eve of 1997, in anticipation of the dire consequences of handing back the colony to China.

David was now a fairly senior employee of Maitland Struthers. He lived a comfortable bachelor existence in the same house half way up the Peak on Hong Kong island, that he had once shared with Felicity. Though he admitted to being a trifle lonely now and then, he appeared to have found his niche in Hong Kong society and was apparently enjoying life to the full. So much so that he had recently given out to family and friends alike that he intended to make Hong Kong his permanent home after he retired.

17

I N the long, hot, glorious summer
of 1976, Cara had her twenty first
birthday. Her parents planned to
celebrate the occasion by giving a
small dance for their daughter. Cara
however, was not at all enamoured
with the prospect of a dance being
held in her honour, and only agreed
to the idea provided she could share the
party with Maisie, who, as Cara pointed
out, would be twenty one herself in six
months time.

If Emily was disappointed at the way
in which Cara had responded to the
suggestion, she understood her daughter's
reticence. Cara had few friends of her own
whom she could invite, whereas Maisie
had any number. By making it a joint
party, the problem from Cara's point of
view would immediately be solved. Emily
resigned herself to accepting that this
was one way around a tricky situation,
and fervently hoped that Maisie would

not be too disappointed at having to share her twenty first birthday party with Cara. Preparations for the occasion duly went ahead. Invitations were sent out, a marquee was hired, a small band engaged, and a firm of caterers called in to provide a buffet supper.

The day of the dance dawned fine and warm, and everything looked set for what Emily hoped would be a happy and memorable evening for both the girls.

Martin and Maisie had arrived from London the previous evening with several of their friends, but in a last minute phone call, Cara informed her mother that she would not be arriving until the following morning. Disappointed, Emily hung up the receiver and went in search of Elsie to tell her not to wait dinner any longer.

The next morning Emily drove into Hurstborough to meet Cara off the London train. She was mildly surprised to see that Cara had brought a friend with her — a girl of about the same age as herself — whom she introduced as Sally Boothroyd.

The girl was pretty in a vapid,

colourless way, with fluffy fair hair, and a limp hand shake. Emily vaguely imagined that she was probably one of Cara's fellow students from RADA, but it transpired that Sally was in fact Cara's new flat mate. She was twenty two years old, came from Bradford, and earned her living as a sales assistant in the dress department of a large store in Oxford Street. All this Emily learnt on the way home. The girl seemed shy and had little to say for herself. It was Cara who supplied most of the answers to Emily's discreet questioning.

When they arrived home some ten minutes later, Emily introduced Sally to the rest of the family. She then drew Cara aside and said in a slightly aggrieved tone of voice, "Darling, why didn't you tell me you were bringing Sally with you?"

Cara shrugged her shoulders, "I knew you would only make a fuss if I did, so I thought it best to say nothing, and just turn up with her." She made no effort to hide the contempt in her voice as she added, "You needn't worry that she's going to upset numbers or anything like that."

Still annoyed, Emily said sharply, "That's not the point. It is a question of where she is going to sleep. The house is already filled to capacity, with some of the young men sleeping on the floor as it is."

"There's no problem," Cara replied cooly, "she can sleep in my room."

"But darling . . . " Emily began, "it's the sheets and blankets and everything . . . "

"For heaven's sake Mother, do stop fussing, we'll manage fine." With that Cara disappeared in search of Sally, leaving Emily wondering why it was that she always seemed to be on a collision course with her daughter.

In spite of the bad start to the day, the evening was a success. The dancing had gone on until midnight, when the three piece band had packed up and gone home. Only one thing had marred the evening for Emily. After dancing with one or two young men, Cara had elected to spend the rest of the evening with Sally. They either bopped up and down to the music together, or sat out, deep in conversation with each other. With a sinking heart Emily recognised

Cara's same possessive attitude towards her friend that she had once shown towards Maisie.

Emily sought out Martin. Slipping her arm through his, she said, "Darling, do you think you could do something about separating Cara from that rather dreary young woman she's brought with her? After all it is Cara's party, and she really should be mixing with her guests instead of spending the whole evening with Sally."

"I'll do what I can, Mum," Martin replied, "but you know what Cara is like . . . Who is this girl anyway? She's a bit different from most of Cara's friends."

"I gather she's her new flat mate." Emily replied.

Martin looked puzzled. "That's interesting. I suppose that means she's split up with Louise."

Emily in turn looked puzzled. "What do you mean by 'split up' exactly? It's a rather strange expression isn't it?"

For a moment Martin appeared a little disconcerted. "Nothing Mum. Really. It was just a figure of speech. Look, I must go. I'm supposed to be dancing with

311

Suzanne. She'll murder me if I keep her waiting much longer." He bent forward and gave his mother an affectionate kiss. "Don't worry Mum, I'll do what I can about Cara, even if I have to dance with her myself!"

In years to come, Emily was to remember that particular evening as the first time that she had entertained any serious thoughts about her daughter's relationship with other women.

For some time now she had considered it strange that, as far as she knew, Cara had no men friends. She was young, attractive and intelligent, and of an age when most girls would welcome companions of the opposite sex. At first Emily had consoled herself with the thought that Cara was perhaps a late developer, but the years went by and there was still no sign of a man in her life. Emily could not help but compare Cara with Maisie. Maisie had a string of young men continually dancing attendance upon her, and although she had never been particularly serious about anyone, her relationship with the opposite sex was normal and natural. It saddened

Emily to think that her daughter was so different.

Towards Christmas Emily received a telephone call. An unfamiliar voice that held a slight American intonation enquired, "Is that Aunt Emily?"

Emily replied in a puzzled voice, "This is Emily Stuart. Who is that speaking?"

"It's Hugh, Aunt Emily. Hugh McNeil."

The penny dropped. "Hugh!" she exclaimed. "Where are you speaking from?"

"London," he replied. "I'm working over here now. I was wondering if I could come down and see you sometime. I have lots of messages for you from my parents."

While he was talking Emily did some quick thinking. Hugh was Teresa and Robert's eldest son. Emily had met the family only once since Teresa had married Robert and gone to live in America. About twenty years ago Teresa had brought the two little boys over to England to visit their grandparents. Hugh would then have been about seven years old, and his younger brother, William, two years his junior.

Gathering her wits about her, Emily replied warmly, "Of course you must come and see us Hugh. What are you doing for Christmas?"

"Well nothing really," he replied. "I've only been over here for a couple of weeks, and haven't got myself quite organised yet."

"Then you must come to us," Emily said firmly. "The family will be home, so you will be able to meet us all at the same time!"

★ ★ ★

Emily stood on the platform waiting for the train to arrive. She felt absurdly nervous at the prospect of meeting the young American. Since she had spoken to him over the telephone she had decided that by now he must be about twenty seven. She wondered anxiously how he would get on with them all. Perhaps he would find the family gathering a bit overpowering. What would he think of a traditional British Christmas compared with their Thanksgiving celebrations held earlier in the year.

In the distance she saw a train approaching, and heard the squeal of its brakes as it drew into the platform. It was Christmas eve, and the London train was full. Several people got out laden with suitcases and parcels. Then she saw him. A strapping young man of medium height, with rugged features and a mop of dark curly hair that protruded uninhibitedly from under his soft felt hat.

For one fleeting moment he reminded her of the man with whom all those years ago she had fallen so passionately in love, and — with such high hopes for the future — had married.

Quickly pulling herself together she raised her hand in a tentative wave. "Hugh?"

"Aunt Emily! Gee it's great to see you again."

On the way home he talked enthusiastically about his family, bringing Emily up to date on the news, and passing on numerous messages from Teresa.

Curious to know what had brought him to England, Emily asked "Tell me what you are doing over here. You said over the phone that you were working in London I think?"

"Well, since I left Harvard, I've been working on Wall Street for a major international bank dealing in investments, and I've just recently been transferred to the London branch. I am absolutely delighted," he went on full of enthusiasm, "for I've always wanted to see something of England. Mother is forever talking about what she still refers to as 'home'! I'm particularly anxious to see Dykes Manor where she was brought up. I was quite small when we came over to England before, and I don't remember it at all."

"That's quite easily arranged," Emily replied, "it's only about twenty miles away from us. Of course it's been sold since your grandparents' death, but we know the present owners, and I'm sure they would be delighted to show you round."

By the time the car drew up outside Wisteria House, Emily had decided that she was going to like this friendly young man who as well as being Teresa's son, was also her nephew.

As she led the way indoors, she turned to him with a warm smile, "Well here we are! Welcome to what I hope you will look upon as your home from home while you are in England."

He grinned back at her, "I think I already do." This time there was no mistaking the family likeness. Hugh had the same infectious, boyish grin, and friendly, cheerful manner that she remembered in his namesake.

He stood in the middle of the hall taking in his surroundings. "The house is exactly as I imagined it would be from my mother's description, only it's so beautifully warm . . . " He sounded surprised. "I always thought that all English houses were cold, damp and draughty, but evidently I was wrong!"

Emily laughed gaily. "You should have seen it a few years ago before we modernised it. It was pretty cold, damp and draughty then, I can tell you! Now come and meet the family," she went on, "they were all busy putting up the Christmas decorations the last time I saw them."

317

★ ★ ★

A few weeks after Christmas Maisie
telephoned from London. Her voice held
a trace of excitement as she asked,
"Mummy, would it be all right if Hugh
came down for the weekend? He's got a
car now, and says he would drive me
down."

"Of course darling," Emily assured
her. "It will be lovely to see him again.
Would you like me to ask him, or will
you give him a message?"

"He is here now Mum, I'll put him
on the line."

Over supper that evening Emily
remarked cheerfully, "Maisie rang up
earlier. Hugh is coming down with her
for the weekend. From what she said, it
sounds as though they have been seeing
quite a lot of each other over the last
few weeks. They were together when she
phoned."

Peter gave an amused smile, "I
thought she was a bit taken with him
at Christmas!"

Over the weekend it soon became clear
that the friendship between Hugh and

Maisie had progressed considerably since Christmas. They were on very friendly terms, and appeared happy and relaxed in each other's company. They spent the weekend either going for long walks together, or exploring the surrounding countryside in Hugh's car. As far as Emily knew, it was the first time that Maisie had shown anything more than a light hearted, affectionate interest in any man, but by the end of the weekend it was evident that Hugh was someone very special to her.

In the months that followed, Maisie and Hugh continued to see each other, until early that summer they became engaged. The announcement of their engagement came as no great surprise to the family, and the following weekend they celebrated the event with a family party, when they were joined not only by Martin and Cara, but Nicholas Frensham too, without whom, by that time, no family gathering would have been complete.

Later the same evening Emily was on her way up to bed, when going past Maisie's bedroom she noticed that her door was half open and the light still on. She heard Maisie call out, "Mummy, is that you?"

Emily put her head around the door. "Still awake darling?"

Maisie was sitting up in bed, her arms hugging her knees. "I'm too excited to sleep!" She patted the bed. "Come and talk to me . . . that is, if you're not too tired?" she added quickly. Emily sat down on the edge of the bed. With a hint of anxiety in her voice, Maisie went on "Mum, you do like Hugh, don't you?"

Emily smiled. "Of course I do darling. I like him very much indeed. So does Daddy, and you know how fond Gran is of him. I don't think we could have chosen a nicer son-in-law for ourselves, even if we had had any say in the matter!"

Maisie's face radiated happiness. "I thought it was all right, but I had to be quite sure. It's very important to me that you and Daddy should approve of who I marry. You've always been such a wonderful example of what a happy marriage should be."

Emily gave a wry smile, "Well don't

imagine that marriage is a bed of roses exactly — you have to work at it like everything else."

Suddenly pensive, Maisie changed the conversation. "It's strange isn't it, that Hugh is your nephew by your first marriage, and I am your niece, and yet Hugh and I aren't related at all!"

"Our family certainly takes a bit of unravelling." Emily agreed. Longing for her bed, she murmured, "Try and go to sleep now, Maisie — you've had a long and exciting day." She bent and kissed her, "Sleep tight, darling."

Just as she was about to close the bedroom door, a small voice behind her said, "Mum — I love Hugh so much that it sometimes frightens me in case something should go wrong. I can't imagine my life without him." She paused, then asked, "Did you ever feel like that about Daddy?"

Standing in the doorway, Emily replied seriously, "Oh yes, I did, I still do." Like Maisie, she was quite unable to visualise her own life without Peter. Their marriage had become closer and more companionable with each year that passed, cementing and enhancing the friendship that had begun when they were both children.

In a tone of mock severity she said, "Now, for heaven's sake go to sleep Maisie! It's after one o'clock. Even if you don't need your beauty sleep, I certainly do!"

Maisie snuggled down. "Mum, I do love you." Emily smiled softly as she closed the door behind her.

During the period that followed the announcement of their engagement, Hugh and Maisie spent several weekends at Wisteria House. Their visits gave Emily and Peter a better chance to get to know their future son-in-law, and they soon discovered that Hugh possessed considerably more attributes and qualities than were at first apparent. He was particularly thoughtful and considerate towards Elsie, making a point of getting to know Maisie's grandmother in the same way he had the parents who had adopted her.

Elsie once said to Emily, "I shall die very happily when my time comes, knowing that Maisie will be cared for by such an exceptionally thoughtful and kind young man. She is a very lucky girl." Elsie, now in her early seventies, radiated a quiet and gentle charm that had captivated Hugh from the start, and his affection for her was genuine and sincere.

Six months later Maisie and Hugh were married in the same small church in Applefold, where thirty seven years earlier Emily had plighted her troth to the handsome young naval officer whose life was to end so tragically in the service of his country.

Teresa and Robert had flown from America for the wedding, and had stayed on at Wisteria House for a few days after the festivities were over. Emily and Teresa spent many hours closeted together exchanging news, and talking over old times. Although they had kept in fairly regular touch by letter, this was the first chance there had been for them to learn in more detail, something of each other's lives over the past three decades.

They were sitting in the garden one afternoon. It was late September and the shadows were already beginning to lengthen as they fell across the wide expanse of lawn, where only a few days before, a large marquee had stood to accommodate the wedding guests.

Teresa leaned back in her deck chair. "Isn't life quite extraordinary?" she mused. "Who could possibly have foretold that after all these years, you and I should be reunited by our children's marriage."

"I know," Emily replied, "it's almost as though our lives have come full circle." She looked at her friend affectionately. Seeing Teresa again evoked so many happy memories. She recalled their first meeting at college. The fun they had together in the months that led up to the war. Their time in the Wrens when they had joined up as carefree, almost irresponsible young girls, and overnight had matured into capable and reliable young women.

The years had been kind to Teresa. She was now fifty eight, a year older than Emily. She had lost her trim figure and her dark hair had begun to grey, but she still retained her old vivacity and sense of fun.

From what Teresa told her, Emily gathered that although Teresa's marriage had been a happy one, it had had its ups and downs. She explained how at first, she had found it hard to adapt to the American way of life, so totally different from her life in England. She was often homesick, and more than once had contemplated returning to the UK when she found that she was unable to accompany her husband on one of his postings.

They had been married for three years before Hugh was born. His arrival was followed quickly by William, and with two small boys to look after, Teresa had her hands full. There were inevitably further separations over the years, but as the boys grew up Teresa had plenty to occupy her, and she learnt to accept the times that she and Robert were separated as part and parcel of service life.

"Hugh was just starting at Harvard, and William was in his last year at high school when Robert was sent to Vietnam." She continued. "That particular period was the worst time of all. I kept meeting wives whose husbands had returned from Vietnam with hair raising stories of what was going on out there. It wasn't like an ordinary posting. This time he was on active service." Lost in contemplation, she paused for a moment.

Then with a shrug of her shoulders she went on. "Well, as you know, Robert was wounded in the thigh and was eventually invalided home. He spent several weeks convalescing in hospital and was then assigned to non-combat duties. I know it sounds an awful thing to say Emily, but I was so thankful." She gave a rueful laugh. "In spite of my upbringing, I don't think I was cut out to be a service wife! All I ever wanted was to settle down in my own home and raise a family, without having to uproot every few years. You've been luckier than me in some ways. You've always had your own home to go back to when you've not been able to be with Peter. That was why when Robert's parents were both killed in that tragic plane accident I was so delighted that he decided to retire. It was wonderful that we were finally able to settle down in the family home in Virginia. It's a most lovely old house Emily," she enthused, "and I adore living in the Southern States. You and Peter simply must come to stay, I know you will love it."

Some days later Teresa and Robert returned to America. Emily and Peter saw them off at Heathrow, promising to pay them a return visit in the not too distant future. On the way home Emily sighed happily. "It's been a wonderful few weeks, hasn't it darling?"

Peter nodded. "Yes it has, Em. Largely due to the extremely efficient way in which you've organised everything," he added generously. In a more serious tone he went on, "Now that all the commotion and excitement of the wedding is over, I think we are going to have to take a firm hand with Elsie. She's been looking very tired the last day or two."

"I agree, but it's so difficult to stop her doing things," Emily replied. Then struck by a sudden thought, she went on, "I wonder if she would consider going to spend a week or two with Mrs. Potter. They've always got on well together. It would be a nice change for her, and would give her a bit of a rest."

"Sounds a good idea to me. Why don't you suggest it to her?"

The car turned into the drive. Leaving Peter to put it in the garage, Emily got out and let herself in through the front door. She was about to call out to Elsie to tell her they were home, when she saw her. She was half lying, half sitting at the bottom of the staircase, in obvious pain and distress.

Emily rushed forward. "Elsie . . . whatever's happened?"

In a weak voice Elsie said apologetically, "I'm afraid I tripped coming down the stairs. I think I may have broken my hip . . ."

An ambulance took Elsie to hospital where she was immediately operated on, and her hip satisfactorily set.

Hugh and Maisie were still on their honeymoon on the Aegean island of Kos and were not expected back for another week. Emily and Peter both felt that Maisie should be informed of her grandmother's accident, but Elsie was insistent that she should not be told until after they had returned home.

Since Elsie appeared to be making reasonable progress, they complied with her wishes, if somewhat against their better judgement. A few days later however, Elsie had a relapse and developed respiratory problems which quickly turned to pneumonia. Emily immediately phoned the small hotel in Kos where Hugh and Maisie were staying, and they caught the next available flight home. Peter met them at Heathrow and drove them straight to the hospital, but by the time they arrived — anxious and travel weary — Elsie, already in a weak condition, had fallen into a semi-conscious state and within hours of their arrival, she slipped peacefully away, dying as she had lived, quietly and unobtrusively.

Her death left the whole family feeling shocked and bereft. The house hardly seemed like home without her, and Emily felt contrite — almost guilty — that they had all taken Elsie so much for granted.

Some days later, Emily attended Elsie's funeral service with the rest of the family. Her mind wandered momentarily as she remembered some of the many other occasions on which she had attended services in the small village church. How as a child she had sat with her parents each Sunday, listening with half an ear to the vicar's long rambling sermon, and wondering hopefully what the next hymn was going to be. She recalled her own war time wedding; her mother's funeral, and more recently, that of her father-in-law.

Her mind returned to the present with a jolt. She thought with a certain irony that it was barely three weeks since the joyous occasion of Maisie's wedding, and gave thanks that at least Elsie had lived to see her granddaughter married.

The family sat in the front pew, tightly squeezed together on the hard, narrow bench. There was Hugh and Maisie, Martin, Cara, Peter and herself. Emily noticed Maisie move a little closer to Hugh. In her despair and unhappiness her small hand sought his for comfort and reassurance. Emily's heart bled for her. Elsie's death was the first real tragedy in Maisie's young life, and coming so soon after her marriage, it had left her devastated.

Emily found herself hoping devoutly that Elsie's spirit was still hovering sufficiently close at hand, for her to know how much she had been loved and respected by them all, and how much her warm and understanding presence would be missed.

Returning home after the service, Emily reflected sadly how empty the house seemed without the quiet, kindly woman who had been her loyal friend and companion for more than twenty years.

18

THE events of the past few weeks, which had ended so sadly in Elsie's death, left Emily feeling tired and dispirited. She missed Maisie and Hugh's visits, when, in the weeks preceding the wedding, there had been so much gaiety and laughter about the house as they discussed plans for the great day. She missed Teresa, and the long heart-to-heart talks they had had together, but most of all she missed Elsie's comforting presence about the place. So much of what was familiar to her had suddenly gone from her life.

Concerned that she looked so tired and drawn, Peter remarked, "Em darling, have you thought about getting someone in to help with the housework? There's a lot for you to manage on your own."

"Well I have thought about it, but I hate the idea of having a stranger about the place."

"I know what you mean," Peter agreed,

"but I wish you would think about it seriously. After all we're neither of us getting any younger!" In the end, common sense prevailed and Emily agreed to find someone who would come in for a few hours each week to lend a hand about the house.

The vicar's wife, hearing that Emily was looking for some help, told her of a Mrs. Webster, who lived on the new estate that had recently been built on the outskirts of the village.

"She's a very pleasant woman — if a bit of a talker," she informed Emily, "and I know she's looking for some part-time work. I could ask her to call and see you, if you would like me to?"

Mrs. Webster turned out to be a cheerful, buxom woman in her early forties. She explained to Emily that now her family had grown up, she had more time to spare, and would welcome a job that would keep her occupied for two or three mornings a week.

She seemed a nice enough woman and knowing how hard it was to get any help these days, Emily decided to engage her.

Nevertheless her tone was guarded as she said, "Well, Mrs. Webster, suppose we give it a months trial, and let's see how we get on together."

As Emily showed her to the front door, Mrs. Webster said a little diffidently, "We were all very sorry in the village to hear about Mrs. Stokes, M'm. She was ever such a nice lady."

Touched by the remark, Emily's face relaxed into a smile. "That's very kind of you Mrs. Webster. We all still miss her dreadfully."

"I'm sure you do M'm. And the poor young lady, just after her wedding and all . . . You never know what's around the corner I always say. Many's a time I've said to Mr. Webster, 'Tom' I've said 'You want to learn to count your blessings,' I've said. 'You never know what's round . . . '"

Fearing that she was about to be subjected to a lengthy discourse on what Mrs. Webster said to her husband, Emily interrupted her by saying firmly, "Yes, well thank you very much for coming to see me Mrs. Webster. I shall look forward to seeing you next Monday."

As Emily closed the front door behind her, she wondered whether she was going to live to regret having engaged Mrs. Webster, after experiencing a taste of her volubility. However on the following Monday morning, her fears were soon allayed. Mrs. Webster arrived on the dot of nine, carrying an enormous black bag from which she extracted a pinafore and a pair of slippers. After satisfying herself on one or two domestic points, she got on with the work quietly and efficiently without so much as opening her mouth, other than to poke her head around the door to enquire whether she should disturb the Admiral to Hoover his study, or wait until he had finished in there.

After so many years of taking for granted the smooth, efficient way in which Elsie had run the house, it was a while before the Stuarts learnt to adapt to the new regime. Mrs. Webster usually arrived while they were still only half way through breakfast. As a result Peter quickly learnt to retire to the study with his Telegraph, instead of reading it at the breakfast table. Emily in turn went without a second cup of coffee so that she could do a quick dash upstairs to make the bed and tidy the bedroom, before Mrs. Webster moved in with her mop and duster.

But, as time passed, Emily grew accustomed to having her about the house, and eventually came to look forward to her mornings with them. Mrs. Webster proved to be a kind, friendly woman if sometimes inclined to be a little too talkative. There were several occasions when, over a mid-morning cup of coffee, Emily had to resort to suddenly remembering an urgent phone call she had to make, in order to bring the conversation to an end without hurting the good woman's feelings.

Taking a cup of coffee into Peter's study one morning, Emily said with a rueful laugh, "You don't know how lucky you are being able to enjoy your elevenses in peace! I've now got to face up to at least quarter of an hour of Mrs. Webster rambling on about nothing in particular!"

Peter grinned. "Never mind darling. It's a small price to pay. She's a very kind, well meaning soul!"

* * *

It was about this time that Cara first began to achieve recognition as a young actress of some talent.

After two years at RADA, she had joined a provincial repertory company, where at the same time as performing in the current play, she was also learning her lines and rehearsing for the following week's production. It was hard work, and after a year in repertory, she auditioned for a small part in a television play. This was quickly followed by other parts, until deciding that she had found her particular niche in the acting profession, she quit the stage to concentrate on becoming a television actress. Over the next few years her career went from strength to strength, and when finally she was given a leading role in a new television series, she played the part with such conviction that before long, the name Cara Stuart became well known to a large number of the viewing public.

Cara was twenty six when she first met Madelaine Gale, another young actress with an aptitude for playing rather guileless, ingenue parts.

On one of Cara's increasingly rare visits home, she brought Madelaine with her for the weekend. Madelaine was essentially very feminine in appearance. Long tendrils of auburn hair framed her pale delicate features in a halo of soft curls. There was a fragile, waif like quality about her that clearly aroused all Cara's protective instincts.

Madelaine was dressed in a long, flowing garment, covered in a mass of frills and flounces, a style of dressing that was in complete contract to Cara's well tailored slacks and open neck shirt.

It distressed Emily deeply to see how completely besotted her daughter appeared to be by this slip of a girl. She was acutely embarrassed and uncomfortable as she observed the long, lingering looks they exchanged; their obvious desire to be alone together, and the cloying manner in which Cara placed a protective, possessive arm around Madelaine's shoulders whenever the opportunity allowed.

Emily was thankful when the weekend came to an end, and Cara and Madelaine returned to London. She was mildly surprised that Peter appeared not to have noticed anything unusual in Cara's behaviour towards Madelaine, but for some reason she felt unable to discuss the matter with him, although of late it had begun to worry her more and more.

Some two or three weeks after Cara's visit, Martin unexpectedly arrived home for the weekend. Peter was away on a short golfing holiday, and Emily and Martin were on their own. No longer able to ignore her doubts and misgivings over her daughter's relationship with other women, Emily seized the opportunity to voice her fears to Martin.

Martin had known for some years of his sister's sexual preferences. He had once discussed the matter with his father. At the time, they had considered it best to keep it from Emily, knowing how hard she would take it if she were to discover the truth about her daughter.

For some time now, Martin had watched Cara drift from one female relationship to another noticing, as his mother had done, Cara's total lack of interest in the opposite sex. Her association with Madelaine Gale however, had lasted a good deal longer than any of her other liaisons and although to Martin, there was something intensely sad about the utter devotion his sister bestowed upon the girl, he hoped for Cara's sake that her affections were returned.

As soon as Emily had begun speaking, Martin realised that his mother already had suspicions about Cara. He decided to tell her the truth without beating about the bush, and was surprised by her calm, prosaic acceptance of the fact that her daughter was gay.

There was a long pause before Emily asked quietly, "Does Maisie know?"

Martin replied in a gentle voice, "Maisie was probably the first to be at the, er, receiving end of Cara's advances. You must remember how tremendously possessive Cara used to be towards Maisie when they were growing up?"

Emily nodded. "And Daddy? Does he know?"

"Yes Mum, but we thought it best not to tell you." Emily nodded her head again.

Then she said slowly, "I think I've always known how things were with Cara — deep down — but ostrich-like, I preferred to bury my head in the sand! I'm glad now that I know the truth," she continued in a matter-of-fact voice. "However unpalatable, the truth is often easier to accept than uncertainty. Thank you for telling me darling, I know it can't have been easy for you."

* * *

The January of 1982 saw the outbreak of the war in the Falklands, when, in a brilliantly conceived and boldly executed operation, British forces were speedily mobilised and transported across the thousands of miles that separated the Falkland Islands from the British Isles.

Overnight the country went onto a war footing. Ships such as *QE2* and *Canberra* were commandeered to act as hospital ships, and to transport troops, vehicles and provisions to the bare, windswept islands in the south Atlantic, where the terrain was formidable and unfriendly, and the troops were under constant attack from the air. At sea, the navy had to contend with Exocet missiles used by the Argentinians, that tore enormous great holes in the side of ships, and inflicted severe casualties on their crews.

However, the losses suffered during the campaign were thankfully, remarkably small, and by June 1982 the campaign was successfully over.

Later in the same year, Martin was married. His bride was a dark haired, attractive girl whose name was Charlotte. She came from a farming family, and was a physiotherapist by profession. She had known Martin for some years, and he had brought her to stay at Wisteria House on several occasions.

Emily found her gentle and uncomplicated, and Charlotte had endeared herself to Emily from the start by her obvious devotion to Martin. Emily both liked and approved of her daughter-in-law, and felt instinctively that her son had made a wise choice.

★ ★ ★

After completing his training, Martin had done two years as a Registrar at a London hospital, before deciding to become a GP and joining a large practice in Tunbridge Wells, where he and Charlotte were now living in a small flat on the outskirts of town.

At the time of Martin's wedding, Hugh and Maisie had already been married for nearly five years, and by then had two children. Fleure — who had been named after Hugh's paternal grandmother — was nearly three years old, and Simon just a year. Fleure was the apple of Emily's eye. She was a dark haired little girl with a mischievous smile, a mind of her own, and a warm and affectionate nature.

Hugh had recently changed his job. He was still in banking, but when he learned that he was shortly to be sent back to New York, he had transferred to another bank, having decided some time ago that he wanted to live in England permanently.

After Simon was born they had bought a modest house in suburban Surrey. The house boasted four bedrooms, and a garden for the children to play in. Much to Emily's delight their home was within easy driving distance of Wisteria House, and Maisie brought the children over regularly.

A year earlier, Hugh's father had died after a brief illness. Hugh had flown home for the funeral, and anxious about his mother continuing to live in the old family house that was much too big for her alone, he gently tried to persuade her to return to England. He felt that there was little to keep her in America, now that he was living in England, and his brother William, who had recently married, was living on the west coast, some 2,000 miles away.

Much to Emily's joy, Teresa had finally allowed herself to be talked into returning home, and was at present engaged in trying to find somewhere suitable to live, that was neither too far away from her grandchildren nor from Emily and Peter.

★ ★ ★

Just when Emily was reflecting on how well everything was working out, tragedy entered her life once more.

She was on her way downstairs one morning when she heard the phone bell ring. Peter answered it. His voice sounded puzzled as he said, "Yes. This is Peter Stuart." After an interval she heard him exclaim, "Oh my God . . . what happened?" There was another longer interval before he said, "I'll come at once," and put down the receiver.

His face was ashen. Panic stricken, Emily said, "Darling, whatever is it? Has something happened to one of the children?"

"It's Cara," Peter replied. "Em, she's in hospital after taking an overdose. That was Madelaine phoning. She says the hospital is doing everything it can, but Cara is still unconscious and in a critical condition."

By the time that Emily and Peter reached the hospital it was all over. Cara had died soon after Madelaine's phone call. The doctors explained that while they had done everything possible, Cara's unconscious body had been discovered too late for them to be able to save her life.

At the inquest, the chief witness had been Madelaine Gale. She presented a sad faced, forlorn little figure as she stood in the witness box, clearly moved as she gave her evidence. She told the court how, for the past two years, she and Cara had shared a flat together in London; how, a few months before her death, Cara had become insanely jealous of Madelaine's quite innocent friendship with another girl. She described the ugly scene there had been between them, when Cara had accused Madelaine of being unfaithful to her, and when no amount of persuasion would make her believe otherwise. The rows between them became more frequent until, unable to stand any more of the suspicions and recriminations, the bitter words, and the quite unfounded jealousies, Madelaine had packed her belongings and moved out.

After that there had been incessant phone calls in which Cara had pleaded with Madelaine to return home, promising to forget the girl in question, although it was clear that she still considered her to be her rival for Madelaine's affections.

Madelaine told the court in a low, subdued voice, that Cara had recently started drinking fairly heavily. One evening a few weeks after Madelaine had moved out, Cara phoned. She was in a tearful, hysterical state, threatening suicide unless Madelaine returned to her.

At this point Madelaine broke down in sobs. It was several moments before she was able to continue.

She told the court how she had not believed for one moment that Cara had meant what she said about taking her own life, adding that she assumed that she had just had too much to drink, and was in a low and depressed state of mind. However, the next morning her conscience began to prick and she put through a phone call to Cara's flat. When she received no reply, she got into a taxi and went round to the flat where she found Cara's limp form sprawled across the large double bed. On the table beside her was a bottle of sleeping pills, an empty tumbler, and a practically empty bottle of gin. Propped up against the bedside lamp was an envelope with her name on it. Opening it, she read, '*Please forgive me. I can't face life without you. Cara'*.

Madelaine had immediately phoned for an ambulance, and after accompanying Cara to hospital, had then phoned Cara's parents to explain what had happened.

The coroner had returned a verdict of suicide while the balance of her mind was disturbed. He expressed deep sympathy with the deceased's family; adding that a tragedy of this sort was all the greater when — out of a sense of despair and loneliness — such a beautiful and talented young woman should have felt compelled to end her life, as the only alternative open to her.

Once Emily got over the shock of Cara's death, she found herself unable to grieve for her daughter in the way she had grieved for the many other people in her life whom she had loved and lost.

She knew that one of the reasons was that she had never been close to Cara in the way she had been to Martin. Yet it went deeper than that. For not only had Cara as a child rejected her mother, but she had continued to do so as she grew older. In her distress and unhappiness at being unable to communicate with her daughter, Emily had hidden her hurt and disappointment behind a curtain of indifference, accepting the fact that their relationship was unlikely to change. Now that Cara was gone, Emily felt little more than an empty sadness that her life should have ended so tragically. Her tears for her daughter had been shed long ago.

Her own feelings apart, she was more than a little concerned about the way in which Peter had taken Cara's death to heart. He reproached himself mercilessly for not having been more tolerant and understanding towards her. While Emily was aware of how much he had disapproved of the blatant way in which Cara had flaunted her relationships with other women, she knew nevertheless that he had a father's deep and protective love for his daughter, and had always been intensely proud of her achievements as an actress.

It tore at Emily's heartstrings to watch him suffer the pangs of remorse and despair he so clearly felt, and to know that there was little she could do to help him.

19

LATE the following year, Charlotte gave birth to twin boys. Charlotte's father was a twin, so that when tests showed that she was expecting a double 'happy event', the news came as no great surprise.

Far from being identical, Paul and Gregory were as dissimilar, both in character and looks, as it was possible for twins to be. Paul, the first-born, was a sturdy, solid child, placid and content. His arrival into the world had been comparatively easy and straightforward and he thrived with each day that passed. Gregory's birth, on the other hand, was fraught with complications, and in a desperate last measure, he had been delivered by Caesarean section. At birth he weighed nearly two pounds less than his brother, and for the first few months of his life he caused his parents considerable concern.

Emily and Peter were equally anxious

about their youngest grandson. There were times when Emily wondered whether the little boy could have suffered slight brain damage at the time of his birth. He was a late developer in every respect, and seemed content to lie quietly in his cot, his eyes the only thing about him that showed any sign of animation.

However, by the time the boys were four years old, Gregory had made noticeable progress physically, although he remained a quiet, shy, sensitive child, content to live in the shadow of his more adventurous brother. He had the added disadvantage of a stutter which manifested itself particularly when he was nervous or upset. In looks he had his father's fair colouring and slight build, whereas Paul was dark like his mother. Paul was a tough little boy in appearance with a cheerful, happy disposition that so much reminded Emily of Martin at the same age.

The devotion between the two small boys was apparent from an early age. As he grew older, Paul became touchingly protective towards his younger brother, appointing himself Gregory's champion and shielding him from the vicissitudes of life whenever possible.

★ ★ ★

Those were halcyon days for Emily as she watched her grandchildren develop from helpless, inert beings into contrasting individuals, each with their own identity and characteristics.

Fleure was now growing up fast. She was an enchanting child who exuded enthusiasm and eagerness in everything she did. Though Fleure possessed little of her mother's delicate, fragile beauty, what she lacked in looks, she made up for in character. From the start Emily felt the same affinity towards her eldest grandchild that she had felt towards Maisie when, all those years ago, Emily had had her first glimpse of Meg's daughter, as she lay in her cot and gazed up at her with dark, beautiful eyes that had immediately reminded Emily of James.

The child loved nothing better than to visit her grandparents. From an early age she had been allowed to stay with them on her own — a privilege that gave her a gratifying sense of superiority over her brother. Simon, two years younger than Fleure, visited his grandparents only when accompanied by his parents. Like most small boys he was noisy, boisterous and completely inexhaustible, and Hugh and Maisie felt that, on his own, Simon would be too much of a handful for his now slightly ageing grandparents.

Since Fleure had begun school, her visits to Wisteria House were, of necessity, restricted to holiday times. She looked forward to the few days she spent each holiday with Emily and Peter with the utmost delight. She loved the old Georgian house with its spacious, comfortably furnished rooms, and large windows that looked out across the distant rolling downs. She loved the garden too, with its sweeping lawns and thick dense shrubberies that afforded ideal cover when playing hide and seek. She never tired of hearing her grandmother tell her how, as a tiny baby, she herself had first come to live there, and of how the old house had been her home for practically all her life.

Fleure was a strange mixture. One moment she was a happy carefree little girl without a care in the world; the next she was capable of displaying a sensitivity and perception far beyond her years. Emily recalled the time when she had taken Fleure with her on one of her trips to see Nicholas Frensham. Nicholas was now an elderly gentleman in his late eighties. White haired, and a little bent, he had none the less retained all his innate charm and courtesy. For the past year or so he had been living in a residential nursing home on the outskirts of Worthing where Emily, and sometimes Peter, visited him each month. It so happened that Fleure's stay at Wisteria House coincided with one of Emily's monthly visits to Worthing. Rather than disappoint Nicholas by postponing their meeting, Emily decided to take Fleure with her.

Fleure was about seven at the time and the outing was something of a novelty for her. She behaved perfectly throughout lunch, and Nicholas was enchanted by the small girl with her mischievous grin and natural, uninhibited manner.

On the way home Fleure asked curiously, "Is Mr. Frensham very old, Granny?"

Emily smiled down at the child sitting beside her. "I suppose he is. He's getting on for ninety now, and that must seem very old to you."

After a short interval Fleure asked, "Have you known him for a long time?"

"Yes, for a very long time — nearly forty years, in fact. He is a very old and dear friend."

They drove in silence for a while before Fleure remarked solemnly, "Mr. Frensham loves you very much, doesn't he Granny?" For a moment Emily was somewhat taken aback, not only by the directness of Fleure's question but also because it reminded her of a time, when not so long ago, Peter had made a similar remark to her.

It was soon after Martin and Charlotte had become engaged. Peter and Emily had been discussing plans for a buffet lunch, to introduce some of their friends to Martin's fiancee. Nicholas' name had been high on the list of guests to be invited, but as soon as his name was mentioned, Emily — quite irrationally — started to raise objections.

"Peter," she began, "if we ask Nicholas, it will mean having to put him up over the weekend when the house will already be full, with Charlotte's parents staying and goodness knows who else. Also one of us will have to fetch him and take him back later."

Peter had replied calmly, "I don't mind running him about in the least, if it will help, but, Em, darling, you really must ask him. He'll be dreadfully hurt if you don't. He still loves you very much, you know."

She raised her eyebrows in surprise. "Whatever makes you say that?"

Peter looked at her with an expression of gentle amusement. "I've known for years that he was in love with you, almost since the time I first met him in Hong Kong."

Although Emily herself had long been aware that Nicholas had once cared for her in a way that was more than just platonic, this was the first indication she had had that Peter had suspected anything. Since the time in

Hong Kong when she had once more been captivated by Nicholas' seductive charm and eloquence, their relationship had never been anything more than that of close friends.

Only once had he hinted at his real feelings for her when, many years ago, he had remarked quietly, "You know, Emily my dear, there has never been anyone else in my life since that time we spent together soon after the war . . . "

Peter's remark had surprised Emily considerably. With a puzzled frown she said, "I didn't realise you knew, Peter. You've never said anything about it before."

"Perhaps I was waiting for a lead from you." He gave a wry smile. "You see, darling, Nicholas was a part of your life I knew nothing about. It became clear to me soon after I met him that there had once been something more between you other than a casual friendship, as you had led me to believe. But you chose not to tell me about it and that was your prerogative."

"I never meant to keep it a secret from you," Emily said unhappily. "After we stopped seeing each other in 1946, I never expected to see Nicholas again. Then when David told us that his father was coming to Hong Kong that Christmas, it all seemed too complicated to attempt to explain what had happened all those years ago."

There was a moment's uncomfortable silence between them before Emily asked curiously, "Tell me, why did you encourage me to see quite so much of Nicholas if you seriously imagined that there had once been something between us? You practically threw me into his arms by suggesting that I should give him a Cook's tour of the colony."

Peter laughed good naturedly. "I admit that at first I had no idea of his feelings towards you. I accepted him as an old acquaintance of yours who, by coincidence, happened to be David's father. It was quite by chance that I discovered how he felt towards you. I caught him looking at you in an unguarded moment, in a way that left me no doubt about what he felt for you. By which time," he added with a rueful grin, "it was too late to do anything about it without causing something of a furore!"

Slightly aggrieved, Emily said, "Yet you still let me go on seeing him day after day? Did you ever stop to think of how I might have felt towards him?"

Peter's voice was grave as he replied, "Oh, yes, I did indeed. I was terrified that I might lose you — that you might still have some feelings left for him." He paused before saying, slowly, "It was obvious from the start that you were attracted to him, and enjoyed being with him — he is after all an exceptionally charming and entertaining companion, as well as being an immensely likeable chap. But however smug or conceited it may sound, I trusted you, Em. It was as simple as that." He smiled at her lovingly. "I knew that whatever your feelings for him, you would never have done anything to jeopardise our family life without first thinking about it very seriously. It wouldn't have been in keeping with your character. Besides which," he added, "Nicholas is an honourable man and I chose to believe that he was sufficiently fond of you not to risk doing anything that would hurt you."

"Oh, Peter." Sorrow and remorse sounded in her voice. Her eyes were misty as she asked, "Were you very hurt?"

He reached for her hand. "I was bloody jealous at the time. But it certainly taught me not to take my wife for granted."

Later that evening, sitting beside him on the sofa, she told him the full story of her first meeting with Nicholas, soon after Peter's departure for Washington. She described how, after a chance encounter at a cocktail party, their friendship had blossomed into one of mutual attraction, until after a romantic evening together when, she laughingly admitted, she had probably had far too much champagne to drink, the evening had ended up with Nicholas making love to her. She described briefly her hurt feelings and wounded pride when she discovered that Nicholas was married, and her outraged and indignant response to his suggestion that they should continue their relationship, regardless of the fact that he was a married man with two teenage children.

"Looking back on it I realised that I probably over-reacted somewhat," she said with a sheepish grin, "and although I know that a lot of that sort of thing did, in fact, go on in those days, we hadn't yet moved into the era of the permissive society, and I was genuinely shocked at the idea of becoming someone's mistress!"

Peter chuckled, "Quite right and proper too, sweetheart!" Then suddenly serious, he asked, "Were you in love with him?"

She considered the question carefully before replying, "I think my feelings towards him were really more physical than anything. I liked him enormously, and enjoyed being with him, but no, I don't think I was ever exactly in love with him. 'Infatuated' might describe it better."

"And that time in Hong Kong . . . ?" Peter asked quietly.

Emily's expression was soft as she replied, "Nothing happened in Hong Kong, Peter. I admit that seeing Nicholas again awakened some of my old feelings towards him. But the situation was quite different. I was a respectable married woman by then, and Nicholas' behaviour towards me was always entirely correct."

At this point Emily stopped abruptly, as with a slight sense of guilt she recalled her last meeting with Nicholas, before he had flown home to England. With frightening clarity the scene flashed before her eyes. She remembered the deep distress she had felt at the sudden realisation that she would not see him again, and how in a moment of emotional weakness she had come so close to betraying the confidence and trust that Peter had placed in her, by allowing her feelings for Nicholas to undermine her self-control. She remembered the bewilderment she had felt at Nicholas' abrupt departure; the look in his eyes as he left her, and finally, his letter explaining his reasons for having abandoned her so suddenly.

All at once she knew that this was something she could not confide in Peter without damaging his self-respect and betraying her friendship with Nicholas. With a shaky laugh she went on, "It was not until after we returned to England and I met Nicholas again, that I discovered, with a feeling of immense relief, that the strong physical attraction that he had always held for me had died a natural death, and that what I felt towards him by then was no more than a feeling of deep affection and respect."

★ ★ ★

"Granny, you're not listening . . . "

Emily returned to earth with a bump.

"I'm sorry Fleure, what were you saying?"

Fleure repeated her question. "I said that Mr. Frensham loves you very much, doesn't he?"

"What makes you say that?" Emily asked curiously.

"Because he looks at you in the same way that Grandpa does, and Grandpa loves you very much too."

Emily laughed in spite of herself. Fleure had seen a look in the old man's eyes that had told her instinctively how Nicholas felt towards her grandmother.

Emily was suddenly reminded of the saying that the eyes were the windows of the soul. Under her breath she murmured with a smile, "Out of the mouths . . . "

"What did you say Granny?"
"Nothing darling, nothing at all."

★ ★ ★

It was Emily's sixty eighth birthday. The whole family were gathering for the weekend to celebrate the occasion, and for some days Emily and Mrs. Webster had been busy making beds and getting everything ready for the invasion.

Throughout the day the family arrived in dribs and drabs. Charlotte and the four year old twins had driven over from Tunbridge Wells in time for lunch, leaving Martin to follow by train later that evening. Maisie, Hugh, Fleure and Simon arrived for a late tea and they were now all seated around the large table in the kitchen, tucking into a meal of scones and chocolate cake, amid a good deal of noise and excitement.

Peter had driven up to London that morning to attend to some business and was not expected home until early evening. It was shortly after six o'clock when the 'phone rang.

Fleure jumped up excitedly. "Can I

answer it, Granny?" A minute or two later she returned to the kitchen. "That was Grandpa," she announced importantly. "He said I was to tell you that he has been a bit delayed. He said he's leaving London now and will be back in time for supper."

Emily put an affectionate arm around her nine year old granddaughter's waist. "Thank you, Fleure."

At eight o'clock there was still no sign of Peter. At half past eight, Emily, with a worried expression on her face, spoke to Maisie.

"Darling, I think we had better start supper. Hugh has to meet Martin at the station in less than an hour's time. We'll keep something hot for Daddy. I can't think what's happened to him," she added unhappily, "he should have been home by now."

Some minutes later they sat down to supper. Emily tried not to let her anxiety show, but she was nevertheless concerned that Peter had not yet arrived home. It was now nearly three hours since his 'phone call and he usually did the journey in well under two hours.

Pointlessly, she kept thinking if only she had spoken to Peter herself instead of letting Fleure take a message.

Maisie noticed her mother's anxiety and said lightly, "Don't worry, Mummy, the traffic is absolutely awful these days. It's impossible to estimate how long it's going to take to get from one place to another."

After they had finished supper, Hugh drove into Hurstborough to collect Martin from the train, while the girls cleared the table, and loaded the dish washer. Emily made some coffee and the three of them adjourned to the drawing room where despite the summers evening a log fire crackled merrily in the grate.

Emily sat down in an armchair. With forced cheerfulness, she said, "It's so lovely having you all here. I do enjoy seeing the children together. Fleure is so good with the boys, particularly little Gregory."

Maisie laughed, "She's a proper little madam, the way she bosses them all around. Perhaps it is something to do with her being the only girl." More seriously, she went on, "Mummy, I know you're worried about Daddy, but I'm sure it's all right. He's probably got held up in some traffic jam." Emily was unconvinced, "It's so unlike him to be so late without letting us know." At that moment there was a crunch of wheels on the gravel drive. In her relief Emily jumped up and hastened to the front door. Opening it she began, "Peter — I've been so worried . . . "

But it was Hugh's car that had pulled up outside. Hugh got out, quickly followed by Martin. Martin kissed his mother affectionately and with a note of anxiety in his voice, he asked, "Is Dad not back yet?" Emily shook her head dumbly.

"Don't worry, Mum — I'll get in touch with the police, just to see if there is any report of a hold up or anything."

Emily was about to close the front door when she saw the headlights of a car coming up the drive. With a sigh of relief she called out, "Martin, it's all right, here's Daddy now."

But as the car slowly came to a halt, Emily realised that it was not Peter's grey Vauxhall that drew up outside. Caught in the shaft of light through the open doorway stood a police car. A police officer got out. With him was a W.P.C. The officer said politely, "Good evening, Madam. Are you Mrs. Stuart, Admiral Stuart's wife?"

Emily froze with fear. She nodded her head. At the same time, she called out in a faint voice, "Martin . . . "

The police officer continued, "I'm afraid that we have some bad news, Madam. Perhaps it would be better if we were to come inside?"

Emily led the way into the hall, still unable to say anything. A dull painful ache gripped her heart.

He went on, "I am sorry to have to tell you that your husband suffered a fatal heart attack earlier this evening, while driving his car down the M23. The car swerved off the road and ran into the side of an overpass bridge. It might perhaps be some consolation to know that the doctor who examined the body was satisfied that the Admiral died before the impact, and would have known nothing about the accident."

20

FOR some weeks after Peter's death the family had rallied around Emily, supportive and caring. Martin had attended to all the necessary arrangements for the funeral and came to see his mother whenever he was able to leave his practice.

Maisie had stayed with her for the first few weeks while Charlotte looked after Fleure and Simon. Later, Teresa had arrived to keep her company. Teresa understood, perhaps better than anyone, what Emily was going through. It was only a few years since she had lost her own husband. She had loved Robert dearly, but she knew that her feelings for him paled into insignificance compared with the lifetime bond that had existed between Emily and Peter.

Teresa had been at Wisteria House for nearly two weeks when Emily experienced a sudden desire to be on her own. She felt that she needed time to think, without her mind being continually distracted by family and friends, all anxious that she should not be left alone. Not wanting to hurt Teresa's feelings, Emily broached the subject with care. She need not have worried unduly. Teresa's reaction had been characteristic.

"Emmy, darling, I know just how you feel. It's a good thing to have people around you at first, but there comes a time when you need to be on your own and start taking charge of your own life again." She gave Emily an affectionate hug. "Don't worry about the family. I'll drop a discreet hint so that they leave you in peace for a while!"

For Emily, the weeks that followed Peter's death were filled with pain and anguish as she struggled to adjust to her new life.

At first she was unable to absorb the full significance of his death. Then, as the reality of the situation began to dawn on her, she faced the world outwardly composed and with quiet dignity, but inwardly her feelings were those of mute despair.

She continued to go about her daily chores almost as if nothing untoward had occurred, keeping her emotions under tight control, and only allowing herself the luxury of giving way to her feelings in the privacy of her own room.

Soon however, she began to adapt to the new pattern of life. She grew accustomed to waking each morning without seeing Peter's long, lean form stretched out beside her; she grew accustomed to the perpetual silence that surrounded her; to the absence of his familiar figure about the place, and to the loneliness of the long winter evenings without his cheerful, comforting presence to keep her company.

Quickly she learnt the necessity of keeping herself fully occupied at all times, and busied herself with numerous tasks about the house and garden, until at the end of the day she was so exhausted in both mind and body that she sank into merciful oblivion within minutes of her head touching the pillow.

* * *

It was some three months after Peter's death, that David Frensham had unexpectedly flown home from Hong Kong on business. His stopover in this country was brief, and after visiting his father, he had stayed for a night or two at Wisteria House.

Emily and David spent an afternoon tramping across the open downlands, buffeted by gusty winds, and drenched by sharp squalls of rain. The combined effect of wind and rain had brought the colour back to Emily's cheeks. As he looked at her, David was reminded once more of the beautiful, desirable woman whom he had first met in the idyllic setting of Hong Kong and its environs, and with whom, all those years ago, he had fallen hopelessly and irrevocably in love.

After changing out of their wet clothes, they were now comfortably ensconced in front of a roaring log fire, each holding a glass of whisky. The whisky had relaxed some of the tension in Emily. For the first time she found herself able to talk about Peter. She spoke of the shock that his death had been to her, and of her inability to come to terms with all that it implied. She spoke of her regret that she had not been with him at the end; of how she felt when later Doctor Thomas told her that Peter had suffered from a heart condition for some time, news which Peter had kept from her.

As she talked Emily could feel herself begin to unwind. She suddenly realised the extent to which she had bottled up her emotions over the last months. She was mildly surprised at the ease with which she could talk to David, and of the relief she felt at finally being able to put into words something of her innermost feelings.

David had listened to her quietly and attentively, understanding all too well her need to talk. He vividly recalled the time when shortly after his mother's death — now many years before — he had felt the same need. He remembered with gratitude how Emily had sensed his desire to confide his troubles to a sympathetic ear, and how she had listened to him — a comparative stranger at that time — with kindness and compassion.

His visit, though brief, had come at

the right moment for Emily. It did much to raise her spirits, and, after taking him to the station the next day, she had returned home feeling a good deal more cheerful. Before he left David had made a point of telling her how grateful he was that she was keeping a weather eye on Nicholas, adding how much his father looked forward to her visits. His remark had left her feeling slightly guilty in the knowledge that now she was on her own, she could afford to spend more time with Nicholas than she had in the past. Accordingly she went more frequently, until her excursions to Worthing became regular weekly ones.

★ ★ ★

One fine spring morning, Emily parked her car outside the nursing home and rang the door bell. After a moment or two the door was opened to her by a pleasant faced woman wearing a neat blue overall.

"Good morning, Mrs. Stuart," the woman greeted her with a cheerful smile. "Do come in. Mr. Frensham is expecting you. He was up bright and early this morning, knowing you were coming. He does so look forward to your visits."

"How is he?" Emily enquired.

"Well, he is becoming a little more frail, but he's wonderful really, considering his age."

As she closed the front door, she said to Emily with a friendly smile, "You know your way, don't you?"

Emily climbed the stairs that led to the first floor room that Nicholas occupied. She crossed the landing and tapped lightly on the door. Inside the room the old man raised his head from his newspaper.

As the door opened he asked, "Is that you, Emily?" He peered at her over the rim of his spectacles. "Come and sit down, my dear, and tell me how you are."

She gave him a light kiss and sat down in the chair opposite him. "I'm very well, thank you, Nicholas. And what about you? How have you been since I last saw you? You're certainly looking well." Indeed, the old man looked a lot more sprightly than on her last visit, when she had left him with the feeling that he was

375

starting to go downhill rather fast. Today, however, he seemed almost rejuvenated, as well as a good deal more cheerful.

"I'm not too bad considering my advanced years!" he replied with a whimsical smile. "A little more deaf, a little more blind, and slightly more doddery, but otherwise I'm well. At least my brain is still functioning — thank God — which is more than I can say for the majority of my fellow inmates!" His sunken eyes still managed to twinkle at her from behind the thick lenses of his glasses. "But let me tell you the good news," he continued. "Since I've seen you I've had a letter from David. He tells me that he has decided to retire from his job with Maitland Struthers and settle down in England."

Emily exclaimed delightedly, "Oh, Nicholas, how marvellous. No wonder you're looking so cheerful!" Her face wore a puzzled expression as she continued, "This is a rather sudden change of plan, isn't it? I've always understood that he intended to remain in Hong Kong after he retired."

"So did I", Nicholas agreed. "However,

his letter goes on to say that he has been offered a seat on the board, which means coming to England more frequently. This may well have something to do with his change of plan, although I know that recently he has become increasingly concerned about the future of the colony, once it has been handed back to China."

Emily nodded silently. "Does he say when he is coming home?"

"Not for some months, I gather. Apparently he has a lot to do before he leaves. There's the house to be sold and so forth."

They talked for a while until Emily noticed that Nicholas was beginning to nod off in his chair. Picking up her handbag she said tactfully, "Well, I must be on my way. I'll see you again next week as usual." She gave him a gentle kiss, and quietly closed the door behind her.

As she drove home, Emily wondered whether David's decision to return to England had anything to do with Nicholas' decline in health. She recalled David's concern for his father on his last visit.

Whatever the reason, she decided that she was delighted that he was coming home, not only for Nicholas' sake, but for her own as well. There had been a strong bond of friendship between David and herself from the time she had first met him as a young man in Hong Kong. Then, her feelings towards him had been more maternal than any other emotion, but more recently she had come to regard him as an old and valued friend — an equal with whom she had many ties, and common interests. Meditating over her feelings for David, it surprised her to realise just how much she was looking forward to his return.

As she put the car away in the garage, she reminded herself to phone Martin that evening and tell him the good news. From the time that Martin and David had first known each other, when Martin had been a small boy of eight or nine, they had always got on well together and had continued to remain friends despite the disparity in their ages. Their friendship was sealed when David had flown from Hong Kong for the sole purpose of attending Martin's wedding.

When in years to come he became Paul's godfather, David had been drawn even closer into the Stuart family circle, until he had taken to spending much of the time that he was in England on leave, either at Wisteria House or with Martin and Charlotte. The twins idolised him. He displayed the same easy, friendly manner towards all four of Emily's grandchildren that he had once done towards Martin and the girls. Seeing David with them, Emily was constantly reminded of the misfortune that he had never had children of his own.

★ ★ ★

That summer David arrived back in England. This time for good.

His return coincided with the first anniversary of Peter's death. It was also Emily's birthday. The day after he arrived, he had delivered through Interflora, a huge bunch of roses with a card that bore the simple message, 'For your birthday. With my love, David.'

Emily was both touched and pleased that he should have remembered her birthday. As she carefully arranged the long stems in a vase, her mind was absorbed with memories of that August day a year ago, when her long and happy life with Peter had come to so abrupt and tragic an end. Casting her mind back over all that had happened during the past year, she knew that she had come through the traumatic experience of Peter's demise with a greater perception and understanding. There was also a growing awareness that though her life with Peter had ended, she still had what was left of her own life to live, to make of it what she would.

By nature Emily was a happy person. The cheerful, exuberant personality that she had inherited from her mother, Victoria, together with her own resolute courage and strength of character, had come to her aid on more than one occasion in her life. It had done so once more on Peter's death. Now, a year later, she felt she was ready to put behind her the sadness and sorrow of the past twelve months, and once more take charge of her own destiny.

Among the many new events and

happenings of the past year, was one that had brought much happiness and pleasure into Emily's life. She acquired a dog. It was the first time since Emily was a child that there had been a dog in her life. The dog was a young black labrador, whom she sentimentally named Sam after his predecessor. Sam was a constant joy and amusement to her. He followed her like a shadow, accompanying her whenever she went out in the car, and sleeping curled up in his basket in a corner of her bedroom. At meal times he sat by her side, an expression of anxious expectancy creasing his face, as he waited for the *bon bouche* with which Emily invariably rewarded his patience.

Letting him out the first thing in the early morning sunlight, she would laughingly watch him chase a marauding rabbit from the lawn as, loose limbed and floppy eared, he all but fell over himself in his efforts to catch the rabbit before it reached the safety of its burrow among the brambles at the bottom of the orchard.

★ ★ ★

At about the time that Emily was beginning to take more of an interest in life, and feel her confidence returning, Martin had inadvertently dropped a bombshell into her lap by suggesting that she should consider selling the house. He had begun the conversation by saying how concerned they all were about her living on her own in a house that was much too large for her.

"Mum, do you not think that it might be sensible at least to consider selling Wisteria House and moving into something smaller? Preferably nearer to us, or to Maisie and Hugh if you would rather . . . ?"

Emily looked at him aghast, "But Martin dear, I couldn't possibly think of selling Wisteria House. It's always been my home — it's part of me. I was brought up here, and Daddy and I have lived here for practically all our married life. It's your home too — you children were all brought up here — and now there are the grandchildren, and you know how they all love coming here. No, Martin, I couldn't possibly think of selling it. I can't imagine how you could even suggest it."

Emily was so adamant that Martin changed his tactics. "Okay, Mum, point taken. But would you consider having someone living in?"

"No, I certainly would not," Emily replied firmly. "I'm perfectly capable of living on my own, and now that I am more used to it, I quite enjoy it. There's really no need for any of you to worry about me, darling," she said more gently. "I do appreciate your concern, but I promise you I'm all right. Mrs. Webster comes in three mornings a week, although I really don't need her that much. But she's so kind, and I think she quite likes keeping an eye on me! Besides," she ended cheerfully, "I've lots of friends around and about, and I've always got Sam to keep me company." She fondled the dog's velvet soft ears as she spoke. He looked up at her, his eyes adoring, his whole body expressing his devotion at the touch of her hand.

At the time Emily had been a little unsettled by the conversation, and after Martin had left she wondered for a moment whether she had been right in dismissing the idea of selling the house in quite such an out-of-hand manner. But she was glad now — some three or four months later — that she had decided to stay on. The house was full of memories, and she felt safe and secure in the comfort of its familiar surroundings.

★ ★ ★

She bent forward to inhale the sweet scent of the roses, before placing the vase in a position where she would most enjoy them. She then sat down at her desk to write a note of thanks to David.

★ ★ ★

Since his arrival in England, David had been staying with his sister Catherine while he set about finding himself somewhere to live.

Catherine lived with her stockbroker husband, George, in an imposing looking mansion in the much sought after vicinity of Wimbledon Common. In looks she bore a strong resemblance to her brother with the same light coloured hair and brown eyes. But in character they were poles apart. Catherine possessed an immense amount of charm and in many ways was very like her father. Yet to Emily, she lacked any real warmth and compassion, and the two women had little in common. David, on the other hand, though equally charming, was sensitive and reserved by nature. All his life he had lived in the shadow of his father's strong, charismatic personality, and beneath his easy going charm and affability he was often insecure and uncertain of himself.

Though Catherine was devoted to her brother, she was nevertheless inclined to be rather too possessive. As soon as she heard that David was returning to England, she immediately put into operation her long cherished plan to marry him off to someone whom she considered would make him a suitable wife. The particular someone she had in mind was her close friend and confidante, Eve Carruthers. Eve was an attractive widow in her early fifties. She was also very comfortably off with a flat in London and a small house in the country.

Catherine lost no time in setting the ball rolling. Within a week or so of David's return, she gave a dinner party. She invited Eve — whom she seated next to David at the table — and two other couples. Watching David out of the corner of her eye, Catherine noted with satisfaction that he appeared to be finding Eve an amusing and entertaining dinner companion.

Later that evening, she asked casually, "Well, David, how did you get on with Eve?" David was well used to his sister's deviousness. This was not the first time she had tried her hand at matchmaking.

Equally casually, he replied, "I found her a very attractive and intelligent woman. But you know, old thing," he continued with an affectionate laugh, "it's a complete waste of your time imagining that you can marry me off to whoever takes your fancy. If I decide to remarry, I assure you it will be to someone of my own choosing!"

Catherine gave him a sideways glance. Since he had returned to England, she had noticed a difference in her brother. He seemed more decisive than usual, as though he had some incentive urging him on. Of late she had found herself wondering what had prompted him to seek early retirement in England when, for years, he had informed his family and friends alike that he intended to stay on in Hong Kong after he retired.

Intrigued by his unusually uncommunicative manner, she asked curiously, "Are you thinking of getting married again, David?"

He replied with a light laugh, "If that's what I decide to do, I promise you that you will be the first to know!"

Slowly daylight began to dawn on Catherine. "David, you old devil, I do believe you are. That's why you've come back, isn't it? Now I'm beginning to understand. Who is she? Is it anyone I know . . . ?"

David said nothing.

"Come on darling," Catherine coaxed. "You can tell me!" Then, with a flash of inspiration, she exclaimed, "It's Emily Stuart, isn't it?"

Catherine had known for years of her brother's devotion to Emily, although he had never spoken of it to her. She had always considered it to be the main reason for the breakdown of his marriages. While she herself had no great love for Emily, she decided that if what David really wanted was to marry Emily, then she would give him her full support. She tucked her arm through his.

"Why on earth didn't you tell me, darling?"

David looked uncomfortable. "Look, Catherine, I really don't want to discuss it. It's far too early to begin to even think about it."

"Then you are serious? You really want to marry her?"

He nodded his head, "It's the reason why I've come back."

Catherine gave a resigned sigh. "Well, darling, if your mind is made up, I'll do anything I can to help of course . . . "

Before she completed her sentence, David forcefully rounded on her.

"Catherine, you're to stay out of this. I know what you are like when it comes to matchmaking, but this is one occasion when I will simply not tolerate any interference on your part. I don't need your help, and I should

388

prefer you to forget that we've even had this discussion." With which he turned and walked towards the door, saying abruptly, "Well, I'm off to bed, it's been a long day."

* * *

Shortly after his conversation with Catherine, David managed to find a modest flat in central London that suited his purposes adequately.

Some days later he phoned Emily with the news of his success. He also informed her that he had now acquired a car.

"Now that I've got this wretched house hunting business behind me," he went on, "I was wondering if I could invite myself for the weekend — that is, if you are not doing anything special?"

"No, David," she replied. "I'm doing nothing special and I would love to see you." Her voice was warm and vibrant as she continued, "I'm so glad about the flat. We'll catch up on each others news at the weekend."

The following Friday evening he arrived in his car — a sedate dark blue Rover.

His pride in his new acquisition showed clearly as he ran a caressing hand over its gleaming bonnet. Emily welcomed him warmly.

"I simply can't believe that you are really back for good! How does it feel to be home?"

"Strange, different, but absolutely marvellous," he replied, as he returned her kiss. "I have been abroad for so long, that I have forgotten what it is like to live in England."

"No regrets at having changed your mind about coming home?"

"None, except for the weather, perhaps. I had forgotten how unreliable our English summers are. It's been cold and wet practically ever since I got back!"

Later that evening David gave her a detailed description of his flat, and expressed his feeling of relief at having finally found a suitable abode.

"I was getting desperate," he ended with a wry expression, "accommodation in London is not easy to come by these days."

"What about furnishing it?" Emily

asked. "How are you going to manage?"

"Catherine is being a great help in choosing the carpets and curtains for me. The furniture should arrive from Hong Kong any time now, and then you must come to see it for yourself and tell me what you think of it."

"I would love to," Emily replied enthusiastically. "It will be a good excuse for a trip to London. I've not been there for ages." After a short pause she went on thoughtfully, "Do you think you will miss going into the office each day, once you have settled into the flat?"

"I don't think so particularly. Being on the board of directors is bound to take up a couple of days a week, I should imagine, and I intend to start playing golf again. Then there's father. I'd like to visit him at least once a week . . . which reminds me, how far is Worthing from you?"

Surprised Emily replied, "Less than an hour, why?"

"Well, I was going to suggest that we had a day out together. Supposing we drive over to Worthing and spend a couple of hours with the old boy. We could have dinner on the way home. There is a rather cosy restaurant I know which I think you will like."

Emily much enjoyed her day out with David. They stopped for lunch at a pub on the way, and after spending the afternoon with Nicholas, they took Sam for a walk along the cliff tops. David had previously booked a table at the restaurant and after a relaxing drink, they went in to dinner. The restaurant was apparently well known for its excellent cuisine and its polite and attentive service, and the evening sped by. It was after eleven o'clock before they arrived home.

Emily was tired but exhilarated. "It's been a most wonderful day, David dear, I've enjoyed it so much." She gave him the same enchanting smile that he remembered of old. "Thank you for taking me out to dinner. It was a great treat. And to think that there is this excellent restaurant, almost on one's doorstep as it were, and in spite of living here all these years, I never even knew about it!" She turned a laughing face towards him as she said, half apologetically, "I'm quite exhausted. Will you forgive me if I go to bed? The whisky is on the table, if you would like a night cap?"

David laughed happily, "No, thanks, I'm exhausted too, if it comes to that. It is all that sea air this afternoon!"

21

DAVID became a regular visitor to Wisteria House. Emily soon discovered that she looked forward to his weekend stays with undue pleasure and anticipation. She was also aware of the extent to which she had come to depend upon him over the past months. As summer turned to winter, their friendship blossomed and matured. There was a growing compatibility between them as they discovered similar interests and mutual pleasures, of which they had hitherto been unaware.

It was not long before Emily found that David had a keen interest in gardening. He once remarked quite ingenuously, "Mark you, I know practically nothing about it. The small patch that was my garden in Hong Kong — where I grew mostly zinnias and gladioli — was the closest I've ever come to gardening, but 'growing things' is something I've always enjoyed doing!"

Whenever he stayed for the weekend, he insisted on lending a hand in the garden. Although Emily had recently managed to obtain some part time help, there was none the less, still plenty for her to do and she welcomed his assistance. His enthusiasm left her in no doubt how much he enjoyed gardening. It pleased her to know they had yet another interest in common.

He also proved himself surprisingly adept in the kitchen. Often on a Saturday night, he would don an apron, roll up his sleeves, and with a drink in one hand and a wooden spoon in the other, he would produce an excellent meal for them both with the minimum effort. Emily would watch him with an undisguised interest and amusement.

"How on earth did you learn to cook like this?" she asked curiously, as she recalled how, for the greater part of his life, he had had a Chinese staff to cater for all his needs.

"Nothing to it!" he replied airily, "I just like cooking."

Apart from David's weekend visits to Wisteria House, for Emily there was also the occasional excursion to London. Her first visit had been to inspect David's new home. Once again she was mildly surprised to discover how domesticated and well organised he was.

On another occasion he invited her to accompany him to the opening night of a new Lloyd Webber show, the tickets for which Emily guessed were almost unobtainable. It was many years since she had been to a London theatre. She was conscious of a feeling of nervous excitement amid the tense, electrically charged atmosphere of a first night. Yet, at the same time, the evening was tinged with nostalgia, as she recalled the many times when she and Peter had attended the opening night of one of Cara's repertory performances.

There was also the occasional concert or a visit to an art gallery or museum. They went to Sadlers Wells for a performance of Los Sylphides and to Glyndebourne to hear The Marriage of Figaro. They were diversions that gave them both immense pleasure and caused David to remark, "I've been away for so long that I had almost forgotten how much culture and entertainment London has to offer."

Sometimes David took her out to dinner in one of London's more fashionable restaurants. His hospitality was such that it prompted her to remark half-seriously, "David, dear, all this is dreadfully extravagant. There is really no need to take me to such expensive places."

He laughed happily. "Well, let me indulge in a few extravagances a little longer. I've not done anything like this for many years. You enjoy it, don't you?" he asked anxiously.

"Of course I do," she replied quickly. "And if it comes to that, I've not done anything like this for ages either! After Peter retired we hardly ever set foot in London. There always seemed to be so many other things to do."

On the rare occasions when Emily needed to spend the night in London, David arranged for her to stay with Catherine and George. While there was no great love lost between Emily and David's sister, they both accepted the fact that they were unlikely ever to become close friends, and for David's sake managed to give a fairly convincing performance of friendliness. Emily had to admit though, that each time she had stayed there of late, Catherine had gone out of her way to make her feel welcome.

★ ★ ★

That Christmas there was a large family gathering at Wisteria House. Martin, Charlotte, Maisie, Hugh and their respective children, as well as Teresa, all assembled under the same roof for the celebrations. It was the first occasion on which there had been such a sizeable gathering since Peter had died, and for Emily, it was a time of mixed emotions.

It brought back memories of Christmases long past, when the old home was filled with the boisterous clamour and excitement of the three children when they were young; of Christmas lunch, with the colourful table decorations, the crackers, the holly, and the candles; of Elsie staggering into the dining room under the weight of a huge roast turkey which she would place on the sideboard for Peter to carve. And how later they would all congregate round the tree while Peter, resplendent in the red tunic and long white beard of Santa Claus, would hand out presents to all.

★ ★ ★

David joined them on Boxing Day. He had driven to Worthing that morning to visit his father after having spent Christmas day with Catherine and George. His arrival was greeted with warmth and pleasure by the older members of the family, and with enthusiastic delight by all four children.

Martin observed with some interest David's relaxed approach to his mother, noticing particularly the warm expression in his eyes whenever he looked in her direction.

In a quiet aside to Maisie, Martin remarked, "Have you noticed anything different about David's manner towards Mum lately?"

Maisie grinned at the tall, fair, immensely likeable man, now nudging forty, whom she had always regarded as her brother. "Of course I have, you idiot! He's quite obviously head over heels in love with her."

Martin was somewhat taken aback by her reply. "Are you sure?" he asked in astonishment.

"Yes, I am quite sure. They've been seeing an awful lot of each other lately. David spends practically every weekend at Wisteria House. Personally I think it's quite the best thing that could have happened for them both. Mum is clearly lonely, in spite of what she says to the contrary, and David is such a darling, I'm sure he'll make her a wonderful husband."

For a moment Martin looked shocked. "You're jumping the gun a bit, aren't you, talking about marriage? Dammit, it's only eighteen months since Dad died . . . Besides, Mum is getting on a bit to think about re-marriage."

"Oh, Martin, don't be such an old fuddy duddy! Mum is only sixty nine, which is nothing these days. She's still a very attractive, young looking woman. She's got years of life ahead of her, years that she will enjoy considerably more," she added seriously, "if she has someone to share them with."

"Well, perhaps you are right," Martin replied dubiously. "She certainly seems to have taken on a new lease of life since David appeared on the scene."

He glanced across the room to where his mother was sitting reading to Gregory, one protective arm around his slight shoulders as he curled up beside her in the big arm chair. She was undoubtedly a remarkably well preserved woman for her years, Martin conceded. Her figure was still shapely, her eyes still held their merry twinkle and though her once golden hair had now turned white, he had to admit that she looked a good deal younger than her years. The lines of pain and suffering were still apparent, yet they served only to add character to her still beautiful, delicately structured face. It was not in the least surprising, Martin decided, that David found her attractive.

He turned back to Maisie. "How do you think Mum feels towards David?"

"She's obviously enormously fond of him," Maisie replied slowly. "Perhaps even more than she realises, but somehow I don't think she's given a great deal of thought to the future. It seems as if she has decided to take life one day at a time." She paused before going on thoughtfully, "She relies on David in a way that suggests he's become very important to her, but whether she feels anything more than just friendship for him, I simply don't know."

"Perhaps she feels it's too soon after Dad's death for her to start making plans for the future," Martin observed.

Maisie nodded her head. "Maybe", Maisie agreed.

★ ★ ★

Shortly after Christmas Nicholas developed a cold which immediately went to his chest and, within a few days had turned to pneumonia. David was summoned by the matron to the nursing home.

"I thought it best to let you know, Mr. Frensham," she began, "although your father is responding to treatment, you never quite know with elderly people . . ."

David's concern for his father showed clearly as he asked anxiously, "How is he?"

"He is very frail, and has some difficulty in breathing, but his condition is fairly stable. I am afraid you will notice quite a change in him since your last visit at Christmas. I would suggest that you don't stay with him for too long as he tires very easily," she warned. "Oh, by the way, Mr. Frensham, your father has been asking to see Mrs. Stuart. Her visit is not due for a day or two. Would you like me to give her a ring or will you tell her?"

"I'll tell her," David replied.

Nicholas was lying in bed propped up by pillows. By his side stood an oxygen cylinder which filled David with a sense of foreboding. It suddenly, and quite inconsequentially occurred to him that he could not remember ever having seen his father in bed before.

"Hello, father," he began quietly. "I'm sorry to hear that you are not too well. Are they looking after you properly? Have you everything you want?"

"Yes, thanks, my boy. It was good of

403

you to come." His voice was weak and his breathing slightly laboured. His long, beautifully shaped hands lay on top of the bedclothes, either side of his gaunt frame. David sat down beside him and placed one hand over his father's. He said gently, "Don't try to talk, father, just lie still and rest and we'll soon have you well again." David sat with him for a while, talking to the old man in a quiet, soothing tone. Then, as Nicholas' eyelids began to droop, David got up from his chair and moved silently towards the door. His hand was on the door handle when Nicholas suddenly opened his eyes.

"David . . . " For a brief moment his face wore its old, amused, slightly sardonic expression. "How much longer do you intend to wait before you ask Emily to marry you?"

David was quite unprepared for such a totally unexpected question. Surprise and disbelief sounded in his voice as he said, "You know how I feel about Emily?"

With a gleam in his eye and a return to his old vigour, Nicholas replied, "Of course I know. Give me credit for a little intelligence. I knew what was in your mind as soon as you told me you were coming back to England for good." His voice had suddenly grown weaker and he began to cough painfully.

"Now off you go, my boy, I'm getting tired . . . And, David, tell Emily I want to see her." His voice trailed off.

"Yes, father, I'll tell her. Now try and get some sleep and we'll both be in to see you tomorrow." He closed the door softly behind him.

Downstairs he knocked on the door of the matron's office.

"I'm just off, matron. I'll be staying the night with Mrs. Stuart — you have her 'phone number. If there is any change in my father's condition, please ring me immediately. I can be here in under an hour. Mrs. Stuart and I will be coming over anyway first thing in the morning."

He let in the clutch and drove at speed through the dark night.

Emily heard a car draw up outside and wondering who it could be at this late hour, she pulled back the curtains and looked out. She immediately recognised

David's car and hurried across the hall to unlock the front door.

"David," she exclaimed in surprise. "Whatever brings you here at this time of night?"

His face looked tired and drawn. In disjointed sentences he replied, "Father is ill. He's got pneumonia. Do you mind putting me up for the night, Emily? I told them I'd be here if I was needed. It's closer than London."

She replied calmly, "Come and sit by the fire, you look absolutely frozen. Have you had anything to eat?"

"No, but I'm not hungry. I could do with a drink though." He sank wearily into a chair while Emily poured him a stiff whisky. Handing him the glass she said, "Now drink that while I make you a sandwich, then you can tell me everything that's happened."

"I must telephone Catherine first. May I? She will probably want to make arrangements to come down to see father."

Early the next morning David and Emily drove to the nursing home. The door was opened by a young nurse who said that matron would like to see them in her office. Emily and David exchanged looks.

After she had greeted them, the matron said in a quiet professional voice, "I am sorry, but I am afraid I have some bad news for you." She looked at David. "Your father died just a short while ago. I telephoned your house, Mrs. Stuart, but you must already have left."

Slowly Emily realised the significance of what the matron was saying. Her eyes welled with tears.

As if from a great distance she heard the matron's voice, " . . . it was very peaceful. He didn't suffer. In the end it was his heart, of course." Emily lowered her head. Two great tear drops spilled over and fell into her lap.

* * *

After Nicholas died, Emily experienced an enormous sense of loss. It was as though all the colour had suddenly gone out of her life, leaving it dull and grey. She had a deep and enduring affection for this man who, for over forty years, had been her friend and companion, as indeed, he had once been her lover.

She still remembered the one night they had spent together. The chemistry there had been between them; his passionate, yet tender love making that had left her with a sense of fulfilment that she had never before experienced. She recalled how, meeting him again some years later, her feelings had been rekindled by his very presence, and how once more she had been drawn to him by the same strong, physical attraction. And she remembered with gratitude, his innate kindness and understanding after Peter's death, as well as the immeasurable comfort she had derived from him.

Since that time, her visits to Nicholas had become an important part of her daily life. He had always welcomed her with warmth and affection, and had regaled her up to the end with his dry humour and witty, intelligent conversation.

Once she was over the initial shock of Nicholas' death, Emily's thoughts centred on David. She knew that his relationship with his father had not always been easy. David had once confided in her some of the problems he had had to face as he grew into manhood in the shadow of his cultured, charismatic parent. But she knew also, that in later years, the gap in their relationship had been bridged to a great extent. With advancing age, Nicholas had mellowed. David in turn had gained in confidence and prestige, until there had been a genuine affection and understanding between father and son. Emily felt even more drawn to David in their shared grief. She did her best to comfort him, gently reminding him of the pleasure and happiness his homecoming had afforded Nicholas in the last few months of his life, and of how peacefully Nicholas's life had finally drawn to an end.

★ ★ ★

It was a mild spring evening. Emily and David had just returned from exercising a now fully grown Sam. They had covered several miles, tramping across fields and through the surrounding woods before the young dog showed any sign of having had sufficient exercise. Emily sighed contentedly as she lowered herself into the depths of an armchair.

"I think that I've done more walking this last year than ever in my life, thanks to Sam," she laughed. "I'm quite exhausted!"

"What about a corpse reviver?" David asked, "Would you like me to pour you a whisky?"

"Just what I need!" she replied. He handed her a glass. She looked up at him with a warm, appreciative smile. "I could easily get used to being waited on like this!" Suddenly serious, she went on, "You do so much for me, David — you look after me so well . . . "

David was equally serious, "It's what I've always wanted to do." For a moment Emily was puzzled. She looked at him, her eyes questioning. He smiled at her, an intimate, tender smile.

"Emily, my beloved, don't you know that I have been in love with you from the time I first plucked up courage to talk to you on board Bob Maitland's boat, all those years ago? I had been watching you swimming with Peter, then you suddenly emerged from the sea like

410

some beautiful mermaid. I can see it all still." He smiled as he reminisced. "You were wearing a pale blue swimsuit that displayed to perfection your tanned, delectable figure; your wet hair clung glistening to your shoulders and as you disappeared from view, I remember how your bare feet left a trail of wet footprints all along the deck! In that split second I fell in love."

Emily gave a soft laugh, "Oh David."

"For years I couldn't get you out of my system. The thought of you haunted me night and day. You were in my mind whatever I did and wherever I went!" There was a long pause before he said slowly, almost painfully, "Do you remember that time when my father came out to Hong Kong?"

Emily nodded.

"I can still recall the shock that I felt when I realised he was in love with you." He gave a short, mirthless laugh. "You certainly seem to have had the most devastating effect on the Frensham family, one way and another."

"I'm so sorry, David dear. I really had no idea about how you felt — that is to say, I do remember thinking at the time that perhaps you were a little . . . infatuated?" She stopped short. She was suddenly filled with remorse that he should have suffered so much heartache and unhappiness, without her having been aware of how deep his feelings were.

She chose her words with great care, "I realise that it was a long time ago, and when you are young those wounds can take a long time to heal, but now it's all over, I hope you can forgive me for having been quite so insensitive, not to have understood how you felt?"

David gave a wistful smile. "You don't understand yet, Emily do you — I loved you then. I still love you, even more. All these years I've never stopped loving you." He paused before asking her gently, "Why do you think I decided to come back to England?"

Emily hesitated. "I always imagined it was because of Nicholas."

He ignored her reply. "After Peter died, I wanted to be near you in case I could do something. I came back on that flying visit last year just for that. I thought you might need someone to talk to, so I concocted an excuse to be with you." In a low voice he continued, "I must admit I hoped that given time I might become something more to you than just a friend." He broke off suddenly. "Oh, Emily, what a hell of a mess I'm making of this . . . "

He got up from his chair and strode across the room and stood gazing out of the window. With his back to her he said quietly, "I never meant to say any of this to you until I was quite sure that you were ready to hear it. In fact, I don't even know how we got on to the subject. But Emily, I love you, with all my heart and soul, and I want you to be my wife more than anything I have ever dreamed of." He turned to face her. His voice held a depth of emotion as he pleaded, "Emily, you do care . . . just a little . . . don't you?"

Although Emily had not known until now how David had felt towards her all those years ago, she had been aware that recently his manner towards her had changed. Over the past months he had been quietly but unmistakably

413

wooing her. His attentions had caused her neither embarrassment nor concern, but had done much for her self esteem. Uncertain of her feelings, she had put aside any thoughts of the future and — as Maisie correctly surmised — had decided to take their growing relationship one day at a time. Somehow she knew instinctively that he was in love with her, just as she had known that he had quietly bided his time all these past months, until he was sure that her wounds were sufficiently healed for her to consider any change in their relationship.

Tears of emotion flooded her eyes as she replied, "Oh, David, of course I care. I'm deeply fond of you and I value your friendship more than I can say. But I am not sure whether I love you."

"I'm prepared for that," he answered gravely. "Friendship is a good foundation for any marriage."

Still uncertain, she said, "You realise that I'm years older than you, David . . . ?"

His smile was tender as he replied with a slight shrug of his shoulders, "What is twelve years at our age?"

414

She was still unconvinced. "What about the children?"

"My dear girl, the children, as you call them, have children of their own and somehow," he added with a twinkle in his eye, "I don't think they will be altogether surprised!"

"Then there's Catherine," she remembered in a panic. "Whatever will she and George think?"

"Don't worry your head about Catherine," he reassured her with a laugh. "She's been wanting to marry me off for years."

For the first time he allowed his eyes to reflect the love and affection he felt for her, as he asked with gentle humour, "Are there any other objections you can think of?"

She looked up into his kind, honest face. Still troubled she asked, "David, give me a few days to think about it? I promise I won't keep you waiting too long. It's happened so suddenly." She got up from her chair and walked restlessly across the room. "I suppose I've known all along that our relationship couldn't continue as it has for ever. But David, dear, I had never contemplated marriage.

I'm just not sure whether I am ready yet
. . . do you understand?"

"Of course I understand," he replied
quietly, "but Emily, whatever your answer,
promise me we'll remain friends?"

Her eyes were soft as she answered
him, "I can't imagine my life without you
being an important part of it, David."

★ ★ ★

It was some time before Emily fell asleep.
As she lay in bed her thoughts inevitably
turned to Peter. Though Peter was still
seldom far from her thoughts, he was
no longer a part of her life. The image
of him had slowly receded to the back
of her mind, where she knew it would
always remain, loved and remembered,
without any of the bitter feelings or
the despair she had known in the long
months following his death. She knew
for certain that whatever she decided she
would have Peter's blessing. He would
have wanted her to take whatever chance
of happiness she was offered.

She lay staring up into the darkness,
turning over in her mind the full

significance of all that it meant to be loved again; to be needed, desired; to share what was left of her life with someone who loved her with a deep and selfless devotion.

She knew that she loved David. Not in the same way that she had loved Peter, but with a love born of mutual understanding, companionship, and an undeniable need for each other.

She had told him that she would give him her answer in a few days. She knew already what her answer would be. He had waited for her long enough, she thought with compassion. She would tell him first thing tomorrow.

★ ★ ★

Outside her window an owl hooted. A sudden gust of wind blew the curtains into the room, letting in a shaft of moonlight. In his basket in the corner of the room Sam yelped excitedly, his limbs twitching in rapid, involuntary movements as in his dreams he frantically gave chase to a rabbit.

Emily finally closed her eyes and slept.

Her face wore an expression of quiet repose. It was as if, after a lifetime in which she had run the whole gamut of human emotions, she had at last found peace and contentment.

THE END

Other titles in the
Ulverscroft Large Print Series:

TO FIGHT THE WILD
Rod Ansell and Rachel Percy

Lost in uncharted Australian bush, Rod Ansell survived by hunting and trapping wild animals, improvising shelter and using all the bushman's skills he knew.

COROMANDEL
Pat Barr

India in the 1830s is a hot, uncomfortable place, where the East India Company still rules. Amelia and her new husband find themselves caught up in the animosities which seethe between the old order and the new.

THE SMALL PARTY
Lillian Beckwith

A frightening journey to safety begins for Ruth and her small party as their island is caught up in the dangers of armed insurrection.

THE WILDERNESS WALK
Sheila Bishop

Stifling unpleasant memories of a misbegotten romance in Cleave with Lord Francis Aubrey, Lavinia goes on holiday there with her sister. The two women are thrust into a romantic intrigue involving none other than Lord Francis.

THE RELUCTANT GUEST
Rosalind Brett

Ann Calvert went to spend a month on a South African farm with Theo Borland and his sister. They both proved to be different from her first idea of them, and there was Storr Peterson — the most disturbing man she had ever met.

ONE ENCHANTED SUMMER
Anne Tedlock Brooks

A tale of mystery and romance and a girl who found both during one enchanted summer.

1	28	121	192	250	308	351	386	417
2	35	123	193	251	310	352	388	418
3	39	124	195	252	311	353	390	419
4	40	132	198	257	312	354	392	421
5	41	136	203	258	317	355	393	422
6	42	148	208	259	318	357	394	423
7	54	149	212	262	320	359	395	425
8	55	154	216	263	321	360	396	427
9	61	157	220	268	322	361	397	428
10	64	160	224	269	324	362	399	429
11	68	164	227	272	326	363	400	431
12	69	166	232	273	327	364	401	432
13	78	167	233	274	328	366	403	433
14	79	168	234	279	331	368	404	435
15	80	169	237	285	333	372	405	436
16	84	172	238	288	336	373	406	437
17	85	174	240	295	337	374	407	438
18	90	175	241	297	338	375	408	440
19	99	180	242	299	341	376	409	441
20	100	182	243	301	344	377	410	442
21	101	183	244	303	347	379		
23	110	188	247	304	348	380		
24	119	189	249	307	350	383		

447	470	493	516	539	562	585	608	631
448	471	494	517	540	563	586	609	632
449	472	495	518	541	564	587	610	633
450	473	496	519	542	565	588	611	634
451	474	497	520	543	566	589	612	635
452	475	498	521	544	567	590	613	636
453	476	499	522	545	568	591	614	637
454	477	500	523	546	569	592	615	638
455	478	501	524	547	570	593	616	639
456	479	502	525	548	571	594	617	640
457	480	503	526	549	572	595	618	641
458	481	504	527	550	573	596	619	642
459	482	505	528	551	574	597	620	643
460	483	506	529	552	575	598	621	644
461	484	507	530	553	576	599	622	645
462	485	508	531	554	577	600	623	646
463	486	509	532	555	578	601	624	647
464	487	510	533	556	579	602	625	648
465	488	511	534	557	580	603	626	649
466	489	512	535	558	581	604	627	650
467	490	513	536	559	582	605	628	651
468	491	514	537	560	583	606	629	652
469	492	515	538	561	584	607	630	653